AF541626

THE
OFF-SITE
TAMASHA
...A COMICAL TALE OF TEAM BUILDING

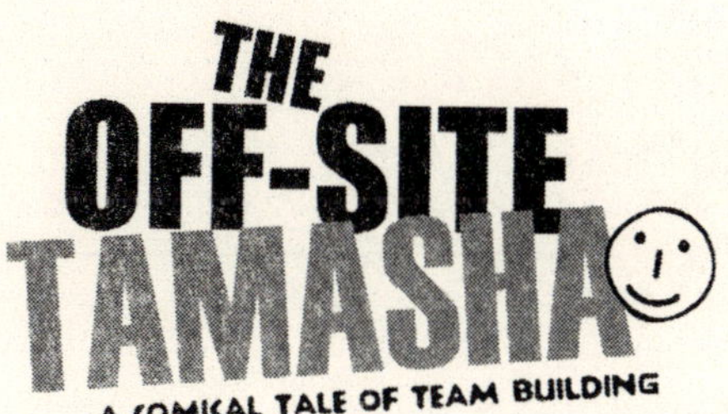

Abhay Nagarajan

Srishti
PUBLISHERS & DISTRIBUTORS

Srishti Publishers & Distributors
N-16, C. R. Park
New Delhi 110 019
srishtipublishers@gmail.com

First published by Srishti Publishers & Distributors in 2012

This is a work of fiction. Characters, places and incidents are either the product of the author's imagination or are used fictitiously, and any resemblance to any actual person, living or dead, events or locales is entirely coincidental.

Typeset in AGaramond 12pt. by Suresh Kumar Sharma at Srishti

Printed and bound in India

For my parents

&

In the memory of my grandfather

Mr. Malayatoor Ramakrishnan

(1927-1997)

Acknowledgements

Thanks to:

My mother for the constant encouragement and for reading my initial drafts patiently.

My father and my brother Hareesh for reading subsequent drafts and for offering valuable suggestions. My brother also took time out of his busy schedule to set up my website.

My 'curd rice' friends from school and college: Ajeet, Santosh, Rajesh, Aditya, Ravi, Ghanu, Nirmal, Meher, Sudheer, Bhomik, Anupam and Kunal for their friendship and interest in my writing.

To the readers of my debut novel, *Corporate Atyaachaar* who gave me their time and valuable feedback.

My publisher for accepting my work and having it published.

And finally, none of this would have been possible without the blessings of God who made it all happen.

PART 1- DEPARTURE

1
RACE TO THE AIRPORT

'We should enjoy this trip. It is very important for us to maintain a healthy work life balance' *the person* told me.

It was early afternoon. We were standing at the car park in the basement in our office building.

'Hmmm' I grunted as usual in complete agreement.

The person in question anyways did not really expect intelligent conversation from me.

'This is a good break for me in particular. Much needed to avoid a burnout.'

Seeing the excitement on *the person's* face, it seemed very hard to detect any burnout signs! What burn out was *the person* talking about?

The person worked only from 9.30 a.m. to 6.30 p.m. on an average. It was probably the most stress free scenario, a boss of a financial setup could ask for! In addition, on most days during office hours under the pretext of a power nap, *the person* dozed off in the conference room in the savasana pose for a gentle 1-2 hours!

'....However once we are refreshed and back, we need to do lots of work. Work is piling up....' *the person* continued planning the vengeance to be unleashed on me, on our return.

The person finished talking.

He then started doing what he did the best. He started itching, twitching, pulling, pinching, rubbing and tugging his body parts lodged comfortably somewhere between his trouser pockets. All was indeed well in his kingdom!

The person in question was my mid thirty something boss, the Human Ball Scratcher (HBS).

The reason for the excitement was because we were leaving for our annual three day company off-site to Kyari, a picturesque tourist spot lodged in the beautiful state of Uttaranchal. Thankfully, despite the state of the economy, the off-site was on schedule and was not cancelled. It would definitely offer some relief from the dry, monotonous office work.

The off-site was planned to be a combination of business development discussions along with some team building exercises.

The Delhi head office had sent us a detailed itinerary which I had briefly gone through. To reach Kyari from Bangalore, we had to first take a flight to Delhi. We then had to take a train to Ramnagar, from the Old Delhi Railway station. The teams from our Delhi and Mumbai branches would be meeting us directly at the station.

I was excited that we were going. The past year had been quite boring.

To begin with nothing had changed in my personal life or in my work life as a financial advisor at Wealth Capital Advisors (WCA) in Bangalore. I had secured a campus placement to join WCA during my final semester of my Masters degree in finance at the University of Delhi. I had left my comfort zone in Delhi where I stayed with my parents and moved to Bangalore. At the office, I was still a financial advisor for a select set of high net worth (HNI) clients in Bangalore. I was not particularly astute or intelligent, but I somehow managed to advise clients twice my age on their investment portfolios!

On the personal front I was as horny as ever. My twenty sixth birthday was approaching in a couple of months. My hormones were still raging overtime. In University, I had been in a relationship with a classmate of mine. Since the breakup, I had not been with any girl. I was slowly becoming a repressed Indian male with an active sex life in his mind and no action in reality. My mother occasionally brought out the marriage threat which I warded off. I was not yet ready to take on the responsibilities of life. I did not want to fall into the matrimonial trap just to escape being lonely. She was however, going all out in her search to ensure a potential match for me to 'settle down'.

I still had no social life.

After relocating to Bangalore, as I began work, I took up an accommodation at a paying guest with a fat aunty who was my landlord. I still stay with the PG Aunty in Bangalore. She has a hot daughter who recently got married to her biker boyfriend. It was a sad, emotional day in my life. When the daughter was around, I could at least stare at her and occasionally exchange mundane pleasantries. I still remember the evening when she met me to get some financial advice. At that time, I had thought that it was an indication that she liked me and the meeting would lead to something.

But nothing of the sort happened.

My parents still stay in Rajender Nagar in Delhi. If they were in Delhi at the moment, I could have spent a few days with them after the off-site. But they seem to have found, some new found zest for life and of late were busy travelling. My father, a chartered accountant finally has realized that there is more to life than his CA firm. He started working part time some time ago. Now he has taken my mother to enjoy the sights and sounds of Namibia. Other trips are also in the offing.

On the professional front, on account of the recession and subsequent modest recovery of the economy, WCA's Bangalore branch had not expanded in terms of new additions to the team. But my waistline certainly had expanded. I still reported to HBS who enjoyed cuddling his privates in public, soaking in the simple joys of life. I was still just another face in the sea of finance professionals with only my visiting card adding a degree of importance to my identity. I was still as submissive and obedient in taking work instructions which certainly had resulted in steady monetary rewards. HBS also continued to compare my intellect with that of his extremely smart, multi tasking young nephew (in terms of age not in terms of accomplishments!) to possibly motivate me to work extra hard!

One aspect of my insipid life had certainly changed.

Telemarketing and banking agents had new found interest in *me*.

I had become attractive to them. They wanted me to purchase their credit and debit card products!

When I had started work a few years ago, I had received phone calls or text messages to buy debit cards. Now it was credit cards! Despite the credit crisis, the banks had great confidence in the credit limits they were offering me on account of my bank balance! The desperate pleas of the credit card executives coaxing me to purchase various forms of cards, made me feel pretty important in the value chain. I really seemed to have moved up the hierarchy. Maybe I was now high net worth for them after my few years of work. In the competitive wealth sales race, the credit card executive is like a little baby monkey in pursuit of a medium sized monkey like me. In turn, I along with a senior monkey like HBS, were in pursuit of the elusive banana-the rich HNI.

From now on, I was clear that my life would be all about chasing the desired financial sales targets -quarter on quarter possibly for the next 100 quarters of my life. Unless of course, the 'quarter on quarter plan' was cut short by an early arrival of a common 'thirty plus', stress induced heart attack! In turn, chasing me to meet their targets would be more executives tempting me to take home loans, car loans, credit cards, mutual funds, personal loans and a whole bunch of other stuff!

From the WCA Founder's perspective, the Bangalore branch was doing well and he had no reason to complain. On account of the good performance, HBS along with a few others was in the running for the 'best financial advisor of the year', an award which was going to be given during the off-site. The Founder was interested only in the revenue which was being generated and the number of clients being acquired in Bangalore. He could not care less if HBS had his hand permanently lodged in his pocket producing Carnatic *or* Western Classical music with his balls as long as the dulcet sound of revenues were flowing into the branch.

One of the unfortunate details in the branch was that the Naval Commander, the new recruit whom I had to mentor in the office, had quit. He had quit citing work differences with HBS. It did not come as a major surprise to me. He seemed the argumentative, confrontational type. A 'type' which HBS had disliked a lot right from the beginning. But I missed the presence of the Naval Commander. I used to derive a vicarious sense of pleasure when he would confront HBS on many work issues. What I lacked in guts, he more than made up for. He often made HBS squirm which was interesting for me to observe. My other work colleague, the Sweet Lady was still around but was on maternity leave after being knocked up by her husband. The news was that she was carrying triplets. I thought three babies in three prams would be cute but also quite a handful. Maybe she would also quit the company.

So for the last several months, it had only been HBS and me managing the Bangalore branch with his 'leadership and vision' and me with my 'clerical execution'! My work load had increased considerably. After the arrival of 'HBS junior'- his chotu son, HBS used to just disappear from office! If not a good boss, he definitely was trying hard to be a good dad. I could imagine him multitasking with a milk bottle in one hand and scratching his privates with the other hand. It would be interesting to note, if little chotu would also develop into a full fledged scratching champion!

A direct impact of this parental love had to be endured by me.

More work of a clerical nature was dumped on as I was unmarried and HBS felt I had no real reason to go home early.

The fact that I could roam aimlessly in Brigade road, see movies in the multiplexes or just sit in my PG room and shag without being disturbed simply did not occur to him.

It was quite a challenging task to do almost everything in the office but I somehow managed with the help of two office assistants who worked in their own styles and with their own problems to deal with.

Without any prior notice to HBS, one office assistant kept disappearing to Nandi Hills located on the outskirts of Bangalore. Days later, the assistant casually entered the office with love bites all over his neck and a love locket in his hand. The locket had his girlfriend's photo in it. HBS screamed at him. He offered him a chance to refocus on work. The assistant was not in the least bit bothered. He proudly announced that he was in 'wild love'. He casually tendered his resignation and also mentioned that he had got a job elsewhere. He walked out of the office! That was the last I saw of him.

To retain the services of the other hardworking office assistant, HBS offered him a marginal pay hike. In addition to the pay hike was also the unsaid matter of the extra office work which he now had to complete! The assistant was sad on many counts-he now had more work to do, he could not quit his job as he had a family to support and above all he had no girlfriend.

One evening, with the Bangalore rains offering the perfect background setting for a genuine heart to heart talk, the hardworking assistant confided in HBS.

I was at my desk completing some work.

The office assistant confessed about the excessive work load and lack of work life balance in his mechanical life. HBS reassured him in a rather curt and not so polite manner. The reassurance was- "Shut up. Do the work. Stop cribbing. Work is worship. Life is not easy. Don't get inspired by the other assistant. You are not a hero. You can never become a hero. Other heroes may have started their careers by being bus conductors, auto drivers or truck drivers. But you are an office assistant. From here on, you can only aim at becoming a better office assistant. Keep working hard. I will give you more work so that you can become a really fast learner and you can get promoted."

The office assistant made a sad face which suggested that he did not want to be a 'fast learner' nor did he want a 'promotion'. Seeing his range of facial expressions, he really did deserve to be in the movies! He also sniffed and a few droplets of 'stress' water from his nose became a permanent fixture of a few dusty HNI client files.

Apart from these incidents, nothing much was happening at work.

It was the *same* boring routine of office, the *same* office files, the *same* desk, the *same* stomach churning stress, the *same* water cooler, the *same* observations on HBS and the techniques he used to scratch his balls, the *same* walk, the *same* talk, the *same* irritation, the *same* excitement when the annual bonus came, the *same* small talk, the *same* office assistant and his *same* 'emotional' sad stories.

The sameness of it all was numbing.

It was in light of this sameness that the announcement of the annual three day company off-site had come as a blessing. For HBS too, the excitement was evident. He told me that the trip was a '2 nights-3 days' package making it sound wonderful like it was some sort of, all expense paid honeymoon corporate package for us!

HBS's driver placed three big VIP suitcases (one of them being mine) and a cricket kit in the boot of the black Honda City. As we were ready to depart for the new airport in Devanhalli, the car was stopped by the parking attendant in the basement of the building.

'The parking rates have been revised to 10 rupees per hour from 5 rupees per hour' the parking attendant told the driver.

'What is this? How come the rates have been revised? I didn't get any communication' HBS screamed at the attendant, rolling down the car window.

'Sir, the notice was put up yesterday evening.'

'I don't care when it was put up. I was not informed. Driver! Did you know about the revised rates?' HBS asked his driver.

The driver said he was not aware.

'But it was put up yesterday' the attendant insisted again.

HBS's pre off-site good mood seemed to have disappeared. He appeared irritated. He was not used to being argued with, especially by underlings.

'Do you know who I am?' he asked the attendant.

'No, sir… I don't.'

'DON'T YOU KNOW WHO I AM?'

'No, sir. I really don't!'

'I am the branch head of Wealth Capital Advisors in Bangalore. We are on the 4th floor. Give me your boss's number!'

'Why?'

'I will take up the matter with your boss!'

'Sir, please don't complain.'

'Ok, I won't complain. But I am paying as per the old rate. Here take the money.'

'Fine!' the attendant replied, looking skywards for help.

As the car merged in the traffic on MG Road, I looked at my office building which was glistening in the sunshine.

Freedom from work for the next few days! Bye-bye ugly corporate building!

'Dear passengers- please use alternative roads to save time and to avoid congestion' a signboard read of the ongoing Metro rail construction on MG Road. Despite having taken an alternative road, we were stuck in a traffic jam which was taking an excruciating amount of time to clear up.

'Why are you keeping the engine running? Can't you see that we are stuck in a jam? Petrol has become so expensive, you damn fool!' HBS screamed at his driver.

The driver muttered something in irritation. His mind seemed elsewhere. He rubbed an itch on his stubble. With HBS away he probably was planning a holiday getaway of his own!

'I can smell alcohol! Are you drunk? You fool!'

The driver muttered something again in his slurred speech.

'If I catch you drinking while driving again…I will cut your salary. I will really cut it. You wait and watch!'

The driver did not respond. *He was probably used to these threats!*

'Did you get my badminton racquet from home?'

'No, sir.'

'What?'

'Sir…sir…. I forgot to collect it.'

'You fool! This time, I am really going to cut it.'

'But, sir…'

'I am cutting it. No more discussion. Just focus on the road.'

The driver would be manhood less, armless, limbless and jobless. It could not get worse. Plus no more magazine subscriptions for him which had already been cut a while ago, when I had just joined work!

'Thank God, I also got along my cricket kit. Just in case we get to play' HBS told me.

I nodded uninterestedly.

In the choked traffic jam, a flexible roadside urchin, maybe all of seven or eight was engaged in a most captivating display of gymnastics. The little fellow was jumping in and out of a circular hoopla while displaying some gravity defying, groin challenging splits in the slightest of spaces on offer between the cars. However competing with him for money and the attention of the vehicle passengers was a Hijra. Circling couples on scooters and on motorbikes, the Hijra was either cursing or blessing the couples depending on whether they paid him money or not. Most people seemed to be paying up.

Meanwhile, having displayed his tricks, the flexible urchin

approached our car to collect his money. I located a two rupee coin to give him. Seeing the glint of the coin, he hurriedly approached my side of the car. He looked at me with an expressionless face which seems hardened by grime and the hardships of poverty.

HBS cautioned me against paying up.

'This is an organized racket. We shouldn't promote begging in any form' he lectured me.

I nodded in agreement.

He was probably right.

I put the two rupees back in my pocket.

I shooed the urchin away who was so near yet so far from the coin.

There was nothing much I could do.

HBS controlled my work life. This was technically office hours! All financial decisions were only taken by him. I could probably indulge in helping the needy during my private time.

HBS asked the driver to roll up the windows, which was centrally controlled. Suddenly on my left, circling HBS's window was the muscular Hijra. Unlike the flexible urchin, he was making a demand and not a request for money. He slammed the palms of his hands aggressively. Though aware of his presence, HBS did not worry too much. Seeing his indifference, the Hijra decided to take some action. With a gentle thrust he placed his hand on HBS's left shoulder through the open car window.

'Oye Chakha!' HBS exclaimed in shock on being gently manhandled.

'Chakha kisko bola re?' the Hijra asked.

He started to thump his hands even more vigorously.

Still clasping HBS, the Hijra cursed his parents, friends and family.

'Put the window up… you fool! Fast!' HBS screamed at the driver, while trying to violently shake himself away. The Hijra however had his manly hand firmly placed on HBS's shoulder. The demand for money also became more vociferous!

'This is total nonsense!' HBS screamed.

The Hijra took one step forward, closer to the car. He threatened to remove the drape of his cheap sari to show us the mysteries of his manly hemispheres that lay beneath.

'Ok....Ok. I am giving money' HBS conceded in defeat.

He seemed rattled. He hurriedly pulled out a note which was stuck to some card. He handed it over.

The Hijra displayed what he had got. He had got a ten rupee note and a visiting card of HBS!

'Oh my God! I gave ten rupees!' HBS screamed in shock.

Clutching his chest, he seemed to be having an on the spot financial heart attack. The Hijra was happy with the money. He circled the note and visiting card around HBS's head and this time, blessed him, his friends and his family. With the note firmly in his hand, the Hijra smiled at us and walked away.

HBS was angry. At being manhandled and being forced to give ten rupees!

He had to vent his frustration on someone. That someone was *me.*

'Why did you want to give money to that stupid beggar boy?'

'Actually....' I replied.

'I don't want any of your stupid explanations.'

Not only financial decisions *but even* explanations were controlled by him.

If I had given the urchin 2 rupees, we would not only have saved 8 rupees as the driver could have immediately drawn up the centrally controlled windows but also the Hijra would not have had the 'pleasurable opportunity' of manhandling HBS!

The traffic pile up finally cleared.

All the cars started in a mad rush to escape the clutter and raced away. Unclear as to whom to remove his further frustrations on, HBS screamed at the driver this time, to start the engine.

The beginning to our off-site could not have begun on a more entertaining note. The driver was screamed at. I was screamed at. HBS was rattled. He was manhandled. He was part molested. But at least a curse was lifted and he was finally blessed! He had also done his bit for philanthropy for the financial year after much confusion and resistance!

2
BIKINI GIRLS

We were finally in the Devanahalli airport after a two hour long drive.

'With great power comes great responsibility…it's your gift…it's your curse'. This is vaguely what Uncle Ben had told the immature Peter Parker prior to his transformation into a completely 'focused' Spiderman in the first installment of the *Spiderman* series.

After we had checked in and after much thought and deliberation, HBS granted me a limited clerical power. The clerical 'power' was to purchase a birthday 'gift' for the Founder whose birthday was on the following day- the first day of the off-site.

He wanted me to go to the airport bookstore to look at gift options.

As he relaxed setting into his la-la holiday mood in the departure lounge, I started to walk towards the bookshop. Suddenly, he seemed to have a quick rethink about whether to accompany me and whether I was capable and competent enough to buy the gift.

'So what are you planning to get the Big Boss?' he asked me.

'Some sort of gift?'

'No…No…No.'

He sounded shocked as if I had robbed a bank or something.

'Ok. So what should I get?' I asked.

'I think you should look at good books on leadership and management. My nephew also reads such books. I think he has got my brains.'

'Hmmm'

'Are you sure you can select good books?' he asked me again.

'I can try.'

'It is important to get a good book. By giving a good book, we will be more intelligent in the Big Boss's eyes. I am sure the others will give him some stupid gift or something. We should never miss a chance to look smart, you see?'

'Ok.'

'I don't think you seem confident.'

'No. I can go get...'

'I shall come!' he said, revoking the power bestowed upon me.

'Why don't you start looking for a book and get my approval? I shall look for a birthday greeting card in the cards section' HBS told me inside the airport bookshop.

I nodded.

In the management section, I found two books on 'leadership and management' which would keep HBS and his nephew happy. Both books seemed full of management jazz. One on 'Corporate Excellence' seemed over 160 pages. The other, on the 'Essence of Leadership for Modern Corporations' was around 600 pages. Armed with both the books, I went in search of him in the cards section.

He was not there.

He was standing all alone in the magazine section located in a corner of the bookshop.

His face was completely hidden and was immersed in a rather oversized magazine. He seemed oblivious to the world around him. He did not seem to notice me, his 'clerical' subordinate, standing obediently with the books, waiting for his approval.

The cover of the magazine he was peering into was very interesting.

It was an extreme delight for my sore eyes too, which had spent most of the previous weeks peering into boring numbers in Excel. Staring at me from the cover was a skimpily clad, two-piece bikini model with a seductive pout and with sand all over her body. Droplets of sand and sweat glistened in her cleavage.

It was a swimsuit magazine.

If the cover was anything to go by, the inner contents displaying more skimpily clad moments of photographic delight definitely justified his immense levels of concentration!

Flipping a page of the magazine, he saw me observing him.

With a sudden violent movement, he tried to put the magazine back in the rack. However the hurriedness of the action did not enable the magazine to nestle back comfortably in the book rack. It seemed like it was a protest from the bikini girls who did not want to be neglected all of a sudden by a staring, salivating mid thirty plus financial advisor!

In a feeble attempt at a cover up, he violently pulled out a *Fortune* business magazine from the rack. He appeared to be completely engrossed in its contents. The swimsuit magazine was still in his hand. He tried to sheepishly hide the magazine under the weight of the thick *Fortune* magazine which had a smiling, bald business leader on the cover.

HBS really must have thought that I was an imbecile of sorts and not as smart as his little nephew to understand what just happened.

'I think we should subscribe to the *Fortune* magazine' he told me, fumbling for words to move past the awkward bikini moment.

'Ok.'

'Good information content. See... a good article on improving the productivity levels. It is by a management guru.'

'Ok.'

'See...another good article on how to enhance the performance of your assets.'

The bikini girl secretly wrapped under the Fortune magazine might approve of that statement.

'See...another really good article on enhancing the bottom line.'

Another point which the bikini girl with her glistening cleavage might approve of!

'Oh....oh...you found a book?'

'I found two actually. One is on leadership and the other on corporate excellence' I replied displaying both the books.

'I think we should present this book' he said, plucking the 600 page leadership book from my hand, while balancing the magazines in the other.

He weighed the book in his hand.

'It's cheaper, thicker and has more pages. Good value for money' he told me.

'Ok.'

'It is also very heavy....'

Trying to balance the heavy book in one hand and the light magazines in the other like a juggler was an impossible task. He made a complete mess of it.

The book and the magazines dropped to the floor.

The truth was out in the open.

On the floor, the skimpy model with her sultry pout was staring at the business leader in his pinstripes on the *Fortune* cover. The smiling business leader on the cover seemed to be marvelling at his good fortune at being checked out by a bikini model despite having the ugliest, bald head any leader could have!

'Oh! How did this magazine fall down?' he asked me.

He probably expected me to be surprised on the unexpected appearance of a swimsuit magazine under the *Fortune* magazine.

'I don't know' I replied, circling my eyeballs in a quick rotation to act surprised.

'I am still surprised how this magazine fell down' he told me, looking upwards at the ceiling of the bookshop.

'Hmmm'

'Why don't you go stand in the counter to bill the book? I shall go get a greeting card. I still don't get it how this magazine came in, inside the *Fortune* magazine.'

I wished he would stop sounding like a guilty broken record.

I began walking to the billing queue.

'I like this birthday card' HBS told me, joining me at the billing queue.

I nodded. I really did not care what he had bought.

'10% of the cost of this card is going towards charity for the clothing of poor children. It is good that the companies are doing something for the poor. It is important to wear good clothes in the cold.'

Would the skimpy bikini girls agree?

'Hmmm'

'Open and see the card, so that you can buy similar cards for future occasions.'

A simple act of buying a stupid birthday card had become a HBS mission to educate me. Hiding my irritation, I opened the card. It was nice and simple with no messages, text or images to offend the sentiments of any age group concerned. It was a plain Jane card with simple border decorations. It seemed like the art work of a young KG kid experimenting with a blank A4 printer size paper, colours and scissors for the first time!

We walked to the departure lounge with the leadership book and the birthday card tucked under my hand.

We finally took our seats in the Kingfisher flight.

'The travel agent shouldn't be sending us on the same flight' HBS told me as he adjusted his seat belt.

'Why?' I asked.

'In case- the plane is hijacked, bombed or something happens…who will run the office? Plus this year we have stiff year end targets to meet. We need less stress.'

I wondered to myself.

It would be nice if the flight was hijacked. HBS would be handcuffed by a terrorist outfit and taking to an undisclosed terror camp location in Pakistan. A press denial would be issued by their government of their role in the hijacking. To avoid the gaze of the international media, HBS would then be covertly moved up the Khyber pass to Afghanistan. There, the actual terror zealots would realize that, HBS was a useless, good for nothing rabble rousing financial advisor who was good only at petty money laundering and in fighting for mutual fund commissions. He was not of any diplomatic significance whatsoever for India! In a surprising act of benevolence, the zealots would have him deported free of cost back to WCA Bangalore!

'Please turn off all electronic devices' the sexy red skirted airhostess instructed HBS as she walked past us.

'I shall turn off my BlackBerry. Very busy you see' he told her with a smile while furtively trying to hide the wedding ring on his finger.

The airhostess also smiled. The cosmetic smile which was plastered 24/7 for a happy customer experience. HBS though did not mind. A normal human while greeting another normal human would try and make eye contact. He however was making eye contact a few inches below...with her breasts. He was staring without a care in the world.

'I like the service. Very efficient and very nice people' he told me about the cabin crew.

The flight captain finally made the announcement that we were about to take off. The flight slowly taxied off the runaway.

We were up in the late afternoon sky. Bangalore receded from my view.

The excitement of the off-site had begun.

3

THE PASSIONATE COUPLE

We reached the Indira Gandhi International Airport on time.

It was around seven in the evening.

We now had to make a dash for the Old Delhi Railway Station which was quite a distance away. En route to the railway station, as we were entering the stretch leading to Satya Niketan (the South Campus, Delhi University area), HBS had this tremendous urge to relieve himself. The cups of free orange juice and coffee which he had consumed on the flight needed an outlet for expression.

Shuffling uneasily in his seat, he could not take it anymore.

'Arre driverji…stop the car' he shouted at our taxi driver. Our white Indica was abruptly halted. The forces could no longer be controlled.

For a man in distress, the God perched way up above in the skies, always provides alternatives to tackle the challenges. Seated in the car, the alternatives on offer for HBS to relieve his tensions were-

1. A typical coffee shop (with a bathroom) which was staring right at us in the face.

2. A public urinal which stated-

FOR NUMBER ONE-ONE RUPEE

FOR NUMBER TWO- TWO RUPEES
Which number do you want?

3. And a good old filthy yet friendly roadside wall which stated-

URINE IS PROHIBITED HERE. DO NOT PASS URINE HERE.
PLEASE PASS ELSEWHERE.
THIS IS THE UNIVERSITY AREA

Standing outside the car in apparent discomfort, HBS started mentally evaluating the pros and cons of each of the options available to him while cross checking with me-

1. Coffee shop- 'It could be very crowded. Plus they could make me buy a cappuccino. Why waste money? What do you think?'

2. Public urinal-'It could be very filthy. More importantly, what if they do not have change for my five rupee coin? What do you think?'

3. Friendly roadside wall- 'I am a financial advisor. If someone sees me pissing, it could affect the brand name of WCA. What do you think?'

After some time- a time in which a chimp could have eaten a banana and a man could have pissed, he finally took a decision.

'I shall go to the public toilet and come' he told me, hobbling in discomfort towards the 'one rupee' urinal.

The job did not seem done.

'Filthy! The Delhi Government has no respect for the tax payer's money. The place is full of flies and shit' he remarked hobbling back in disgust.

I nodded sympathetically.

'THIS IS TOO MUCH! I CANNOT CONTROL IT ANYMORE!' he screamed in anguish.

He stomped angrily towards the friendly roadside wall- the last option in the 'alternatives' hierarchy. Like water gushing rather menacingly through a dam, which has burst open due to a crack on account of years of Government neglect, he pissed right onto the dirty roadside wall lining the South Campus University Area.

'I really have this new found *extra* respect for women. I think they have this power' he told me after having relieved himself.

'What power?' I asked.

'We are guys. We can go on the road but women cannot. Public toilets are also so filthy. I think they have this magical holding power which allows them to control for much longer than us. Maybe it is scientifically proven. I need to check.'

At the signal at Satya Niketan, we passed a road side sign of Castrol, the lubricant oil manufacturer which perhaps summed up what HBS was trying to tell me, of what separates women from the men with regards to their magical holding powers-

It's More Than Just Oil. It's Liquid Engineering.

We got stuck in another traffic jam near Sri Venkateswara College just past the South Campus stretch.

In an auto next to our taxi, a young passionate couple probably just in or out of college were busy expressing their love for each other oblivious to the stares of the outside world. A well lit street light offered a good view. The slender fingers of the girl's right hand had surreptitiously made its way through, to the top of her boyfriend's shirt button and was engaged in a bit of tender stroking of a tuft of his curly chest hair. The boy's left arm was tightly wrapped around his girl with his long, hairy fingers sliding below the lines of her frayed top merrily caressing the ampleness of her disproportionate, cellulite laden left hip.

This curvy, non-size zero left hip was on display to the four of us- our taxi driver, their auto driver, HBS and me.

While we were all enjoying the bodily sights on offer, it offended HBS's moral brigade 'sense and sensibilities'. 'Our generation has lost all its values! This is not in our Indian culture!' he told me. It was pretty hypocritical hearing that given that he was staring the most.

He certainly deserved to become a member of the Taliban or at least a financial advisor for them!

Not conforming to any traditional rules was our taxi driver.

'Yeh...dilli hai mere yaar...bas ishq, mohabbat, pyaar...' the driver hummed the song merrily to himself from the movie *Delhi-6*.

It seemed like he wanted something more than just deriving mere, vicarious pleasure from observing the passionate college love on offer. He removed his mobile phone, a pretty nice looking Samsung from his pocket and put it on camera mode. Conveniently turning around, while holding his camera phone at the right angle to capture the steamy moments on offer, he started talking with his counterpart-the driver of the auto. The auto driver generously moved his auto just a bit ahead. Our taxi driver smiled at him, his partner in this mission.

Our driver seemed to have got a perfect angle for a perfect 'college-auto' You Tube video which could catapult him towards internet riches! With the angle in place, the drivers started muttering to each other in Hindi possibly working on a revenue sharing agreement from the sale of this passionate romantic video clip!

The signal turned green after a while. Our taxi was slow to get off the blocks.

'Driver, jaldi chalo...' HBS screamed at the driver in Hindi.

'Arre saab, picture abhi baaki hai merai dost.... ' the driver replied SRK style.

He turned his head around in true filmy style and smiled at us. He was happy with the work he had done.

Our taxi finally moved, taking a left leading towards the ring road.

The couple's auto took a U-turn entering another loosely populated, long stretch to merrily continue their passionate indulgences. Seeing this, I could now probably place in context, the famous poem "*The*

Road Not Taken" by Robert Frost-

".....Two roads diverged in a wood and I-
I took the one less travelled by,
And that has made all the difference."

4
THE TEAM

We finally reached the Old Delhi Railway station at around 9 p.m.

The station was buzzing with activity.

'Keep the change' HBS magnanimously told the old porter who laboriously lifted his two suitcases and his cricket kit (I carried my own suitcase) across four platforms including an overhead connecting bridge. His coarse hands and sweaty armpits spoke of years of toil. He asked for 45 Rs. HBS haggled with him as though his life depended on it and gave him 35 Rs. The porter thought he could use his old age as an emotional mechanism to bargain for more money. Unfortunately it was not to be. 'Kanjoos aadmi' he remarked. He grudgingly put the money in a secret pocket in his sweat soaked vest inside his red shirt. He then rubbed his coolie badge with his sweaty hands and walked away.

We greeted the team from Mumbai and Delhi.

They were standing on the platform in comfortable groups waiting for our train, the Ranikhet Express. This was the first time I was meeting them. Barring HBS and the Big Boss-our company Founder, all the others were strangers. The off-site would hopefully change all of that. All of them were guys. Most were in their late thirties and forties.

They looked tired and quite indifferent to the off-site. Obviously the experience of a company off-site was not new to them. I wondered what had happened to all the women of our company.

The branch heads of the Mumbai and Delhi teams were in serious discussions. After all, the best financial advisor of the year award would be decided from one of the smart men standing on the platform in front of me. I thought to myself that I had to stop acting immature and flippant about work goals. I had to adopt a more focused, serious outlook to life like them, if I ever aspired to climb the corporate ladder and join their ranks.

'Hi, you're the team from Bangalore right?' a rather effeminate voice asked us. It belonged to a man who was dressed in Reebok track pants. He carried a notebook in his hand and wore a black marker pen in a circular loop around his neck.

'Yes' HBS replied.

'I am the coordinator and the HR Trainer of the off-site. Welcome' he said.

The Trainer extended his hand for a friendly handshake. He spoke to the group in the most mellifluous of voices. His Adam's apple seemed to have been misplaced in transit during puberty. He seemed to have suffered from an estrogen overdose while growing up resulting in this dainty, bambie deer like characteristics. Most of the financial advisors seemed to have enjoyed a testosterone overdose during puberty, resulting in alpha male sort of features like the living example-HBS!

HBS exchanged quick pleasantries with the groups without mingling with them. He was busy fidgeting with his BlackBerry, acting busy and desperately trying to disengage himself from any possible small talk with the team members. No one sought his company either. Clearly others also disliked him. No wonder he did not have friends his age and enjoyed dominating me all the time!

He moved towards the Founder.

Obviously the 'Big Boss' was important enough in the hierarchy for him to speak to! I had also met the Founder a few times and on each occasion I had found him to be affable, enthusiastic and pleasant. He was in his late forties. He had an imposing presence. He certainly was a true team leader for WCA. I still remembered how he had taken my job interview and the effort he had taken in coming to Bangalore to celebrate our year end success.

'How was your game of golf?' HBS asked the Founder.

'It was good. I have come straight from the golf course. But I need to practice more to bring down my handicap' the Founder replied. He was smartly dressed in his golfing trousers and t-shirt and was carrying a solitary golf club.

'Given the amount of rain in Delhi nowadays, it must have been quite a challenge to get a game of golf?'

'Well…the course was a bit damp. But there was no water logging like in the city. The Delhi Golf Club has one of the best drainage facilities.'

The Founder spoke with evident pride about his preferred golf course.

'That's what I thought…the outfield must have been wet.'

'Well yes. The greens were a bit damp but it was still in good condition. This is golf not cricket…greens *not* outfield.'

'Oh.'

HBS excused himself to attend to a call.

'How have you been?' the Founder asked me.

I was finally noticed. I felt happy that I was recognized.

'Good. I am enjoying the challenges' I replied insincerely.

'Can I just talk to you for one second?' HBS asked me, abruptly interrupting my conversation with the Founder. His voice had assumed a sense of significance. He probably feared that my conversation with the Founder could lead to a bigger role for me at WCA. His authority could be compromised.

This was the height of insecurity!

'Any idea what was the closing value of the Sensex today?' he asked.

'I didn't check.' I replied. *He had a BlackBerry. He could access the info for himself. Why did he want me to check?*

'Oh, no. It is important to know. One more thing....'

'What?'

'Was that one crore cheque deposited this morning in the high value transfer?'

A high value transfer was a transfer of funds of a high denomination.

'What *transfer*?'

I was all confused. What transfer was he talking about? To the best of my memory, I had completed all pending work related tasks.

'Just call up this number and see if the high value transaction has gone through.'

He showed me a number on his phone. *It was his driver's mobile number!*

'Why don't you call up the bank and confirm?'

'But this is...'

'Just call up and confirm. Keep me posted' he commanded in his 'emergency' tone as if someone was in the ICU.

I moved to a side of the platform and called up his driver.

'Did you deposit the high value cheque of one crore this morning?' I asked him.

The driver did not seem to know it was me on the line. He informed me that he hated being disturbed during the evening and night time! His speech sounded slurred. In a combination of broken Hindi and English he muttered that his boss-a stupid, stingy bastard has threatened to cut his body and his salary!

The driver was definitely inebriated. He told me he had *never* seen more than a few hundred rupees in his wallet at any given point in time! This was because his boss was a stingy bastard who never gave salary increments!

He cut the call.

I came back to inform HBS about the situation.

'Did you call? Did the high value transfer happen?' he asked me expectantly with the Founder within earshot.

'I called but actually....' I replied. I was confused with where this discussion was headed.

'So the high value was done? Great! More business for team Bangalore' he stated, cutting short my explanation.

'But...'

'Good work.'

He patted me on my shoulder.

'In Bangalore, I always tell my team to be extremely efficient and proactive in dealing with client business matters' HBS told the Founder.

'Good going. What business?' the Founder asked excitedly.

'Well, I am working on a big transaction for a new client.'

'Good work! Fantastic enthusiasm even now during the off-site! Keep it going!'

All the other advisors standing around the Founder looked at HBS with irritation. Talking about work at the beginning of an off-site would certainly not please anyone.

'Well thanks! Bangalore is a performing team.'

'No wonder you are in the running for the best financial advisor of the year award. Well done!'

'Thanks. I always push my team to its limits.'

He certainly made me slog like an orphaned donkey.

The Founder walked away to talk to the others.

HBS looked at me and winked. He was a man on a mission even during this off-site!

I suddenly realized that the entire telephone call had been a bullshit drama staged by him to show his might! By forcing me to make the call and then praising the efficiency of the team, he wanted to show the kind of premium that was attached to his time and the nature of 'big ticket transactions' we executed for clients! And to top it all, the kind of efficient subordinates *like me* whom he had at his disposal to get these little jobs done!

'I think I should take up golf. It is a good platform to network with

HNI clients' he told me, while shaking his body.

I nodded.

'I should check the procedure to be *legible* for the club membership at the KGA golf club in Bangalore. I want to be *legible* as a corporate member only. I shall speak to the Delhi office.'

'You should.'

The Ranikhet Express arrived.

'Three of the team members are yet to come' the Trainer told the Founder.

'Don't worry. Two of the women from our Delhi team have come. There they are-' the Founder said, pointing in a direction behind me.

I turned and looked around.

Two lady advisors from the Delhi team had arrived. They were dressed in almost matching light blue salwar kameez suits. Their dupattas were also colour coordinated in a bright pink colour. They were aunty types in their mid to late thirties. Not hot. But at least there were some females around. The Aunties exchanged brief pleasantries with their Delhi team members. Aunty no 1 was holding a mutual fund fact sheet of all things! Aunty no 2 seemed to have walked straight out of a regressive saas-bahu serial with her garish jewellery, faint traces on sindoor on her forehead and a thick film of makeup covering the bags under her eyes.

They huddled together and kept to themselves.

Aunty no 1 was reading data aloud from the fact sheet to herself. The fact sheet was a monthly document containing details on the various mutual fund schemes. It was the sort of document which could keep a very keen mutual fund investor without an interesting social life busy over an entire weekend.

Aunty no 2 was busy glancing at her wrist watch and was irregularly blinking her eyes. Dark circles encircled her eyes like bags of charcoal. Maybe she had run out of cucumber as a part of her daily face pack regimen. Maybe she was sad that she was missing her quota of TV serials for the next few days. Hopefully she had Tata Sky Plus to record her TV serials.

The Trainer struck names off a list in his notebook.

'A Delhi advisor is missing. He will come at the end. He is invariably late. There is nothing to worry. We can start boarding if you wish' the Founder continued.

'That's better. Plus we can make more room for the luggage in the coach' the Trainer said.

'There he is!' the Founder exclaimed.

The final member- the Delhi colleague for our off-site had arrived. He was walking towards us.

'Finally! He should learn to value people's time' the Trainer said, glancing at his Timex wrist watch.

'Oh! There comes the idiot. He is late as always!' Aunty no 1 told her friend, who was standing in front of me.

'He can do anything he wants. After all, his uncle is the biggest HNI client of our Delhi office. He gives us the maximum business' Aunty no 2 replied.

'I know. No wonder the Big Boss tolerates him. If I owned WCA, I would fire the idiot right now!'

'I wish that day would come soon.'

'But I don't think anything will change. The after effects of the recession are still being felt. Everyone needs his uncle as a client for the business.'

'That's true.'

'I hate him. He is such an idiot!'

I turned to look at the much *reviled* idiot.

Fast approaching us was the Delhi colleague who was around my age. His Man Friday of sorts- a typical Ramu kaka type, was carrying his suitcase by his side.

Four distinctive features separated this guy from the rest of us.

The first was the set of prosperity lines which ran across his broad, expansive forehead seamlessly, like a series of moist-white parallel railway tracks. The moist whiteness was on account of the merry union of the white ash mark which was smattered across his forehead and the generous droplets of the Delhi sweat. The second image was the manner in which he had worn his trousers. In this day and age of dangerously 'low waist-low rise' trousers, his black trouser was dangerously 'high rise', bunching up merrily way up above his belly button, closer to his chest! He did not dress like the average twenty something Indian male. But his clothes and belt looked new and expensive. The top brands seemed to rest easily on his rich, under toiled shoulders with the same ease with which the snake skin covered Mallika Sherawat in *Hisss.* His red GAP t-shirt looked quite impressive. His stylish shining black Bulchee belt looked liked it was a recent purchase. He obviously was an expensive shopper unlike the cost conscious me, who always shopped in Karol Bagh or in Sarojini market. In Bangalore, on weekends, time permitting, I would rush to the discount factory outlet stores in Marathahalli to shop. The third image of the guy was of the index finger of his right hand which was in his right nostril. This finger was quite stubborn and was refusing to come out during the length of his walk across the platform. And finally, he had what none of us in the group had- he had a black mole on his right cheek. Disgusting strands of black hair peeked out of the mole like an attention seeking marigold protruding out of a basket of assorted flowers.

'Theek hai kaka. Mein samaan rakh lunga. Teen-char din baad miltai hai' the Delhi colleague said to his kaka. He had a loud booming voice with impressive clarity. It was as if he had a baby Bose speaker for lunch. He removed his finger from his nose and removed 100 rupees from his pocket and gave it to his kaka. The kaka in turn hugged him and walked away.

The Delhi colleague walked towards the Aunties. He greeted Aunty no 2.

'Hello' she told him rather forcefully. She seemed like she did not want to have a conversation with him.

'Sasuma pranaam' he replied jokingly. He seemed unaffected by her indifference.

'Stop it, you idiot! Don't make fun of me like you do in office.'

'Theek hai. Mujhse galti ho gayi. Maaf kar do.'

'Shut up.'

'Kyon shut up? Kya aaj, aap merai liye off-site ka vrath rakhenge?'

'That's it! One more word out of you and I will complain.'

'Ok, I am sorry again. Gussa kyon hoti ho?'

'Tum bewakoof ho isi liye.'

'Nahi! Mein bewakoof nahi hoon! Mein lover hoon. Mere dil mein dard ho raha hai.'

He rubbed his chest vulgarly.

'Saala nautanki. Total namuna. Drame baaz' Aunty no 2 concluded with irritation.

The Trainer arrived.

'Welcome to the off-site. So you finally arrived…on time' he told the Delhi colleague rather sarcastically.

'Got delayed' the Delhi colleague replied, without a hint of an apology.

'We should all now board quickly. The train is about to leave.'

The Trainer went back into the train to check the arrangements.

'Hi, you are from Wealth Capital Advisors, right?' the Delhi colleague asked me.

'Yes, I am from the Bangalore team' I replied.

We shook hands though I really did not want to after having seen his finger in his nose.

'Who is he?' he asked about the Trainer.

'He is the off-site Trainer' I replied.

'What happened to his voice? It sounds like that of an item girl.'

'No idea.'

'Get IDEA.'

He laughed at his own version of the mobile service provider advertisement.

I checked the reservation chart to find my seat number. A large part of the AC three tier coach had been booked to accommodate our entire WCA team. Me, HBS, the Aunties and this crazy Delhi colleague were all in one compartment.

We entered the coach.

The Aunties had already put their suitcases in our compartment. They were not there. They must have gone to the restroom.

'Aahhh…I think I have stretched a muscle' HBS winced in pain, all of a sudden, placing his suitcases under the seat.

'Why? What happened?' I asked.

'I think I twisted my left hand. I am also feeling pain in my back.'

'Your hand is paining but why are you rubbing your ass?' the Delhi colleague asked him.

'You mind your own business! I know all about you' HBS replied, rather curtly.

'It's good that you know all about me. But what happened to you?'

'I have been having a lot of *tits* with my wife. I also had a *tit* yesterday. By mistake she twisted my hand. It is hurting now.'

'What *tit*? Was it a big or a small one?'

'It was nothing too big or small. It was just a casual *tit*.'

HBS's BlackBerry rang. He walked away to attend to the call.

'What did he mean by *tits*?' the Delhi colleague asked me excitedly.

'I guess he meant tiffs' I replied.

'Or maybe he had a *tiff* over the choice of tits.'

The colleague broke out in a crazy laugh. I also smiled.

'He occasionally interchanges words and meanings. Just now, before boarding, he got confused between *eligible* and *legible*. But it does not matter to him' I told him.

'That's interesting. Have you noticed another interesting thing?'

'What?'

'He scratches so much. Do you know why?'

'How will I know?'

I wanted to play it safe.

'Bangalore mein, itna garmi to nahi hai na?'

'No.'

'Ye banda bahut khujli karta rahata hai. Yeh toh insaan se KKR ban gaya.'

'What's KKR-The IPL cricket team?'

'No…not the cricket team. This guy has become a khujli karnewala rakshas!'

I started laughing.

HBS was back. I stopped laughing.

'What is the laughter all about?' he asked.

'We were talking of men and their personal body problems' the Delhi colleague stated.

HBS nodded vaguely.

'We should all learn to respect our bodies and check for body problems, immediately' he said. He then scratched.

The train started to slowly move.

The off-site was now well and truly underway.

5

THE VIRGIN

'Welcome all of you. Hope you all enjoy this off-site. We will be reaching the Ramnagar station by 5.15 in the morning' the Trainer told us as he entered our compartment. He seated himself on the lower berth.

'We will surely enjoy' Aunty no 1 assured him on our behalf.

'I selected Kyari for this off-site because it is a lovely secluded spot. With its cool temperature it will be a great break from city life.'

'I am quite surprised how come it hasn't been used for film shootings so far. Or has it?'

'Good point. I don't think films have been shot there.'

'Once when I went to Switzerland, I had witnessed a movie shooting' HBS chipped in.

'Wow. Was it a Yash Chopra movie?' I asked excitedly.

I quite liked masala Bollywood movies.

'No. I think it was a Kannada or Tamil movie' he replied.

'Where?' Aunty no 1 asked, glancing up from her fact sheet.

'In a place called Lucerne. It was a song sequence I think.'

'All songs filmed in Switzerland are pretty much the same' the Delhi colleague remarked.

'I would disagree' HBS replied strongly.

'I still maintain all songs filmed there are more or less the same.'

'They are not.'

'Guys, it is not worth fighting and losing your cool. The whole purpose of this off-site is relax and enjoy' the Trainer said.

It looked like his unspoken role was to soothe ruffled feathers and prevent ego clashes as and when they arose during the off-site!

'The best part of the trip was that I also accidentally bumped into a celebrity' HBS continued.

'Celebrity?' I asked quite excitedly.

'Guess.'

'Was it an actor?'

'No. Guess again.'

'Was it a diplomat?'

'No. That's also wrong. Guess again.'

This game of twenty questions could go long into the night!

'Footballer?' Aunty no 1 asked.

'No. But you are getting close.'

'Was it a tennis player?' the Delhi colleague asked.

'Yes! That's correct! I met Roger *Fredericks*.'

'You mean Roger Federer!'

The Delhi colleague had a look of absolute disbelief.

'Ah...yes! Federer or *Fredericks*....it is just a name. How does it matter?'

Was he kidding? Was Roger Federer just another name? This was just, yet another installment in HBS's lack of knowledge in all matters non-financial!

'Where did you meet Roger Federer?' the Delhi colleague questioned.

'I met him in Basel, towards the end of June 2006.'

'It has to be a mistake. It cannot be possible.'

'What do you mean? Why can't it be possible?'

HBS seemed hurt by the accusation levelled against him.

'In June end 2006- Federer was at Wimbledon en route to winning the championships!'

'But I met him in Basel and took his autograph.'

'I don't think it is possible. I think you are mistaken.'

'I am correct!'

'No. You are not. I watch tennis-especially Wimbledon. I don't think *Fredericks* or Federer would leave Wimbledon, fly down to Basel, sign an autograph for you and return to Wimbledon and win the trophy.'

The Delhi colleague had rather clinically put the sequence of events in place.

'Well said' Aunty no 1 chipped in.

She was smiling. So were the rest of us.

'Well maybe I shook hands with some one else by mistake and took an autograph' HBS replied meekly.

'I am sure that is what happened' the colleague concluded.

'Sorry to cut the discussion short. I have been informed that the dinner will be served shortly. Guys enjoy the off-site. Party like never before. I will be coming back shortly to make an announcement' the Trainer told us.

He walked out of our compartment.

'We are going to meet the others' the Aunties told us.

They also trudged out of our compartment.

'Next time don't you dare cut me like that' HBS told the Delhi colleague rudely.

'Cut you regarding what?' he asked.

'You cut me when I said that I saw *Fredericks* in Switzerland.'

'Are you stupid or what? It is FEDERER!'

'Mind your language. Just because your uncle is a big client, don't act over smart with me.'

'I can do anything I want. You mind your business and I shall mind my business.'

HBS looked very irritated.

No one had spoken to him like that! Ever!

As we were sitting, a woman out of nowhere, possibly from another coach, came and occupied the lower side berth. She was hot. She started unpacking some stuff from her suitcase. Her black lacy bra accidentally popped out of her suitcase and fell on the aisle passageway. She looked at us, without a trace of embarrassment. Out of the corner of my eye, I saw that it was the Lovable lingerie brand. If my underwear had fallen out in front of a girl, I would have squirmed a little bit and looked askance out of the window or at the chain in the compartment to stop the train.

'Look at that chick, man' the Delhi colleague muttered to me.

'Hmmm' I grunted as HBS was around.

'Do you like her fine legs? I don't know about you but I also like her big breasts, man.'

I remained silent.

'Rate her on a scale of 1-10. Think of her as a mutual fund and see if she fits in your investment portfolio.'

The Delhi colleague was unstoppable.

I still remained silent.

'Is this how you talk about a woman?' HBS whispered to him with his eye firmly fixed on the black bra. After picking up her bra, the woman put it in her suitcase and walked away towards the wash room.

'Yes. I will talk about chicks the way I want to. What will you do?' the Delhi colleague answered loudly, since the woman was not there.

'Why don't *you* rate her? You seem to be an expert' HBS asked him.

'I will give her 12/10. Nice body. Nice ass. Her ass fits in her body nicely like a 14 inch TV would in the budget of a middle class family. Actually I would give her 14/10.'

'Are you mad or what to talk like this about women?'

'No, I am not mad.'

'Then why are you talking like this about women?'

'I will talk the way I like. The Indian Constitution has given every citizen the freedom of speech.'

'Are you a horny virgin or what to talk like that?'

'No. For your information, I am a South Indian Iyer Brahmin.'

'What relevance does that have in this context?'

'I am a horny virgin Brahmin. I think of chicks all the time. I appreciate mostly external beauty but deep down, I also seriously respect internal beauty. Having said that, every woman I see, I assess and evaluate. Do you have a problem with that?'

The colleague was funny. He spoke with remarkable candour!

'Are you serious?'

'Yes I am. You are pretending like you don't think of women all the time. I am sure even you check them out, just that you are hypocritical and will not admit to it!'

'What do you mean? Are you drunk? I am a married, committed man. I also have a small son.'

HBS was *shocked* by the insinuation. He showed us the marriage ring which was on the ring finger of his right hand.

'I am not drunk. You look like the type who would love to have many extra marital affairs.'

'You better think before you talk. I am just not like that! I seriously think you are being rude.'

'I don't care if I am being rude. I speak my mind. Take it or leave it. You also scratch a lot. That is not a right as per our Indian Constitution! I don't like you one bit. I don't get good positive vibes from you. YOU DON'T TALK TO ME!'

The last sentence exploded out loud.

Our small compartment soon became engulfed in silence.

The rating game had gone too far.

HBS had met his match!

Thankfully a full blown altercation was avoided by the arrival of the Trainer. The Aunties also were with him. Thank God, the Aunties had missed this altercation.

'I want to make one more announcement' the Trainer said, entering our compartment.

'Regarding what?' HBS asked.

'I will be conducting a general quiz during the off-site.'

'I love quizzes!'

'To begin with, pair up in teams of two and decide upon a team name.'

'Ok.'

'Even the prize money is very good. It is being sponsored by a fund house.'

'Wow! What is it? Is it going to be movie tickets?'

'No. Not movie tickets. It is even better. The winners get a home theater system!'

The Trainer left our compartment to make the announcement to the other team mates as well.

'So let's register as a team' HBS told me immediately.

'Yaar, how about us?' the Delhi colleague-the Virgin Brahmin asked me.

'You are late! We just registered' HBS stated assertively.

'We should start preparing for the quiz seriously' HBS told me.

'Well to be honest, I am not much into quizzing' I remarked honestly.

'No problem. Don't worry. We shall meet during the off-site and plan for it.'

'Ok.'

'I used to be pretty good in my college quizzes. I am so excited. Let's work as a team and we should WIN.'

'Win? As if! You might win in your dreams' the Virgin muttered.

Our dinner trays arrived to offer some respite from the juvenile altercations.

'So, excited about the off-site? Your first one I guess?' Aunty no 1 asked me.

It was our first proper conversation in the compartment. Both of us were feasting on a cup of sour curds served in the dinner tray.

'Yes. I hope it will be an interesting experience' I replied.

'This food is good. I didn't have breakfast and lunch today. I was fasting' Aunty no 2 chipped in.

'Good woman. Ideal susheel pavitra bharatiya nari. Which vrath did you keep today?' the Virgin asked.

'Keep quiet. Don't make fun. It was for my husband' she replied.

'You shouldn't skip breakfast. It is the most important meal of the day' HBS interrupted, joining in on the discussion.

'I generally skip breakfast. I don't get the time' she replied.

'Missing meals is not a good practice. Today, even I missed my breakfast and as a result I had a very heavy late lunch before my flight. It has impacted my body.'

'No wonder, so many weird noises were coming out from your mouth' the Virgin said.

HBS glared at him.

'I shall ignore that comment. Also if possible, it is very important to have a glass of milk-preferably direct milk. Also the milk should be fresh.'

What on earth was direct milk? Was it milk to be had straight from a Swiss cow's udder rather than from a carton or packet of milk?

'Having milk is important for you women as it helps reduce the chance of ostentation' HBS continued.

'Ostentation?' Aunty no 1 asked.

'Yes. I was reading about it. As women get older, they suffer from ostentation.'

'What has direct milk got to do with a display of wealth?' the Virgin asked.

'Pay attention. What display of wealth? I am talking about ostentation.'

'That is what I am also asking...what has wealth got to do with milk?'

'I am talking about ostentation-the condition in which women suffer from brittle bones' HBS explained.

'One more mistake! That is osteoporosis *not* ostentation!' the Virgin exclaimed.

'That is what I was meant. It's all the same thing.'

'You are paagal, man. A total dhakhan! First you call Federer as '*Fredericks*'! Then you term osteoporosis as '*ostentation*'. You think everything is the same for your paagal brain. And you just told us that you are good in quizzing! You have zero general knowledge!' the Virgin taunted HBS.

Sensing a major showdown the Aunties stood up.

'If you would excuse me, I am just going out' Aunty no 1 announced.

'I am following you' Aunty no 2 said.

The Aunties trudged out of our compartment.

That ended our dinner.

Unlike other groups who were either busy playing cards or were chatting, our group called it an early night. We turned off the lights. The Aunties were on the lower berth. I was on the middle berth and the Virgin was on the upper berth above me. HBS was on the other middle berth.

I got up in the middle of the night.

I saw droplets of water on the right shoulder of my shirt. I looked up. The Virgin was sleeping. His mouth was at an angle, hanging outside his pillow, with drool falling down on my shirt! *Yuck*. He was mumbling something to himself. '*Baarish ho rahi hai...its raining its raining its raining...mere dil ro raha hai...*'. He sounded like Anu Malik in full flight.

I was now fully awake.

With difficulty, I got off the middle berth so as to not stamp Aunty no 2's face.

I walked to the washbasin to wipe the filth off my shirt.

As I was entering back into the A/C coach, all of a sudden, HBS entered from inside and pushed me to a side.

'Thank God you are awake' he told me as we stood next to the washbasin.

'Why?' I asked. I feared the worst. *Was it some emergency?*

'We need to talk about the quiz. I was thinking about it, the entire time.'

Was he mad?

'You want to talk right now?' I asked.

I had to listen. It was not like I had a choice. I glanced at my watch. It was 2.15 a.m. We anyway had to be up by 5 a.m. to pack and get ready.

'I have come up with a team name' he told me.

'Oh. What is it?'

'*Amirchand Express.* What do you think?'

I kept silent to act like I was in thought.

If nothing else, one definite positive of having such a team name was that we might at least win a prize for the oddest sounding team name!

'I thought a lot before reaching this name. *Amirchand* captures the current mood in the markets. Everyone wants to be rich.'

'But what does *Express* stand for?'

'I simply added it!'

'Or maybe *Express* can mean all the investors in a train just like we are all in a train right now.'

'Good observation. A train which moves only upwards with no stops like the Sensex index of 2007.'

'Hopefully no bear market stops!'

'Also keep our team name confidential. Think of it like a non disclosure agreement we sign with clients for confidentiality purposes. Don't disclose anything to him' HBS said, alluding to the Virgin.

'I will not.'

We walked back to our compartment to catch up on some sleep.

MUMMY! DADDY! I SEE DEAD PEOPLE!' the Virgin screamed like a madman waking all of us up. His pillow which was full of his saliva fell out of his berth and sailed through the air and fell on the floor of our compartment.

I glanced at my watch.

It was 4.15 am.

'I MISS MY GRANDFATHER!' he screamed again.

'You bloody fool! Is this a joke or what?' HBS shouted. His hair was all dishevelled. He adjusted something under his white sheet, which a railway attendant had provided. He looked like a scratching ghost.

The Trainer rushed into our compartment. He turned on the light.

'What happened?' he asked the Virgin.

'I think I had a bad dream. A nightmare' the Virgin explained.

'*You* are the nightmare!' Aunty no 2 screamed from the lower berth.

'Ok. Now relax. Try to get some rest' the Trainer said gently.

He walked away.

'I STILL SEE DEAD PEOPLE' the Virgin continued. This time, I think he was pretending just to irritate us. He partially covered his face with the white sheet. He reminded me of Bruce Willis's patient, the small boy in *Sixth Sense*.

We finally reached the Ramnagar railway station at 5.45 a.m.

Our train reached a bit behind schedule.

The early morning sun was fast rising through the picturesque foothills of a mountain range which could be seen in the distance.

The Trainer was right. The temperature was at least a good ten degrees lesser than at the Delhi station. It would hopefully only get cooler and better.

We all got off at the station with our luggage.

PART 2-OFF-SITE-DAY 1

6
ZEROES DIFFERENCE

At the station, the Trainer gave out the list of rooms and room mates.

The Virgin was my room mate. I had to tolerate his psycho tantrums and outbursts for the next three days.

Taxis had been organized to drive us down to our lodge, which we were told was around ten kilometres away.

I was with the Virgin in a taxi which had more pieces of luggage than humans.

We were the only two in the taxi. It was the perfect setting for getting to know the funny psycho better.

'Yaar, so how long have you been in the Bangalore team?' the Virgin asked me as our taxi sped away from the station to the lodge.

'For the last three years and a bit' I replied.

'Fuck. That is a lot of time to tolerate that asshole, man.'

'I guess. He is difficult to get along with but overall it is fine.'

I tried to remain diplomatic.

'Do you want me to speak to the Founder and ask for your transfer to the Delhi office?'

'No…no…not needed. Thanks.'

'Just fight him. Never be scared of him. Darna mana hai. Don't tolerate injustice.'

'Easy for you to say that, man. Some of us have to earn a living.'

'Why? What gave you that impression?'

'I heard your uncle is a big client in the Delhi office?'

'He is not just a big client. He is the baap of all clients! Half of the bloody revenue of the Delhi office comes because of the business my uncle gives.'

'Then why are you even working here at WCA? You can quit whenever you want. Why don't you work with your uncle itself?'

'No, yaar. I want to do my MBA in finance so I want some relevant work experience.'

'Ok.'

'Plus I work only from 9-5. Others work late into the night.'

'Oh.'

'I am not very popular in office.'

'I could make that out.'

'People think life is easy for me, man.'

'Isn't it?'

'Ok, fine. My life rocks. But it is only from the outside. I have three Mercedes, two houses in Jor Bagh, just finalized an investment in GK-2 and I have a flat near the DLF Golf course. I don't think it makes me super rich. But I am mighty comfortable.'

Was he showing off? Well, only a few significant zeroes in the bank account separated him from me.

'Oh. What is missing?' I asked sarcastically.

'Life is not easy for me, man. I am serious. I have to tolerate a lot of things.'

'Like what?'

'My parents died early in a car crash, leaving all this wealth for me. Ever since my parents left me, I have had very low self esteem. I am constantly compared to my business family friends. No one really likes me.'

'Oh.'

'I am not respected for the individual I am. And also, in general I am poorer than others my age.'

'Dude, you are kidding right? You are like the richest among all of us!'

'That's true. I was kidding. But more seriously, in spite of my wealth, chicks don't talk to me. They never want to date me or go out with me.'

'That's surprising, man. I thought you would be quite the 'catch' in the Delhi social circles?'

'No I am not. Chicks don't dig me. I have been rejected many times by girls solely on the basis of my looks. I am aware that I lack clothes sense even though I wear branded stuff.'

'Dude, you have enough money to go for a fashion makeover and for cosmetic surgeries.'

'How many surgeries and body treatments can I have?'

He sounded serious.

'What do you mean?' I asked curiously.

'I used to have a hairy chest like Anil Kapoor and Akshay Kumar. I went for hair removal.'

'Oh.'

'I used to wear thick glasses. To correct that, I went for the lasik eye treatment.'

'Ok.'

'I wear leather shoes specially imported from the US but still no chick notices me.'

I gazed at his stylish moccasins.

'I am short. I am over looked by people in a crowd.'

Yes....he *was* short.

'I once tried to wear heels to look taller.'

'You did?'

'Yes. Everyone made fun of me.'

'I thought as much.'

'I have this mole on my cheek which makes me look bad. I used to think that I look cool like Enrique Iglesias, the singer.'

'Why don't you go for a surgical removal of the mole like he did?'

'I did try but doctors think it is connected to some nerve ending or something. They will not remove it because of possible complications.'

'Oh.'

'In school once, on Valentines day, I gave a girl a card. She threw it back at me calling me a really ugly version of Enrique who incidentally was also the heartthrob for all the chicks at school.'

'Hmmm'

'She also modified that dialogue from the cult classic *Deewar* while insulting me.'

'What did she say?'

'She said tere paas maa nahi hai par mole hai aur mere paas maa hai par mole nahi.'

'Oh.'

I had to control myself from laughing. I found it really hard to believe that a girl would give such a cheesy line to reject a guy.

'I felt really bad. I cried that day. I took back the V day card and tore it to pieces. I threw it in a school dustbin. I still remember the exact moment.'

'Hmmm'

'On another occasion, I tried to sing *Aati kya khandala*...for a girl. I also moved a handkerchief around my neck like a hero.'

'What happened?'

'The girl ran to the department to make a complaint.'

'Oh.'

'And then once during a college fest, on stage, like Salman Khan I started to sing *Oh...Oh...Jaane Jaana...* shirtless, with a guitar in my hand. All the girls who were there, saw me and started to disperse quickly.'

'Hmmm'

'I was left only with my guitar and my shattered confidence.'

'Relax, man.'

'I am ugly. I know it.'

'Dude, it is ok. Relax.'

'Girls want decent looks plus money. I have money but no looks. I have to live with that fact.'

The Virgin turned emotional.

He was silent for a bit. He put his hand on his heart. He touched the mole on his cheek. Was he going to sing a song now like Enrique? Maybe that song-'*Let me be your hero...*'

This gave me a chance to think about my ex-girlfriend from college. I felt I was moderately good looking but I had no money. So were Indian girls hard to please? They seemed to want everything before the guy even turned thirty. What did they offer? Most women became fat after one kid. From what I had heard from some of my married college friends, the new age Indian woman did not look after the in laws, did not cook at all, unlike many of the women of our parents generation. One friend told me that his wife, as part of her initiative to explore the world of culinary adventures, had tried to prepare some yellow dal for dinner. He remarked that it was very watery like what it used to be in his college hostel mess. The wife felt offended. She stopped cooking as he did not appreciate the effort she had taken. As a result, he was forced to eat plates of Maggi which he secretly liked as it reminded him of his good old bachelor days. A cook was then hired. The husband started praising her cooking. And with that began a serious of fights with the wife on what seemed like frivolous issues.

The interplay between a not so evolved Indian male and the new age Indian woman was indeed a subject which authors could definitely explore through their writing.

'I want a woman to appreciate me for my true self' the Virgin continued.

'Don't we all? What is your true self?'

'I am a sensitive, emotional fool. I am not this confident, aggressive person my Uncle's family and people in my society want me to project. I project a rich, arrogant image to cover my insecurities After all, how much importance can an investment in Jor Bagh, a golf villa near the DLF golf course and 3 Mercedes buy right?'

The Aunties were right. He was a total drama queen! A show off with emotions!

Maybe the Virgin suffered from the short man syndrome like Napoleon, in which he used his aggression and monetary might to act as a cloak for his insecurities about his height and other self esteem issues.

'You just told me that like two times!'

'I don't like to show off. I am just stating the facts- Money can't buy true love.'

'Perhaps it can.'

'I just wish sometimes I was middle class like the rest of you.'

If he were middle class, the chances of getting a girl would be even more difficult! His life and times was worth exploring on celluloid. The movie could be titled the '4th Idiot'!

'Hmmm'

'You know what? You have been pretty honest with me. I appreciate that. In office, people are either excessively nice to me or hate me big time.'

'Thanks.'

'Having a good honest talk with someone is hard these days. Either people have no time or they listen to you with some ulterior motive.'

'I guess so.'

Our taxi motored along at a fair clip. The taxi driver drove in a disciplined fashion unlike HBS's driver in Bangalore.

I was feeling sleepy but my attempts at catching a quick cat nap was thwarted thanks to the Virgin's prolonged confession and display of honesty with me. He treated me like a church Father with the taxi seat as some sort of confession box.

'So yaar, are you also a virgin?' he asked me all of a sudden.

'Yes.' I replied. I was taken aback by the direct question.

'Did you ever have a girlfriend?'

'I had one in college. She dumped me.'

'Didn't things happen with her?'

'No. It didn't.'

'Arre I am sorry for the personal questions. Don't worry. Our time will come.'

'Hopefully it will.'

'I want chicks to love me, man. I want some hardcore action.'

'Even I desperately want some action!'

The Virgins of the world would unite and would be led by this rich, rabble rousing Virgin!

'Dude, you were mumbling in your sleep this morning in the train' I said, changing the topic.

'I know.'

'You were talking about seeing ghosts.'

'I know. I keep getting recurring dreams of my grandfather.'

'Oh.'

'I am very attached to my grandfather. He came to Delhi from Erode in Tamil Nadu, many years ago. He was the one who established our family textile business. When my parents died, he raised me. When he died, I started living with my Uncle who now also manages our family wealth, a part of which is invested with WCA.'

'Ok.'

'I had a protected upbringing. Chicks were not allowed to come to my house. I had no interaction with them. It is totally my loss! Even in school and college, chicks stayed away from me. Bedtime was at nine. My life was really disciplined. Can you imagine?'

It was hard for me to think of the Virgin as a stickler for rules.

'I actually can't.'

'As I would get up every morning at 4 a.m., I was greeted with religious hymns playing loudly with my grandfather and my Uncle doing the morning prayers after waking all of us up in our three storied house. I know MS Subbulakshmi's *Suprabhatam* by heart by just listening to it…day in and day out right from my childhood. After the prayers, I had to attend Hindi classes to improve my grasp of the language as my Uncle felt it would help me better when I eventually would join the family business.'

The Virgin's hindi teacher would have taught him shudh hindi. But he seemed to have forgotten everything and instead had become an excellent Hindi song, slang and gaali expert!

'Oh.'

'Also, my grandfather was the one who taught me to put this ash mark on my forehead. Actually, I am not that religious. But if I stop putting it, I feel like I am defying him. So I put it every morning and I often have to suffer ragging from people who don't know the sentimental significance of it.'

I wanted to tell him that the ash mark mixed with the Delhi humidity made a very unholy mess and was a sure turn off with the women. But given his mood swings, he might take offence to what I might want to offer as a suggestion and act pretty caustic and nasty.

Live and let live.

It was better for me to be silent on this matter and join him instead as a silent partner in the HBS bashing!

We passed a small football field, a Montessori school, a stream and villages which were glistening in the morning sunshine. Our taxi finally reached the lodge at our off-site location.

I looked at the lodge. It was a nice looking place of five floors. It was located in the midst of greenery in the middle of nowhere.

It was quite aptly named, *The Paradise in Heaven.*

The rest of the team who had reached just before us were standing in the reception area.

A person from the lodge took my suitcase and greeted me by putting a shawl around me.

The Virgin draped the shawl around his neck like it was an Anaconda.

He also started coughing like he was being strangled. He was a total attention seeker.

I walked to the reception area.

'Welcome all of you. This is officially the beginning of your off-site' the Trainer announced. He asked all of us to stand in line as he jotted down some points in a blue coloured notebook. He was carefully judging everyone's moves and was making notes in his note book. We all stood in a line, like we were in some beauty contest, making ourselves subject to official scrutiny by the others.

'The various activities during this off-site are intended to allow each one of you, to get out of your skins and to put you in a situation where in, your designations, official roles, and ranking do not count. Rather, qualities like team work are necessary to finish the tasks…' the Trainer continued to explain.

'What a dialogue' the Virgin told me.

He was standing next to me.

'….As a team I want all of you to remember that the whole is always greater than the sum of the parts….'

'It is easy for him to say- he is a 2 in 1- he can work under all conditions.'

I was pretty sure that the Virgin with his observations and comments would get me into trouble before this off-site was over.

'….A good team should work in synergy. It should make two plus two equal five and more and *not* just four…'

'He must have failed Maths in school. No wonder he has become a Trainer.'

'….This off-site will teach you to get out of your comfort zone, face challenges, face fear, resolve conflicts and teach you that money is not everything. Money is only a byproduct for a happy life. Above all, it is only a medium to make all of you better human beings….'

'Kya lecture de raha hai?'

I smiled. The Virgin was funny with his observations.

'….Why don't you all, go freshen up and we shall all then meet for breakfast? Post breakfast, we shall have a session of yoga followed by a game of football.'

The gathering dispersed.

The Virgin and I approached the receptionist to collect our room key.

A mountain dog was chained to a table near the reception table. It growled at us welcomingly. The Virgin fearlessly started patting the mountain dog. The dog licked his face giving him a mini bath, making him two tones fairer like what was promised in the fairness cream ads!

HBS arrived.

He collected the key to his room. He was in room 105. Being the Bangalore head, he got a single room on the same floor as the Founder, the Delhi branch head and the Mumbai branch head. The Virgin and I were allotted room 309. The receptionist told us that we were the only ones on the third floor. The rest of the team had been allotted rooms on the ground, first and second floor.

So much for team building!

I was alienated from the big wigs and from everyone else and was rather unwillingly thrown in the company of the Virgin!

'Room partners, eh?' HBS asked me tauntingly as he collected his key.

I nodded.

'Be careful of him. I don't want any damage to you. Lots of work is piling up when we go back.'

'Ok.'

'You mind your tongue' the Virgin told HBS while patting the dog.

'I can tell him anything. We were discussing work' HBS replied.

I kept quiet.

I thought to myself. Maybe my situation was not that bad. The Virgin was obnoxious but it was not like I knew anyone else.

I had to grin and bear his company over the next few days.

Even though it was an off-site...all the teams were pretty much keeping to themselves and to their own friend groups. The Virgin was the only one I was talking to. He was entertaining with his various observations. I quite liked the blunt, aggressive way in which he spoke to HBS. It was something I could never imagine doing. It was similar in style and manner to that of the Naval Commander in our Bangalore office before he had quit.

'Excuse me, sir. Would you like to have some complimentary biscuits?' the receptionist, a tall lanky guy, asked me and HBS.

We nodded.

A young waiter approached us with a tray of biscuits.

He placed two plates of biscuits- chocolate biscuits for us on the table and dog biscuits in the dog bowl for the chained dog.

'Welcome once again, to *The Paradise in Heaven*. Please help yourselves to some crisp chocolate biscuits' he told us.

'Tastes different...it is quite nice. Must be Swiss made' HBS said, munching on the biscuit.

'Wait! Stop! Don't have the biscuit!' the receptionist cautioned us, all of a sudden.

His face looked tense.

'But why?' HBS asked.

More than half the biscuit was already in his mouth.

'It is a dog biscuit not a chocolate biscuit!' the receptionist replied in a shocked manner.

'What!' HBS roared.

The silly waiter had interchanged the plates of biscuits, by giving us the dog biscuits and keeping the chocolate biscuits in the dog bowl beneath us!

Thankfully my tongue had just grazed the edge of the biscuit. HBS was however not that fortunate. A combination of hunger and over eagerness to enjoy the free complimentary biscuit had made him munch on more than half of the dog biscuit!

I was happy.

'I am so sorry, are both of you all right?' the receptionist asked us. He looked really concerned.

We both nodded in the affirmative.

With his cheeks puffed up like a little greedy Somalian refugee boy's first rendezvous with food, HBS did not seem *alright*. The ingredients in the dog biscuits seemed to have caused some sort of reaction in him. He was panting and making a weird sort of moaning noise. While research studies have proved that dogs over time tend to look like their owners, this was probably the first instance of a financial advisor looking a lot like a mountain dog!

'Shabbash ladke!' the Virgin patted the young waiter on his back approvingly.

'Sorry, sir' the waiter replied. He had tears in his eyes. He thought the Virgin was being sarcastic.

'Kuch nahi! Koi load na lai. Tumne kutta ko hi, kutte ka biscuit khila diya hai.'

The Virgin tipped him hundred rupees!

The waiter walked away. He had a look of complete bafflement on his face.

'What is this? Is this a joke? Do you want me to complain? Don't you know who I am?' HBS screamed in irritation at the receptionist.

He was making a slow recovery from his biscuit munch.

'Sorry, sir. It was a genuine mistake' the receptionist pleaded.

'What if something happens to me?'

'Who gives a fuck?' the Virgin commented.

'You keep quiet. Don't act over smart with me. And also mind your language' HBS warned him.

'I won't. Tere baap ka rajya nahi hai' he replied defiantly.

HBS lost his cool. He also resorted to Hindi.

'Baap pe mat ja' he warned the Virgin again.

'I can say anything I want. I told you this earlier also.'

'You can't.'

'Yes, I can. Main tujhe, kutte ki tarah kaid kar lunga.'

The Virgin pointed his finger at the dog leash. This was juvenile but the image of HBS chained like a dog was funny.

HBS was furious. He stormed off with his room key.

We walked up to our room on the third floor.

I did not see any 'Do not disturb' sign on any of the room doors. No other guests seemed to occupy any of the other rooms on the floor.

The entire passageway was eerily silent. It was like a horror movie set in which, even after the cremation of the dead body, the spirit still lurked around in the hallways!

Our room was the second last room on the floor.

We entered our room- Room 309.

The room was quite nice and spacious with 2 single beds. There was no TV. I guess the idea was, for us city dwellers, to be cut away from civilization! In a corner were a set of potted artificial plants. The room also had a balcony. The view from the balcony was stunning. It offered a scenic view of some mountainous range. However pretty scary was the deep drop from the balcony into a steep ditch straight down below.

'Just look at the view' the Virgin remarked, pointing outside our balcony. I nodded in approval.

'Anyways let's unpack. We have to go for yoga and then play football' I told him.

'I don't play football nor do I want to learn yoga from some old yoga guru. A total waste of time and energy! I want to relax.'

He jumped onto his single bed and pretended to sleep.

7
FLEXIBLE YOGA

The Virgin and I were at the recreation room in the lodge.

Black coloured exercise mats were already placed on the floor.

The Trainer dressed in black tights had organized the session of yoga to demonstrate the benefits it could have in calming down, our stressed minds- the hardworking financial advisors! He was followed by an old Yogi who was wearing a loosely tied mustard coloured loin cloth. The Virgin said that he got a feeling that the *langot* baba was a friend of Baba Ramadev. He didn't offer any reasons as to why he felt so. The old Yogi was followed by his assistant, a petite woman probably in her early twenties. She had Shilpa Shetty's yoga DVD in one hand. She placed it on a table in the corner of the room.

'Can yoga cure stress?' our Founder asked the Yogi.

'It cannot cure but can help you handle stress with confidence' he replied.

'I have been doing yoga for many years but I still feel stressed.'

'Maybe your technique has been wrong.'

'So what can be done?'

'Let's go through the basic techniques again. If you do it correctly, it will integrate your body, mind and soul.'

'Ok.'

'Let's restart with the pranayama breathing technique which can cleanse your system.'

Each of us positioned ourselves on our exercise mat placed on the floor.

'My assistant will demonstrate' the Yogi explained.

The petite Yogic Girl took center stage in front of all us.

'I hope all of you are observing me' she stated.

Of course we were observing her!

'Observe me carefully. Don't take deep breaths.'

'She does have big breasts' the Virgin told me, sitting on a yoga mat next to me.

'She said breath *not* breasts. Concentrate!' I replied.

'Loosen your body. Leave it free. Calm yourself.'

'Look at her body, man. She looks so flexible' the Virgin told me, with saliva oozing out of his mouth.

'I know.'

'She must be quite a gymnast in bed also. Just look at her move, man. I want to learn all about tantrik sex. Do you?'

'Of course, I would want to know!'

'Every move she makes…every breath she takes… I will be watching her!'

'That is some English song right?

'Yes.'

'Ok. Let's concentrate, dude.'

The Yogic Girl was in full flight giving us a demonstration.

I observed her to understand the correct breathing technique as her body arched through the air in a series of rhythmical breathing movements.

'Class, since I have now explained it to all of you, why don't all of you try it out?' she asked us.

We all nodded in agreement.

'Be slow and steady. Keep your body loose. Slowly breathe in....' she instructed.

I inhaled.

'Slowly breathe out...'

I exhaled.

'Class are you all feeling better?' she asked us.

'Yes!' we replied.

'Mazaa aa gaya' the Virgin told me, making noises out of his nostrils.

For the next half an hour we practiced some basic yoga techniques with the Yogic Girl helping us with our postures. Whether or not more sessions on breathing would cool down my stressed nerves was a matter of debate. *But I was sure of one thing.* The Yogic Girl and the images of her general calm and her effortless breathing had left an indelible impression on my mind. I was sure that in the future, it would give me confidence to focus on work despite the unwanted, unnecessary clutter caused by HBS.

The old Yogi took center stage again.

He moved one leg over the other, with his hairy leg curving in from an angle! He was some sort of weird flexible man, with his hands also moving under one of his legs and emerging masterly from the side of the other leg! Even attempting these complicated postures seemed rather stressful.

'So complicated, man' the Virgin told me, shifting uneasily on his yoga mat.

'I know.'

'My balls are getting crushed.'

I was stumped for an answer. This was the first time I had heard of such a problem while doing yoga. *Did the yoga DVD on the table have a solution for such a problem?*

'Anyone needs help with their postures?' the Yogic Girl asked.

'I need help! I am confused' the Virgin screamed, thrusting his hands vertically to get her attention.

'Sure' the Yogic Girl replied.

She approached us.

'Shall I help you instead?' the Trainer asked the Virgin. He was sitting on a mat in front of us.

'No. Your help is not needed. Let the professional *langot* baba help me. Or let her help me. She is a professional' the Virgin replied.

'Why bother her? I shall help you.'

The Yogic Girl walked away. The Virgin was sad.

'The idea of this yoga session is to challenge the mind as well as the body and see how the body can react to the brain stimulus' the Trainer explained to the Virgin.

His hands were on the Virgin's hips. He helped him into the bone crunching yoga position.

The Trainer took his position back on his mat.

'Why was he holding my hips for so long?' the Virgin asked me.

'No idea. Maybe he just wanted to help you.'

After a while, the Virgin disengaged from his posture and collapsed on the yoga mat in the convenient savasana corpse pose like how HBS usually did in office, under the pretext of an afternoon power nap.

He refused to get up.

Minutes later, our yoga session concluded.

And with that, the first official activity of the off-site was complete.

8
FOOTBALL

Post the yoga session, our entire team assembled in the football field near the lodge.

The field was uneven with wild grass growth. It was suitably converted for tourists like us, by erecting the goal posts.

The Trainer explained the rules of football. This was a football game with a *difference*. It was going to be played 'HR style'.

Our entire team was divided into 2 teams called 'TIGERS' and 'LIONS'. The Trainer decided on these names after a final shortlist which also included names such as- 'Panthers' and 'Cheetahs', 'Panthers' and 'Jaguars', 'Cheetahs' and 'Jaguars', 'Cobras' and 'Anacondas' and also 'Vultures' and 'Eagles'. Rather quietly, the Virgin suggested a set of team names to me. His names were 'Protruding Penis Papads' and 'Victorious Vagina Vegetables'. Another suggestion was 'Scratching dumb fucks' versus 'Non-scratching dick heads'.

I nodded silently digesting the suggestions.

The TIGERS team was led by the birthday boy for the day- the Founder while the LIONS team was led by the Mumbai branch head.

I was in the TIGERS team which also included HBS. As per the Trainer's instructions, in each of the teams, three individuals had to play the following roles-

1. One had to be a 'handcuffed' guy.
2. One had to be a 'chained leg' guy.
3. One had to be a 'blindfolded' guy.

'Each' of these outcasts had to be accompanied by two others from the same team. This was some sort of team building exercise in which each of these outcasts also had a role to play and contribute despite their limitations. The rest of the team divided themselves as defenders, midfielders, attackers as per a normal game of football.

Seeing other new recruits from the Mumbai branch opting for these outcast roles, I volunteered to be the 'blindfolded' guy in the TIGERS team. Since I did not know to play football, this was the best role which could hopefully shield me. The Virgin opted to play the 'handcuffed' guy in the LIONS team.

The game commenced with the Trainer's blow of the whistle.

Since I was blindfolded, I was helped by two people to kick the ball. The role of the people accompanying me was to inform me, on the arrival of the ball and help me kick it to a concerned team person.

'Kick to your right' one of the colleagues accompanying me, screamed.

By the time I had lifted my leg to kick, the ball had already gone past me. In a matter of a few minutes, the ball had passed me a few times and I had missed out, on at least three opportunities.

I felt a sense of helplessness.

Not knowing how to play the game and being blindfolded had made me truly handicapped.

'Let me help him' a voice said.

It sounded like a familiar voice.

'Be ready' the voice told me.

It was the voice of HBS!

'The ball is coming!' he screamed.

'To my left or right?' I asked.

'To the right' he replied.

I moved my leg to the right. Too late! The ball seemed to have already gone past me.

'Why don't you listen to my voice?' he screamed in frustration again.

'I am trying' I said.

'The ball is coming again. Kick!' he commanded.

I lifted my leg to kick but I kicked air instead and not the ball. The ball again had gone past me.

'Can't you understand English?' he screamed again.

I remained silent.

'Look at that handcuffed boy in our team! He is kicking so easily.'

How could I see? I was the blind man!

'I am not able to see anything' I said meekly.

'At least try...'

I remained silent.

'The ball is coming. Don't miss it this time' he shouted right into my face.

'Where is it?' I asked.

'To your right....'

I started moving to my right.

'....No! Move to your left.'

'Left?'

'That's right.'

I was confused. *Did I have to move to my left or to my right?*

'What the hell are you doing? What is the problem with you?' HBS screamed right into my ear.

I was blind not deaf.

The ball had moved past me for the umpteenth time!

The Trainer blew his whistle. The short game of 'HR style' football had ended. My team had lost.

The LIONS had won.

I really did not care. I was thankfully out of my misery. I only wish I had a solitary hour alone with the Yogic girl to make me relax after this stupid game of tension football.

'You should learn to kick properly' HBS told me. He looked irritated.

The ideal scenario right now would be to blindfold him and kick him.

It was time for the post match analysis.

'I have analyzed each individual's performance through this game of football on the basis of the following parameters....' the Trainer remarked, reading out from his note book.

"Behavioral patterns, Performance in the game, Enthusiasm levels, Energy levels, Motivational aspects, Leadership qualities, Team building skills and finally, Lateral thinking skills."

He had analyzed eight parameters.... all in a game of football in just twenty minutes! An impressive way indeed, of justifying the fees he was charging!

He followed up his analysis with detailed explanations.

According to him- the objective of the game was to see how well the teams as a unit had performed given the constraints it faced in terms of the 3 outcasts it had-

1. The *'handcuffed'* guy represented an individual brimming with ideas which were unconventional and which were maybe not being heard or implemented by the management. As a result such an individual felt stifled in the organization.

2. The *'chained'* guy represented an individual who was over dependant on others to execute tasks. Such a person lacked the clarity to be a self starter and execute tasks independently. As a result, such an individual felt over burdened with work in the organization.

3. And finally, the *'blindfolded'* guy represented an individual who was directionless and needed extra mentoring by his seniors in the organization. Such an individual needed nurturing and constant

feedback for self improvement in the organization.

HBS looked at me.

I looked back at him.

Maybe I fitted the bill as the 'blindfolded' guy, with him being my self imposed mentor for all things-financial and non-financial!

'For each of you present here, I shall send my feedback directly to the Delhi office based on the eight parameters. I would like to however point out a specific incident' the Trainer explained. 'Can you please step forward?' he asked me and the blind folded guy from the other team to come forward.

From the corner of my eye, I could see the Founder giving me a very unpleasant look.

Maybe everyone felt I was the reason my team had lost.

My blind folded companion from the other team was blinking his eyes repeatedly. He must have done a really good job in the game as his retina was taking so much time to adjust back to the bright sunlight!

'Among all the three roles, this was the toughest and they did it well. How about a round of applause for them?' the Trainer said.

The teams clapped for me and my blind folded companion.

That came as a relief.

The Trainer again made some notes in his note book.

'Using my inputs and feedback, how about playing a real game of football without the constraints?' he asked us.

As we had lost our earlier game to the LIONS, HBS decided to give us a pep talk. 'Come on boys! Let's play with energy. We have to win. This is a battle. It is now or never' he told us emphatically.

'Yes, we will fight!' we replied as a team in unison.

'It is us versus them. We are TIGERS-the king of the jungle. They are LIONS…what are they?'

He fumbled on the lion description to complete the sentence. We all spent a moment in thought but to no avail.

'Grrrrrr' he growled trying to make it sound like a serious tiger war cry.

Following suit, all the members of my team also give a tiger like roar which reverberated across the small field. More than a war cry, it sounded more like a sexual mating call!

The Trainer blew his whistle.

The game was on.

With an immediate opening attack, the attackers of the other team sped past us. Within seconds itself, the football in an impressive elliptical curve swerved in mid air, passing my team mates and lodged itself in the goal post.

It was a goal to the LIONS. They had taken the early lead.

The speed with which they were dribbling the ball past us seemed to have made our captain- the Founder unhappy. 'Come on, boys! More passion, more energy' he shouted.

A few minutes later, the ball dribbled its way into our goal post again!

In comparison to their team no one in our team either had the skills or the passion to compete.

The only thing our team could do was to engage in bull-shit motivational talk.

'Come on boys. More energy! We are TIGERS!' HBS screamed again.

The other team did not seem to be even talking.

They were going about our demolition in a clinical manner. They were like FC Barcelona in full flight and in complete control.

Since the outcome of the game was more or less certain, it was now more important to show the people who mattered how involved I was.

It could have a significant bearing during a future appraisal time!

'Ahhhhhhhh....' I screamed out loud, nearly bursting the air pockets in my lungs. This was the best way to redeem myself for the 'failed' blindfolded act.

'Good energy levels' the Founder encouraged me further.

For the remainder of the game, I decided to trail HBS and the Founder.

I realized it was more important to run behind the people in power than the ball in play.

An athletic opponent from the LIONS came to tackle our Founder to take possession of the football.

The Founder kicked the football gently to the side, possibly in fear that the opponent might just kick him! He then quickly moved out of the way. A young girl removing her Barbie dolls out of her doll house would have been more confident than him. He was probably good at golf but hopeless at football.

In comparison, the Mumbai head was running like a man on a mission to win.

Impotent at kicking, the Founder resorted back to his theatrics. 'We might be losing…but boys, let's go down fighting' he stated.

The athletic opponent kicked the ball which flew straight into our goal post.

The Trainer blew his whistle.

The LIONS had won their second match in a row.

The Trainer made notes again in his note pad.

It was time for further football analysis.

'I want to point out a couple of things before we wrap up the session. Irrespective of the results today, the game of football was the real winner' the Trainer told us. He sounded like the regular set of Indian cricket commentators who resorted to the customary clichés at every possible opportunity.

'Firstly, it is also important to find victory in defeat. Secondly, I would like to thank him for uniting the TIGERS and keeping their morale high, despite the loss' he said, about the Founder.

The Founder seemed happy with the critical acclaim.

We all clapped-A customary clap despite the fact that the

TIGERS had been *comprehensively thrashed* by the LIONS in both the games.

'Bloody loser' the Virgin screamed at HBS. Given that he had been pretty silent till now, he had all the energy to scream.

'You mind it! Don't talk against me. I have told you earlier as well' HBS replied.

'L-O-S-E-R'

'I am warning you. I am putting TT "on" right now.'

'What the hell is TT? What will you do?'

'I will do this-'

HBS lost his cool.

He picked up the football lying on the ground and threw it straight at the Virgin, who was standing a few feet away. The ball smashed into his nuts. HBS did not seem apologetic.

The football rolled away merrily.

'TT is testicle torture. TT is now switched "off". You deserved it!' HBS shouted.

'I thought TT was table tennis. You bloody chucker!' the Virgin screamed in agony as he collapsed onto the ground.

'Oh no, let me see what is the damage on offer' the Trainer screamed, rushing towards the Virgin. He was ready to pull his pant down in front of everyone to see the damage.

'What the hell do you think you are doing? Stay away from me! Don't touch me!' the Virgin screamed at him.

The Trainer backed off.

'I don't think you can become a father' HBS announced rather confidently seeing the Virgin squirm on the ground.

'I can't feel my balls. Will it impact my ability to play ping-pong? I was a high school champion in the sport' the Virgin asked screaming in pain.

His voice had lost the booming quality it had earlier. He was now sounding like an amplified version of the Trainer! Maybe he could start singing songs at music concerts.

'No more ping-pong. I am sorry to say this, but on account of limited flexibility in that region, I think you are going to suffer from slow ding-dong' the Trainer stated rather grimly.

Despite the delicate situation, all of us had a laugh.

With the football having been wrapped up, we all trudged back to the lodge for a much needed break.

A few minutes later, the Virgin joined me.

He was doing various stretching exercises to ensure his body was flexible in the important places. He started rubbing his crotch area like a cave man rubbing stones together to get a fire started.

'Dude, are you all right?' I asked him.

'Somewhat. I hope I can become a father. I am in pain now.'

'Oh.'

'I have lost sensation in my balls. I am feeling weak and vulnerable right now. I feel like an emotional woman. Only God can help me now.'

'Why don't you go to the room and take rest? I am going to the cafeteria to relax and have a cup of tea.'

'Ok. I am going to teach that guy a lesson. Something he will never forget in a hurry.'

'Forget it, man. This is an off-site. Plus you only taunted him first.'

'I don't care. I never forgive or forget.'

'Ok.'

'You wait and watch. I love all Indians. This fucker however belongs to a different state itself. I am not talking about Indian states such as Andhra Pradesh, Madhya Pradesh, Arunachal Pradesh or Uttar Pradesh.'

'Then which one?'

'This fucker belongs to a small backward state with no electricity in his brains called *Chutiya Pradesh* which incidentally is also not on the official Indian map.'

'Hmmm'

After having provided me with a geographical lesson and sounding rather ominous in his new voice, the Virgin hobbled rather uncomfortably towards the entrance of the lodge.

Only time would tell as to who would finally come out on top.

I went to the cafeteria to have a cup of tea.

9
BEDROOM & BOARDROOM

'Men are born for the boardroom and women are born for the bedroom' the first line of the article read.

Sipping on some tea, I was reading this potentially combustible article on the battle between the sexes in a lifestyle magazine, in the small cafeteria in the lodge. I had made myself comfortable on the plush leather sofa seats. The seats were a bit sticky and were clinging onto my backside, making a slight muffled noise each time I moved.

The article traced the evolution of the modern day working woman. From being treated as mere objects of male desire, the modern day working woman had now well and truly evolved at the work space. She had created her own unique identity and had made rapid strides in breaking the proverbial glass ceiling. She was no longer content being a mere home maker. She was strong and independent with a mind of her own. The article also synthesized the complex interplay between man and woman in issues pertaining to the bedroom, boardroom, trust, fidelity, instant gratification, money and morality. After reading this succinct article, the male reader could aspire to hopefully achieve everlasting matrimonial bliss!

Two women came into the cafeteria and occupied seats in front of me. They were definitely not from WCA!

One of them was an attractive dusky Indian beauty with her sexy kohl lined eyes and a very inviting smile. She wore what seemed like the world's tightest faded blue Levi's jeans! Body hugging would be an understatement. She also had a slender waist. She wore stilettos which made an interesting tip-top sort of noise. It was something I quite liked. The top button of her red shirt was open. She stretched as though she had just woken up from her sleep. Just by looking at her, I got all excited. Generous droplets of sweat started to line my collar.

The other woman, the taller and bustier of the two was pretty but not as good looking. She definitely seemed the busier of the two. She had a permanent frown on her face. She was scrolling through her mobile which seemed like an extended limb of her body. She had ugly bands of fat bulging out from all the wrong places.

But she got my attention.

She wore a loose black top. She had multiple tattoos, the most visible of which were two, one under each of the collar bones. Under the left collar bone was a scorpion tattoo to possible indicate aggression. Under her right collar bone was some sort of religious Sanskrit chant tattooed to possible offer a 'calming' influence. As a unit, the tattoos seemed to signify the constant life long battle between good versus evil.

Going by the stereotypes in the article which I was reading, the women seemed to fit in quite conveniently with the names- Bedroom and Boardroom.

The first woman seemed like perfect marriage material for a moderately conservative Indian male, who had not yet fully kept up with the changing gender equations of our times. She seemed the sort who would make the sacrifices and the compromises to keep the man and his family happy. She seemed like the one whom the man would like to whisk straight from the marriage hall to the dark, exciting confines of the bedroom.

The second woman seemed like definite competition for the insecure

Indian male in both the Bedroom and the Boardroom. Seeing the way she was clutching her phone, she seemed extremely busy in negotiating and maneuvering deals in the corporate boardroom with little time for the bedroom. She seemed target oriented which was ideally suited for the Boardroom.

Closely observing the women had derailed my train of thoughts. I still continued to pretend to read the lifestyle magazine. Actually, I was looking at Bedroom-the attractive one. She seemed more feminine and desirable. She was staring at me with her sexy eyes. Maybe God had chosen this as my lucky day. Would the staring lead to something more substantial?

I then overheard a conversation between the two women.

'....As I was saying, you have these real big ones don't you? It must be really difficult for you to maintain them, right?' Bedroom was asking the busy one, Boardroom.

'Yes. They have actually grown in size in the last few months' Boardroom replied.

I was shocked. *Was it some hormonal outburst?*

'It must also be quite tiring for you to look after them right? That too, day in and day out?'

'Yes it does take a lot out of me. Too much stamina and patience is required.'

'What do you feed them?'

This was weird! What was there to feed? They were as big as they could get!

'Nothing...I give them the usual food and lots of pampering.'

'Tommy also requires a lot of pampering. He is also very fussy about what he eats.'

'Tommy? Your brother's dog right?'

'Yes. Tommy is a St-Bernard. He is a very friendly little fellow but needs to be constantly pampered.'

Oh! The women were discussing dogs! Not something else which my horny mind was thinking about!

'I can totally understand. At least these dogs unlike men are consistent in their love for us.'

'I agree. By the way, how are the little ones?'

First it was the big ones and now it was about the little ones- it could not be about dogs again, could it?

'They are fine. Thanks for asking. I enjoyed baby sitting them for my sister in law when she was travelling.'

'That's nice. It is always good to help out the family.'

'We always have so many engagements to attend to. In this trip, we better finish our *fig leaf collection* before we return to Delhi.'

Boardroom checked her list of appointments on her mobile.

What was this *fig leaf collection*? It sounded interesting.

'We should finish it. Our deadline is fast approaching. We need to find a replacement quickly.'

'That's right. Just one minute. I am getting a call.'

Boardroom glanced at me. I think she noticed me hanging on to every word.

She then walked off.

I looked away.

'Excuse me…Hi…Are you from WCA?' Bedroom asked me, all of a sudden.

I still pretended to read the magazine. I thought my eyeballs would fall out after so much of odd staring out of the corner of my eyes.

'Yes…yes' I replied, trying to act composed.

She smiled at me.

This did not happen to me often. I also smiled back.

I was happy. It was not everyday that a pretty woman spoke to me.

'But how did you know I am from WCA?' I asked her.

'The guy at the reception was telling us' she replied, pointing in the direction of the receptionist.

'Oh.'

'He said your team has come for some sort of company off-site.'

'That's correct. By the way, I am a financial advisor.'

'Nice.'

'Can I give you my visiting card?'

'Sure.'

HBS had always taught me to exchange visiting cards.

He felt that it could be a source of potential business opportunities. Little did he know, that most prospective clients I met just chucked or misplaced it!

As I got up from the seat to give her my visiting card, the seat under me made a not so pleasant 'suspicious' noise. The rich leather stuck to my ass like it was some sort of adhesive! Bedroom looked at me and smiled.

'It was not me. It was actually the sofa' I said defensively.

I gave her my visiting card with as much dignity as I could muster.

I wanted to rip the damn sofa for having botched up my chances. It did nothing to enhance my reputation as a financial advisor or as a guy who had the cool moves to charm and impress women.

'Ok. See you around. Have fun' she told me.

'Hopefully, I will' I replied.

Bedroom walked away, slowly out of sight but certainly not out of my mind. She was joined by Boardroom.

Someone who was definitely back in sight was HBS. He was walking straight towards me.

'I noticed these women around here earlier, just after our yoga session also' he told me.

'Oh, is it?' I asked.

'Those women didn't seem very impressive to me. What do you think?'

'I didn't see them properly' I lied.

'One of them has a scorpion tattoo. It looked vulgar. A woman shouldn't do such things.'

'Hmmm'

'Anyway let us meet during the evening party. Also get the gift which we have got. Hopefully, the Big Boss will like it.'

HBS walked away.

I was pretty sure he enjoyed staring at the women and at the tattoos! He must have assessed and analyzed them thoroughly. He was just not admitting it.

Bloody hypocrite!

In the airport, he had happily stared at the swimsuit magazine. In the train, he was the one who enjoyed the rating game the most and now this! At home, he probably tried to act like a devoted husband and father by engaging in an overdose of 'Jaanu' and 'Chotu' antics to keep them happy!

I knew him well by now. His behavior was not something that surprised me anymore.

I walked back to my room.

I took the gift out of my suitcase and kept it ready for the evening event. I did not want to forget it and get blamed by him in front of the Founder!

10
SOCIALIZING

'Good evening everyone. Thank you all for coming! This is a truly memorable day' the Trainer dressed in a bright floral shirt stated with excitement in his voice.

The entire team had gathered in the small party hall in the lodge to celebrate our Founder's birthday.

Team members were handing over their gifts to the birthday boy, the Founder whose huge grin suggested that he was quite enjoying the attention like a six year old would.

He wore a new crisp suit and as usual looked every inch a power dresser.

When it was my turn, I handed over the book on leadership and the birthday card.

I thought for a minute about the excitement I could have created if I also handed over the swimsuit magazine which HBS had loved so much at the airport!

'The book is on leadership' HBS remarked with pride. He was standing by my side.

'Thank you so much. WCA does need to groom leaders for the future. I can maybe use tips from this book during my leadership session tomorrow' the Founder replied.

'Yes. Plus the best financial advisor award will definitely give clarity on the future leaders.'

HBS really wanted the prize which was slated as the final event of the off-site! I walked away as he pushed his case for future career growth.

The Virgin joined the celebrations in his casual style. He did not have to prove a point to anyone. I did not see a gift in his hand. After having spent most of the evening rubbing his various body parts, he seemed to have finally recovered from his football knock.

'Look at the Trainer. He looks so funny' he told me.

'I know.'

'Just tell me, which man will ever wear such bright colours?'

'No idea. It must be a fashion statement.'

'It is not a fashion statement! Look at him! He is a joker. He should come on a show like the *Laughter Challenge*!'

I thought to myself.

If the Virgin could comment so much on *others* sartorial sense, why did he not wear *his* expensive pants properly?

'As we bring in the evening of fun and frolic, I have also prepared a brief ice breaker game' the Trainer told us in the gathering.

'Another bullshit game' the Virgin sighed.

'As a tribute to the efforts taken by our birthday boy in setting up this company, I request each one of you to step forward and tell us why WCA is your preferred employer.'

'Oh God! Please save us from this torture! Now everyone will begin to add extra makhan. Talking of butter, I feel like eating butter chicken, man. Also I want some daaru' the Virgin muttered.

'I thought you were all principled-no non-vegetarian and no drinking?' I asked.

'No man. I booze and I occasionally eat chicken. Before I sleep, I talk to my grandfather. I confess all my vices to him. I don't hide anything from him.'

'Good for you.'

'Also as far as possible, I try to eat a meal of curd rice with rasam or with Priya pickle every day. My grandfather used to tell me that eating curd rice keeps the body cool and in control. While I may lose my self control while talking about women, curd rice certainly keeps me in check!'

'Hmmm'

'The idea of this game is to test your creative skills while making the introductions' the Trainer continued.

'Ok. Can I start?' the Virgin asked innocently.

'Sure, go ahead.'

'I work here because my uncle gives the maximum business as a client in Delhi.'

All laughed.

I admired his guts, positive arrogance and his honesty. This was what the intoxicating mix of power and money could do.

'I am sure all of us are working here, out of choice and not out of compulsion' the Founder immediately jumped in, to defend the company which he had set up so industriously.

'Well not really. But if you say so' the Virgin said.

'WCA has given me good opportunities for growth. It has also given me a chance to win the best financial advisor award' HBS said, rather honestly in his turn.

'Why don't you give your reason?' he asked me.

'I like working here at WCA. It is challenging and at the same time entertaining. I like the goals and the team' I said, with appropriate insincerity.

'Well said' the Founder stated. He was smiling ear to ear.

'A complete answer' the Trainer added.

'Great learning curve' Aunty no 1 said during her turn.

'Yeah right' the Virgin muttered to me.

'I love the work environment. Such good people,' Aunty no 2 said during her turn. 'I love working late nights. Luckily I have a good support system at home. I would do anything for the happiness of my team mates. I love it when it is really *hard* even after regular work hours.'

'Does she even know what she is blabbering?' the Virgin asked me.

'I don't think she does' I replied.

'Give it to me you ugly aunty. Ah…Ah…even you will do. Raat mein andhera hai! Who was the great man who said that all cats are grey in the dark?' he remarked.

He started making moaning and other low decibel sexual noises.

'Control yourself, man.'

Rather inadvertently while praising the company, Aunty no 2 had also had raised the sexual hopes of the male advisors in this testosterone tank called WCA! She was unaware of the sexual innuendo. Maybe she just wanted to work hard which would keep the team and higher ups happy, which in turn would help her get a bigger bonus during appraisal time.

The rest of the team mates spoke about the challenges and the joys of working at WCA. The usual, feel good corporate drivel which made the Founder very happy indeed. He could not have asked for a better birthday gift! A bunch of super talented, super sycophantic financial advisors praising him and the company with not a word out of place!

'Thank you all for your participation. One more announcement- All of you please be ready by 5.30 in the morning. We have to drive down to the Jim Corbett National Park for a jungle visit. So don't drink too much!' the Trainer announced.

The bar counters opened up.

The entire team was by the bar for the booze session. The makeshift bar provided the finest liquor which was specially organized for the evening. I sipped on a beer while the Virgin sipped on a glass of scotch.

The party though was not at all rocking. The DJ was playing English music with desi beats. He played *The Summer of 69* in different versions including a thumping Punjabi version.

The evening though had some interesting sights on offer.

At a table by the bar, in front of me, a couple was sitting. They were probably tourists on vacation. They seemed to be in their early twenties and did not have any ring on their fingers to indicate any sort of matrimonial commitment as yet. But the 'love filled' manner in which they were conversing seemed to suggest that they were ready to take their relationship to the next level.

'Here baby, eat this' the girl said.

She rolled up some noodles in the fork to feed her boyfriend.

The boy seemed visibly embarrassed by this public display of affection but nevertheless positioned himself to be fed.

With the noodles hanging in a mangled loop on the tip of the fork, the girl moved forward to feed her boyfriend. For some strange reason, the boy moved violently to a side. This action caused a reaction in the girl's hand as well. The noodles twirled out of the fork, completed a few summersaults in the air like an Olympic swimmer and fell down on the boy's expensive looking, white coloured designer shirt.

'What have you done?' the boy asked his girlfriend angrily.

'I am really sorry, baby. I didn't mean to' she replied.

The boy did not respond.

'I said I am sorry, baby' she repeated again.

It was unfortunate that a memorable moment was thus lost in a noodle mishap.

'Yaar, when will our time come when chicks care for us?' the Virgin asked me as we looked on at the couple.

'No idea' I replied.

'This evening is so bloody boring.'

'I know.'

'But guess what? I think God has listened to us. Look man…chicks finally!'

I turned around.

The Virgin pointed in the direction of a set of perfectly sculpted legs which had made an appearance.

It was Bedroom followed by Boardroom!

They looked hotter than in the afternoon. If their dressing could not increase the excitement levels of the party, nothing could or would.

Bedroom was in a shimmering red sari which was sliding along the curves of her body in a seductive sort of way. Her blouse was tied in a loose knot at the back which seemed precariously positioned to give way at any given moment!

I seriously hoped for a wardrobe malfunction.

Boardroom also looked quite hot. She was in a black gown which smartly hid her bands of loose fat. Her gown was slit up to her thigh displaying her sleek yet chubby legs.

They walked towards the Founder.

They exchanged air kisses. They then engaged in what looked like small talk.

'What are they talking to the Big Boss? Are they dancers? Cabaret ho raha hai kya?' the Virgin asked me, sipping on his scotch.

'No man. I don't think so' I replied.

'*Piya tu ab toh aa ja…aa ja*' he muttered, shaking his hips and thrusting his other body parts vulgarly and suggestively.

'Dude, control yourself.'

'*Ruk ruk ruk…oh my darling….give me a look…Chumma chumma de de…* I have lost all self control! I can visualize myself dancing with those chicks under a waterfall. We should be item boys and dance with these items girls.'

'I know.'

'Look at those two tattoos on that fat chick. It is too awesome.'

'It is.'

'Guess their vital stats.'

'I don't know. You tell me.'

'I think their vital stats are "36-24-36" for the thin one and "56-46-56" for the fat chick.'

The Virgin explained his estimates by drawing curves and shapes in the air like a tailor who had been thrown out of his job for improper conduct with women but still worked on a freelance, project to project basis.

'"56-46-56"? Too much of an exaggeration, don't you think?' I asked.

'No, yaar. I think she looks like that. Indian men like fat women. Do you think she will appreciate my observations and honesty?'

'I think she will slap you for your honesty. She might even pluck that mole out from your face.'

'I think you're right. That could be dangerous. Nowadays no one appreciates honesty.'

'That's true.'

'We should go meet them.'

'I actually met them briefly this afternoon.'

'What! When? Where did you meet them?'

'I had gone for tea. They were sitting in the cafeteria discussing something.'

'Oh! Did you get their room number or telephone number?'

'Dude, what do you think? I am not so confident and savvy as you, ok?'

'Ok, I'm sorry. Ladkiya item hai item' he remarked.

With his glass in one hand, the Virgin forked out his other hand and graphically described their bodies and breasts.

The Aunties were also next to us at the bar counter to refill their drinks.

Both the Aunties were well dressed in chiffon saris. They looked good and dignified. But they were in no way as attractive as Bedroom and Boardroom.

They seemed a little sad that no one was complimenting them.

'Who are these bitches?' Aunty no 1 asked Aunty no 2.

'No idea' she replied.

'Look at all these men from WCA. All are staring at them! This is too much!'

'I just know these women are up to something. My eye is twitching. I saw something similar happening once in a saas-bahu episode.'

'Sasuma pranam' the Virgin chipped in.

He placed his glass on the counter and folded his hands in a prayer like gesture.

'Don't start off again' Aunty no 1 said, springing to her friend's defence.

She scolded the Virgin.

The Aunties then walked away.

A while later the Trainer came to the bar counter to fill up his drink.

'Who are these hot women?' the Virgin asked him.

'Well, they are artists or painters or something like that. They have been staying here for the last few days.'

'Oh, ok. Nice!'

Wow! Bedroom and Boardroom were creative artists! That sounded really exciting!

'They are from Delhi. They wanted some creative inspiration away from the city.'

'That sounds really awesome!'

'I had met them during the day and I invited them over.'

'The best thing you have done all off-site.'

'Excuse me?'

'Err…nothing! Have a great evening.'

The Trainer had a surprised look. He walked off.

Bedroom was watching us from a distance.

I also looked in her direction. I tried to make eye contact. I tried to give my killer smouldering look to get her attention. A few minutes later, HBS also arrived at the bar for a refill of his drink.

'How are you feeling?' he asked the Virgin sarcastically.

'You scratching street dog. Mind it!' the Virgin replied. He looked angry. He had not forgotten the damage to his balls.

As HBS and the Virgin were locked in a mini verbal fight, a waiter passed us carrying an empty tray. He left the tray by the bar in front of us. The Virgin moved a bit and picked up the tray. HBS tried to move away.

The flurry of activity resulted in an accident.

The metallic tray gently collided with HBS's head. The sound of metal on a human head had an interesting ring to it.

'Aahhh…' HBS screamed out in pain.

'Are you ok?' the Virgin asked, feigning concern.

'I know you did it deliberately. Why are you asking?'

'It was a mistake. But it serves you right for what you did to me!'

'I am sure you have deliberately involved the waiters as well. First they gave me dog biscuits and now this has happened!'

'Relax. There is no real conspiracy to torture you.'

HBS walked away rubbing his head.

I was happy. The act of revenge had happened!

As we sipped on our drinks, other advisors had already hit the dance floor.

HBS joined the Founder and had started talking to Bedroom and Boardroom. He had criticized Boardroom's tattoos but did not miss an opportunity to talk with them!

'Yaar, let's also go meet the chicks and then get onto the dance floor' the Virgin told me.

'Sure.'

'Let dance with them. Look! Other guys have already started dancing.'

We joined HBS and the Founder.

They were in the middle of some discussion with the artists.

'...Global warming is a real concern these days' the Founder explained to HBS and the artists.

'That is where alternative energy like wind power fits in. It is low on carbon emissions' HBS added.

'I agree' Bedroom remarked.

She sounded impressed. She adjusted the knot of her blouse. An effective wind power source could easily overpower the loose knot resulting in a rather embarrassing, pristine state for her.

'Oh! You guys are here?' HBS asked, sounding surprised.

He looked at me and the Virgin curiously.

'No, it is our ghosts' the Virgin replied with sarcasm.

'Stop it, you two!' the Founder said.

'Why don't all of you keep the energy talks going? I need to energize myself with a drink,' the Founder stated, heading to the bar for a drink. 'Also can I have a word with you in private right now?' he told the Virgin.

Both of them walked away.

'By the way, I don't think you have met my subordinate. I lead the Bangalore team of WCA. I am the boss' HBS said, introducing me to them.

Not that I needed an introduction! I had just met them a few hours ago!

I stared at Bedroom.

Would she settle for an average looking, hardworking financial advisor like me?

As long as I was included in all matters related to money, property and page 3 parties, I had no problem in being the backend support for all domestic chores! I could be a modern day house husband and she could be a corporate high flier if she chose to be one and attend meetings in Paris, Tokyo and New York! If gender roles were fast changing in modern India, I did not mind being part of it.

'A pleasure to meet you' I muttered sheepishly as I stepped forward for an air kiss with Bedroom, like how the Founder had done. I made a small pout of my lips in anticipation of a kiss. Instead, all I got was a cold handshake and a cold look from her. HBS also looked quite shocked at seeing my courage. He surely did not expect me to pout!

My dreams of my first air kiss crumbled!

I was embarrassed.

The moment had passed.

I also shook hands with Boardroom. Her hands were manly and seemed hardened by the passage of time unlike Bedroom's feminine hands which were soft, non-scaled and adequately moisturized. She also gave me a cold look. This was rather strange. Both of them showed no sign of remembering me. Maybe they were drunk. Or maybe I was just plain unattractive.

This upset me a little.

'I practice the salsa sometimes. Want to dance?' HBS asked them suddenly.

'That's interesting. Let's go for it' Bedroom replied.

'I shall join you later. I am off to get a drink' Boardroom stated.

She walked off.

I walked towards the men's room.

In the passageway leading to the rest room, a couple was passionately kissing each other.

It was the noodle twirling tourist couple! They did not notice me. I walked nonchalantly towards the rest room. When I came out, they had disappeared. Clearly...the angry boyfriend was definitely going to get lucky tonight!

I observed a private moment of self pity. When would my luck turn?

I returned to the main area.

HBS was dancing pretty well. He was trying his moves to burn up the dance floor. He was doing the salsa with Bedroom. He was holding her slender hips. Her sari was sliding rather tantalizingly as she swayed to the music. Her movements were also getting a bit raunchy. She did not seem to care about the salivating advisors who were staring at her with their mouths open. I wondered why she was an artist. Given her hot figure, she should instead have been spending her time modelling for figure hugging clothes which accentuated the hips, thighs and ass!

Overnight fame, stardom and pots of money would be guaranteed!

I saw the Virgin heading my way.

'Yaar, I am back. The Big Boss gave me gyaan on not fighting with that asshole.'

'I think he is right. Enjoy the off-site. Don't fight' I said.

'Right....fight...off-site...wah...wah... it is rhyming and all! You should become a poet.'

'No, man.'

'That asshole dances pretty well.'

'Yes, he does.'

'I think I am also going to dance.'

'Sure. Go ahead. I will watch from here.'

The Virgin started dancing.

He engaged in an attention seeking sort of dance which took the focus away from HBS and Bedroom. He danced like he was a vulgar Indian fast bowler who desperately wanted to keep the shine intact on the cricket ball by rubbing it vigorously around the crotch area! Maybe he was taking a dig at HBS! He then screamed in his loud, drunk voice-'*Dil mein merai hai dard de disco*'. He looked at the disco lights which had taken effect. He then rubbed his chest, to show the immense love *and* pain in his heart!

He certainly got everyone's attention.

The Trainer also joined him on the dance floor.

He had two left feet. He moved his hands sideways and then vertically like an IPL umpire who signalled a wide and then a six of consecutive deliveries. He continued this mechanical motion. It reminded me of the way I had danced in my high school farewell party many years ago!

The DJ upped the beats.

On the dance floor, the Virgin, HBS, Bedroom and the Trainer were dancing in close proximity.

The dance movements were getting exciting to watch.

All of a sudden as HBS did a salsa move with Bedroom, the lights went out.

The hall was engulfed in darkness.

The generator came on a few minutes later.

The position of the four of them was hilarious!

HBS had his hands on the Trainer's hips. The Trainer had his hands on the Virgin's ass.

Bedroom had moved away and was standing by the side of the dance floor!

The entire team burst out laughing. I could not control myself. The situation was embarrassing for HBS, the Trainer and the Virgin.

'I was immersed in the music. I always give 100% to my work or in my dance' HBS offered as a feeble explanation before moving away.

'Move your bloody hands away from my fucking ass!' the Virgin screamed at the Trainer.

'I was also carried away by the music. My hands just got stuck. It was like I got an electric shock from your body. I am sorry' he explained.

'You got an electric shock from my ass? Are you mad? Are you gay? You stay away from me' the Virgin warned.

The Virgin made some obscene, insensitive and rather unwanted remarks about the Trainer's lack of upbringing. He then expressed his views on the Trainer's sexual orientation, said bad things about his parents and also shared really graphic views on how he was possibly conceived. Views which involved a horny horse and a stormy Swiss barn!

The Trainer was quite unruffled and handled the situation with dignity and like a true professional. He did not react. He took charge once again.

'That was an entertaining outburst! Ok guys, all of you have dinner. Rest well. Tomorrow we have a hectic day coming up. We have a jungle safari and other activities lined up. All of it is for your team building' he announced and walked away.

The dance for the night was over.

All of a sudden while I was having my dinner, the Virgin collapsed and fell on the floor.

He was drunk. Maybe he had lost his footing. All the scotch on the rocks had conspired in giving him the ultimate knockout! The rest of the team continued boozing or eating.

I felt a bit bad on seeing the general apathy among the team for the Virgin's condition.

This also spoke volumes of his not so popular status.

I volunteered to drop him to the room.

Not because I wanted to but because the Trainer and Founder had unnecessarily extolled the virtues of showing good team spirit and being there for each other.

I made the Virgin stand and supported him with my shoulder. He was deceptively heavy for a short man.

I started walking back with him to our room.

11
THE ARTISTS

With difficulty I lugged the Virgin back to the room. Needless to say, I was sweating and out of breath by the time I pushed him onto his bed.

Once in the room, he seemed to recover dramatically.

'*Dhak dhak karne ne laga...*' he chanted, thumping his chest like a drunk gorilla.

Interspersed with the thumping were vivid descriptions of the hot artists which left little to the human imagination.

It was interesting to hear his cave man like raw emotions.

'*Pappu can dance saala....pocket mein rocket hain...*' he muttered, adjusting something under his blanket.

Then he mumbled, 'Thata, I hope you understand and you love me.' I remembered that he had told me that he confessed all his drinking bouts to his grand father.

He then abruptly started to snore.

I walked towards the balcony to get some fresh air. The room reeked of alcohol. I opened the balcony door.

A cold draught blew inside. I felt good and the beer I had consumed made me a bit reflective and romantic. I thought of my ex and the time we had spent outside her hostel room one cold night…just holding hands.

As I stood, I heard voices- Female voices. The voices were coming in through from room 310. The room was not empty after all! The voices sounded somewhat familiar.

It was the artists in animated conversation!

I got a bit excited.

But how come they were back so early from the party?

Maybe they were tired.

Eavesdropping was something I had perfected to an art. The stillness of the night would definitely help me get a better listen of their talk. Even their balcony door was open. Our room balconies were separated by a narrow ledge of just a few feet in width, with the intimidating deep ditch down below.

I stood near a flower pot at the side of my balcony to listen better.

'Can you tell me if my thighs are firm?' Bedroom was asking Boardroom.

'Of course they are darling. I see no problem with them' was Boardroom's reply.

'Then how could my ex-boyfriend have a problem with me?'

'It is difficult to understand that.'

'How difficult is it to get an Indian male who is willing to treat a woman on par-financially and emotionally?'

'Good point. Remember how I told about my alcoholic boyfriend who used to cover his insecurities by calling me fat. Look at me. Am I fat?'

'Not really. But you can look at losing about five kilos.'

'So what if I am a little fat? I am a woman of substance. I am unique in my own way. How can a man dare to think I am fat and out of proportion?'

'I know. Men…I tell you are a complicated lot. They want perfect bodies.'

'Why can't they respect us for the size of our brains?'

'I agree with you completely! Our love failures have also impacted our *fig leaf collection.*'

'We better refocus and complete the sketches.'

What was this collection? They were talking about it even when I had met them for the first time in the cafeteria.

'Our deadline is approaching- we are running behind schedule.'

'I know.'

'Anyway can you please put some lotion on my back?'

'Sure.'

'Let me get undressed.'

Aunty no 2 was right! She had said during the party that the artists would be up to something. They were!

Within a few seconds, a black bra flew from their room onto their balcony like a missile which had crashed in Iraq! This was getting too exciting. I wanted to see what was going on. I leant against my balcony railing. The flower pot next to me obstructed a better view.

I moved it a little.

As I moved it, a sound was made.

'Did you hear a noise? What was that?' Boardroom shouted.

'Let me go check' Bedroom replied.

It was too late to retreat. Bedroom entered the balcony. She was in a towel draped around her body.

She had come to pick up the bra.

She saw me standing like a robber, shivering slightly with embarrassment.

'What are you doing here?' she asked, looking at me in shock.

'This is my room' I muttered.

'Were you eavesdropping on us? Did you overhear anything?'

'No.'

'That's a lie!'

'Ok. I did hear a bit' I finally admitted. I was completely embarrassed.

'Come to our room and let us sort it out.'

I locked my room with the key and knocked on their door.

'Come in' Boardroom told me, opening the door of room 310.

It was a spacious room. It was better furnished than the one I occupied with the Virgin.

She ushered me to a huge double bed.

'Have a seat' she ordered.

I sat down tremulously on the bed near the bedside lamp. The bed was covered with a soft, silken, light pink bed sheet. The mattress was soft and inviting unlike the fairly hard mattress in my room.

I looked around with all my faculties on full alert.

Bedroom was in the buff except for a loosely draped towel and a whip hanging around her neck! Boardroom was dressed in a loose spaghetti top and hot pants. On the floor, a suitcase was open with a whole bunch of props including a black coloured toy gun which looked like an AK-47! Two best selling paperback reads on '*You are your own boss when it comes to weight loss*' and '*How to become size zero and fall in love with a hero*' written by a celebrity Bollywood fitness trainer were on the floor. Two sets of kinky handcuffs were on the floor. A box of condoms was on the floor. A vibrator was on the bed! A hardbound, oversized sketchbook of sorts was on the bed. A stationery kit with pencils, black markers and erasers were strewn carelessly by the sketchbook on the bed. A Polaroid camera was also on the bed. A bottle of lotion was open on the bedside table.

I had seen all of these items only in low budget porn movies! Yet, it was right in front of me here, in a room in a lodge in the middle of nowhere in Kyari!

They approached me and sat down.

We sat in a single file on the same side of the bed. I was sandwiched between both of them.

Sitting like this, a definite crick in the neck was guaranteed.

This was the first time I was sitting like this in a room...that too with two stunning women who were so hot!

I could smell the perfume they wore.

I saw Boardroom's scorpion tattoo from really close quarters.

Were they not concerned, that I being a stranger was in their room, in the night?

What was going to happen to me?

'It is time for the interrogation' Boardroom told me, rather curtly.

'Ok.'

'What were you doing overhearing us on the balcony? Don't you think it was inappropriate to eavesdrop on our conversation?'

'It was. I will not mention the conversation to anyone.'

'That is an easy way to get out. What else do you have to say?'

'Well...you two are probably the prettiest women I have seen.'

'How dare you talk like that?'

'I am telling the truth. I have nothing to hide.'

All of a sudden, Bedroom slapped a handcuff on the wrist of my left hand chaining me to the sturdy bedside table. Boardroom took an instant photo of me with the Polaroid camera, with naked Bedroom in the background. She had wrapped a scarf over her face so that it would not be clear.

'Hey, what's this for?'

I was shocked at the turn of events.

What were they going to do to me?

'Is this a sting operation? Are you going to blackmail me? Are there any video cameras?' I asked.

'Yes...we might blackmail you.'

'Please don't. I am poor. I am at the beginning of my career. My mom will kill me.'

At the very moment, my mobile rang.

I took my mobile out of my tight jeans pocket with my right hand. It was my mom calling up from Namibia! Talk about maternal instincts. I looked at my watch. It was early evening in Namibia (there was a four and a half hour time difference). I spoke to my mom. Thankfully she did not detect anything different in my tone. She told me she was enjoying the trip. She asked me how I was, if I had seen any of the photos of the girls she had sent for my approval, if I was eating properly, if I had eaten my favourite snack (which was sandwiches), how the off-site was progressing, if any pretty girls were there and a whole lot of other mother-son talk.

She hung up after a few minutes.

I wanted to tell my mom that I that I had not eaten a sandwich but was most certainly sandwiched between two pretty women!

'So that was your mom, eh? Now you return to reality, my dear boy. You will pay… you eavesdropping idiot' Boardroom continued.

I put the mobile back in my pocket. I was beginning to get scared of these hot women right now.

'Do you want money? Are you robbers?'

'No. But show us your wallet.'

'Here take it. Take all the money' I said.

I put one hand in my fairly tight jeans pocket with some discomfort to remove my leather wallet which was frayed along the edges.

'Hey, check out his wallet. He has a photo of his parents' Boardroom told Bedroom.

'I told you. I am a good homely Indian boy.'

'You stingy man…I don't care if you are homely but you have no money. You have only 175 rupees. What will you give us?'

'I also have a debit card' I defended myself.

'What do you do?'

'This is too much! Both of you don't remember me or what? I had met both of you in the cafeteria earlier in the day. I am a financial advisor with WCA. Our company has come here for an off-site.'

'Financial advisor...right...right!' Bedroom remarked, piecing together the events from the earlier part of the day.

'Can I leave? I have apologized. Matter should be over. Discussion closed.'

'The matter is not closed. You go around carrying *this* in your wallet?' Boardroom asked me.

The scrutiny of my wallet was in progress.

Boardroom pulled out a condom. She looked at me questioningly.

'Well let's put it this way- I don't get too much action off the stock market' I said.

'Oh! So you always want to be ready if the opportunity comes by?'

'Yes, I do.'

'Also look what I also found inside his wallet.'

'What?' Bedroom asked excitedly.

'I found a passport size photo of a pretty girl. Who is she?' Boardroom asked me.

'She is my ex-girlfriend. She was married off a while ago.'

Her wavy hair and sweet smile could still make my heart race.

'Ok, so you are a heartbroken lover boy who still keeps his ex's photo?'

'Yes. Her parents wanted a typical IIT-IIM guy for her. They got one through a wedding web site and she was married off. I hope the degrees will give her the love which I would have anyways given her.'

'Oh poor baby, don't feel sad. We also have had choppy relationships. Give me a hug if you want' Bedroom told me.

I was happy to oblige and I got a bear hug. She also patted me on my thigh.

I was aroused instantaneously.

I hoped that my erection would get her attention.

This interaction was unreal. The excitement levels were straight out of a B-grade porn movie made of the lowest of budgets!

These artists seemed crazy, kinky and drunk! Had Indian women become less inhibited and willing to experiment in more ways than one?

Was I going to get some action…finally? Was this the reason for calling me to their room?

After a pause, Boardroom spoke to me.

'You know what? I think you are perfect for something for which both of us have been planning' she said.

'What's that?' I asked.

Was she referring to an orgy?

I was excited.

Maybe my self indulgent moment of self pity at the dance party had been rewarded. Maybe my luck was turning!

'We are painters. Actually more than painters we are sketch artists. We are planning on sketching the *fig leaf collection*.'

I was excited about the possibility of having sex. They clearly were talking about something else.

'I heard you talking about it earlier also.'

'When did you hear me?'

'I heard both of you in the cafeteria as well.'

'We know! We saw how your jaw dropped and how excited you were, when we spoke of our big and small ones and then about the *fig leaf collection*.'

'I feel cheated. Is this some sort of a setup?'

'Well not exactly. But in a way, it is.'

'What!'

'We are creative artists. We came here to Kyari to get some creative inspiration to complete our *fig leaf collection*. We had come a few days back to this lodge. The receptionist told us that financial advisors were coming for an off-site for 2-3 days. We needed a male model to pose for our collection. So we thought we could get a model from your group. This was our opportunity. Today was the day. We saw you men arrive this morning. In fact, I saw you entering your room.'

'How come, I didn't see you?'

'I think you were busy discussing something with your room mate, that drunkard. He is quite crazy, by the way. We observed you during the dance party and after he collapsed, we followed you almost immediately.'

'Oh!'

'We then had a conversation in our room and we deliberately kept our balcony door open to set it up perfectly. We knew sooner rather than later you would hear us.'

'What! So...you had all of this planned? I feel so used. I thought I was guilty. I don't think I have nothing to fear anymore. Let me go!'

'You are right, barring a loss of reputation and possibly no work for the next few years of your life.'

'Please don't. Plus you have no proof.'

'You want proof? A guy in a woman's room, in the middle of the night in a quiet location! All I have to do is to scream right now. Plus I just took a photo of yours, right?

'Do you want me to circulate it? Do the math.'

'Ok, you win. What do you want?'

'We want your cooperation for the *fig leaf collection.*'

'What the hell is this *fig leaf collection*?'

'It is a series of sketches. It is the tragic journey of a love struck, young man just out of college.'

'Oh. So what do I have to do?'

'We want you to pose for a few sketches which I have in mind.'

'Just pose?'

'Yes. You are something of a night time muse for us.'

'But why did you do all this plotting and planning done? You should have just asked me. I would have agreed immediately.'

'Well it is a bit more than just a normal sketch. It is in the nude.'

'WHAT! Are you crazy?'

'A little bit.'

'I think I am going to scream. Both of you are crazy. I am a financial advisor. Not a porn star. Let me go!'

'Drop your pants.'

'What! Right here? Right now?'

I was shocked. I had not expected such a direct command.

'Yes. Then when?'

'I mean with the lights on?'

'Yes. Do you think I can sketch in the darkness?'

I guess…I did not have a choice. I dropped my pants. This was an awkward moment. There was nothing pleasurable when things are done under coercion. The last time I had dropped my pants under tension like this was during a brief ragging session during my college time.

'Oh, wow!' Bedroom gasped, seeing me in all my glory.

'What is it? Hit me with it' I said.

'It has surpassed expectations. I think you were born to be the *fig leaf boy*.'

'Oh, thanks. I feel worthy. It has boosted my self confidence.'

I felt important and glanced southwards to check the reason for the new found appreciation.

'By the way, I am talking about the expressions on your face *not* that!'

'Oh!'

I pulled up my pants silently. I felt disappointed and humiliated.

'But why am I, the chosen one to pose as the fig leaf boy? Why not some one else? I am sure they can do a better job' I asked Boardroom, in an inquisitive manner.

'One of our friends, a professional model was to join us from the art school but he cancelled at the last minute' she replied.

'Also the reason we zeroed in on you is because, all the other advisors in your team seem arrogant and cocky. They also have pot bellies. You are young and you are one of the fairly good looking ones in the lot' Bedroom added.

Some praise finally!

'Thanks. But where is this art school of yours? Are both of you even real artists? Do you have any online presence? Any web site? Are you on Facebook?' I probed further like an investigative journalist.

'We are artists. Our school is a private one located in Saket in Delhi. I can't tell you more' Boardroom continued.

'But what if you had not trapped me today?'

'We would have found someone else. If we didn't know a team full of advisors were coming, I would have bribed the receptionist to pose. I see that excitement in his eyes when he looks at me.'

My confidence levels were abysmally low now.

'So I was not your first choice? I just happened to become the choice by default?'

'Yes. But thinking about it now, you are perfect to be the fig leaf boy.'

'Are you serious?'

'Yes. Well…you want some praise is it?'

'Well why not.'

'You seem repressed, frustrated and dejected in your life.'

'How is that even praise?'

'Well despite the frustrations, you have a sense of spirit and you look fairly handsome.'

I realized that this was about what I could expect to get. Very weird praise indeed from very weird women!

'If you put it that way…then well thanks!'

'You want to ask any thing else or can we start our sketches?'

'You want to sketch right now?'

'Yes.'

'But what if you blackmail me after tonight? How will I know you will not tell anyone?'

'We won't, man. Trust us.'

'One more thing- I saw you guys socializing with my company people in the party. Do they know anything?'

'You ask so many questions. You should have been a lawyer instead of a financial advisor. They know nothing. But yes, we were talking to them.'

'What was that all about?'

'The usual time pass talk. We were telling them we are artists *not* nude sketch artists.'

'Also in the dance party, why did both of you not recognize me even though we had met earlier in the cafeteria?'

'We didn't want to arouse any suspicions and put you in trouble.'

Well... that explained the aborted air kiss!

'How thoughtful of you,' I said sarcastically. 'For all my help, you will not sneak on me, right?'

'We promise we will not.'

'But what if my colleagues come to know?'

'Oh, they won't. This night is a little secret between the three of us.'

'Would you be interested in giving me a massage after we finish the sketches? My back tends to get very stiff and very dry' Bedroom asked me, all of a sudden.

I was silent for a moment. This was too tempting an offer! I would be a fool to refuse.

'Of course I want to! This is magical. This is supposed to be my company off-site but right now it *really* feels like a porn site.'

I was now really excited.

'So are you satisfied? Remember this is a strictly professional engagement. Don't get other ideas. If you aren't comfortable posing, we shall search for a replacement-your drunken roommate, perhaps?' Boardroom said.

She sounded irritated with all my questions.

The thought of the Virgin getting the offer I was getting right now made me very insecure. Midnight rendezvous' with hot artists, an opportunity to be a part of some kinky creativity, an opportunity to offer my services as a masseur and the exciting possibilities that lay beyond that!

I had to grab this chance.

'No.....No. I want to pose' I reacted instinctively.

'So we do have a deal?'

'Yes, we do.'

'How come now, you have no fear of being blackmailed by us?'

'I trust both of you.'

I did not. But I first had to comply with their requirements to enjoy the add-on benefits.

'But if you don't mind me asking what is that vibrator doing on the bed?' I asked Boardroom.

'That is to pleasure ourselves if you know what I mean' she replied.

'I get it. One more question-What if my room mate or someone else from my team gets up in the middle of the night and searches for me?'

'The drunkard drank so much during the party. I am sure he is not going to get up in the night. To answer the second part of your question, I frankly don't think anyone in your company really cares about your worthless existence, to actually take the effort to search for you, especially at night.'

Boardroom was rude but what she said was pretty true!

'Ok. I am ready to pose. Let's finish it fast. How long will it take? I am here for only two nights.'

'That's fine. I will be sketching. I will finish it fast. There are totally ten sketches.'

'Ten? That's a lot.'

'Don't worry. Each sketch will take only around 20-40 minutes. We should wrap it in around 3-6 hours including the time taken for costume changes and other delays.'

'What do you mean *costume changes*?'

'Well, the fig leaf boy goes through various stages of evolution. For instance, in one sketch, we need you to shave your chest hair.'

'What!'

'Well yes…to get the metro-sexual look.'

'But the hair on my chest has taken years to grow.'

'Don't argue. This is a requirement of the sketches.'

'Looks like the sketches will take a lot of time. I have to leave by 5.30 in the morning for a jungle trip to Corbett to hopefully spot a Tiger.'

'Forget that Tiger. I am quite impressed by your crouching Tiger' Bedroom remarked, looking at me closely.

'Err…..thanks.'

'No wonder the Tiger population is dwindling in the real jungles. You are an insensitive poacher. You are a bad man.'

'Stop it, both of you! We have work to do' Boardroom interrupted in a cold manner.

'Yes! Let's get down to business!' I said, gritting my teeth.

'I shall sketch five tonight and five tomorrow night.'

'Ok.'

'I am unlocking the handcuff.'

I rubbed my wrists. I quite enjoyed being handcuffed!

'Read the pamphlet which I have prepared with great interest. The *fig leaf collection* is meant to depict love in its true form.'

'This seems unreal. Like a dream sequence straight out a movie.'

'Well let's just say- tonight is your lucky night.'

12
THE FIG LEAF COLLECTION-1

I glanced through the pamphlet which Boardroom had handed over to me. The *fig leaf collection* had ten sketches in all. Each proposed sketch had a detailed narration attached which gave me a good idea of what I needed to do, to be a good model.

Clearly the artists had thought this entire thing through!

The ten sketches listed were as follows-

Sketch 1- *The Act of Recognition*

Sketch 2- *The Act of Preparation*

Sketch 3- *The Act of Observation*

Sketch 4- *The Act of Passion*

Sketch 5- *The Act of Disruption*

Sketch 6- *The Act of Defiance*

Sketch 7- *The Act of Sacrifice*

Sketch 8- *The Act of Nervousness*

Sketch 9- *The Act of Union*

Sketch 10- *The Act of Cowardice*

Boardroom placed a chair by the bed in all readiness. She took out her oversized sketch book to sketch.

'Shall we start with the first sketch?' she asked me.

I nodded. I was ready.

I read through the contents of the first sketch from the pamphlet. It read as follows-

"*The Act of Recognition* is a sketch of a young boy readying himself for an interview of sorts. He is holding an apple in one hand and a college degree in the other. The boy is not clad except for bright red sneakers which he is wearing and a fig leaf which is the only piece of clothing which covers his modesty."

'Here wear your props- the red sneakers, carry this paper as your certificate, carry the apple in your right hand and cover your modesty with this fig leaf' she instructed me.

She handed me the props including a grey coloured cloth meant to be the fig leaf!

'Ok. You know what? The sneakers fit quite well. I am surprised' I said.

'I told you. You were born to be this fig leaf boy' Bedroom chipped in.

'Are you ready?' Boardroom continued.

'I am. Can I ask a question?'

'Yes, go ahead. But stay still while I am sketching. You can ask your questions as I sketch. I am starting, finally.'

'Where did you, get all of these props from? Delhi?' I asked.

'It is none of your business.'

'Did you buy it from Janpath, Palika Bazar or Paharganj market?'

'No.'

'Why are you so secretive about your art course?'

'Well let's put it this way-we don't get support from our parents or from society in this endeavour of ours.'

'But that is not entirely true. Lots of Indian artists are into nude art. What is there to hide?'

'Nudes of women are common. The typical Indian male mentality is always to look at women from a stereotypical point of view. Do you know the challenges I had to face to convince people when I decided to become an artist let alone a nude artist?'

'Is it so? So your parents, family don't know what you guys really do?'

'They don't! They think I work in an office and she is a good dutiful girl about to get married.'

'That's right. They think I am an obedient little school girl' Bedroom said, with a naughty smile.

'Creativity is not like some instant two minute noodles. It takes time to develop. It takes days or maybe even years to emerge.'

'True.'

'Good to see a male agreeing for a change. I am used to resistance at every step of the way.'

'So, how did the two of you meet?'

'We met at the art school and became good friends. The school helped us blend our interests together especially when we had our difficulties.'

'What difficulties?'

'I cannot tell.'

'Ok. But what is this great urgency to complete the *fig leaf collection*?'

'You want to know?'

'Yes. I want to know. After all, this is only between the three of us.'

'We are racing against a deadline.'

'What kind of deadline?'

'The nude art and sketches from our school is a great hit among a few lonely wives in some of the elite colonies in South Delhi.'

'What? You are serious?'

'Yes. They purchase our nude sketches. Our work is appreciated by them.'

'So is this why, you are keeping your entire art course and the details a secret?'

'Yes. We have an exclusive clientele. Just like you have your investment clients, we have our art clients. This time, we are selling this entire set of ten sketches to one rich client in Defence Colony, who is paying us a really good amount. She wants to gift it to her divorced friend on her birthday, which is coming up next month.'

It would be a good idea to get the client's contact details to also make her a client for investment purposes. HBS would definitely be happy with my multitasking abilities! But why the hell was I thinking of work and HBS? What was wrong with me?

'Nice.'

'Our client suddenly advanced our deadline. She wants us to submit the entire set of sketches by the end of the week. That's why this urgency to complete.'

'Ok.'

'I am almost done sketching this first one. You have done a good job.'

'Wow! Thanks.'

'Don't get too excited. We have a long way to go. From this sketch, I am already able to derive a few artistic interpretations of your state of mind.'

'Like what?'

'Well the uneaten apple in your hand, it is seems like a sign of nervousness before the interview.'

'For that matter, I think I will always be nervous before any job interview.'

'Your branded sneakers reflect total disregard for a corporate job.'

'Well not really. I am quite well settled as a financial advisor at WCA. It pays fairly well.'

'But are you truly satisfied?'

'No idea.'

'Your nakedness to me reflects the fig leaf boy's search for true recognition. To be accepted for what he is.'

'Hmmm'

'Ok, I am done. You can relax. Go through the requirements for sketch 2- *The Act of Preparation.*'

Boardroom went near the balcony and took some deep breaths. I began to read the sketch requirements.

The sketch details read as follows-

"In this sketch, the same fig leaf boy jumps out of a closet with his hair gelled in spikes. In one hand is a pay cheque and in the other is a briefcase."

'Here, put some hair gel' Bedroom told me.

Her soft fingers running through my hair was a big turn on.

I had to focus.

'Now what you need to do is to stand in our room closet and jump out' Boardroom interrupted.

'Ok.'

'Also carry this briefcase and this paper as the pay cheque.'

I stood rather awkwardly with the briefcase outside the closet.

'I like this sketch. A young man of today who is confident of his sexuality. It is a very impressive take on the metro sexual man.'

'By the way, your Trainer who has organized this off-site event of yours, is very effeminate' Bedroom chipped in.

'Yes, he is. Every one makes fun of him. His voice, mannerisms and the shirts he wears' I said.

'I know. What was that bright floral shirt he was wearing today at the party? Is he gay? Is he out of the closet?'

'I have no idea.'

I thought she could be right…given the way the Trainer was clasping the Virgin's hips rather merrily during the party and the Virgin's subsequent aggressive outburst.

'This sketch is done' Boardroom announced.

She got up from her chair to stretch a bit.

'What is your background, by the way?' Bedroom asked me.

'My father who is a CA told me not to view college as one big bang fest. He told me to study hard and get maximum output for the time spent. He told me life is not all fun and games. Post my Masters, I joined WCA and have been in finance ever since.' I ended on a sad note.

'Oh, poor baby' she told me in her soothing tone.

'I am neither getting the bang nor making the really big bucks!'

She looked at me and smiled.

Hopefully I would finish the sketches with a big bang!

I really felt Boardroom was indefatigable and completely focused on what she was doing.

'Start going through the requirements for sketch 3- *The Act of Observation*' Boardroom interrupted.

The sketch details read as follows-

"In this sketch, the fig leaf boy is silently munching on the apple as he observes from the corner of the bedroom, his sweetheart lying naked on the bed. Her hips along with a strategically placed tattoo (on the hip) are glistening in the radiating morning sunshine, which is streaming in, through the bedroom window."

'So who is going to be playing my sweetheart for this sketch?' I asked.

'Who do you think?' Bedroom replied, dropping her clothes.

She lay on the bed. Nude. She looked at me and laughed.

I wanted to act professional and not stare at her with my mouth open. But I couldn't control myself. She was so well proportioned and so sexy, that I had difficulty breathing. I had doubts whether I would have the required control and focus which the sketch demanded.

'Are you getting turned on?' she asked.

'A little' I replied, trying to cover my piercing projection which was protruding out.

'Keep your excitement in check' Boardroom told me. She did seem to make out that I was getting incredibly excited.

'This night is unbelievable. Let's do it' I remarked, wiping drops of sweat off my forehead.

By "do it", I meant the sketches and the thoughts of some *steamy sex.*

'I want you to stand near the balcony door. Let the table lamp offer the stream of light' Boardroom told me.

'Ok.'

'Also munch on the apple. It is time to concentrate. I am starting to sketch.'

'Aren't you feeling a bit conscious being in the buff?' I asked Bedroom.

'No. True artistic creativity is all about separating the selfish human flesh from the spiritual self. If you understand your inner spiritual self, then the flesh seizes to exist' she replied.

'This is complicated. I can't understand.'

'It's ok. You will learn with time.'

I observed Bedroom. Though she was nude, there was a certain innocence attached to her and she did not seem vulgar. It was like she was just doing her job and she was being thoroughly professional about it. She was a complete natural without any fake mannerisms. She seemed to trust me completely and that was refreshing to notice. I felt I had to grow up and act more mature. *I had to forget about the steamy sex (for sometime!) and focus on the sketches.*

'Nice strategically placed tattoo. I didn't know you also had a tattoo. What is it?' I asked, looking at the small tattoo on her hip.

'Obviously you would not know. It was concealed till now. The tattoo is a small cricket bat' she said.

'But why a cricket bat?'

'So that I can then play with the balls... if you know what I mean.'

'Yes...of course. It's nice and naughty.'

'Anyways nowadays all that men care and crave for, apart from sex is the stupid T-20 cricket.'

'I also love T-20 and Test cricket.'

'I personally like the tattoo. It is the sign of an empowered woman and a progressive society' Boardroom remarked.

'But don't you think this sketch is a stereotypical, regressive display of a naked woman lying on a bed?' I asked. *I was mature once again with my pertinent question.*

'Good point but no. I rather interpret it as a shy woman who is exposing her modesty to the outside world but someone who is unaware of the harshness around. And looking at the way you have munched on the apple, it is a sign of your sexual hunger building up.'

'Oh!'

I had munched on half the apple!

'Keep your hunger in check.'

'Yes…yes.'

'Even *he* was like that.'

'Who are you talking about?'

'I am talking about my ex who dumped me.'

'Can I ask what the problem was?'

'It doesn't concern you. This sketch is done. I shall go to the washroom and be back.'

Boardroom walked away to the washroom.

'What's up with her? Why is she so pissed off and grumpy?' I asked Bedroom, who partially covered herself with the silken bed sheet.

'I shall tell you later' she replied, playfully tempting me from the bed.

'Please…I want to know, now.'

I really wanted some good night time gossip.

13
LATE NIGHT REVELATIONS

'She dislikes men' Bedroom said.

'That seems obvious. But what's the reason?' I asked.

'According to her all men are dogs. She feels that all of them only think only about sex and are on the constant lookout for sex 24/7. She feels all men want to get into her pants without understanding her true inner self and beauty.'

'Oh!'

'She has suffered jolts both professionally and personally.'

'How has she suffered personally?'

'She was in a relationship with a guy. He was two timing her primarily because of her weight.'

'Oh!'

'Apparently once when they were making love and she was on top, he started screaming Oh God...Oh God! She thought he was enjoying the action that he was getting and was thanking God. But it turns out, that he was shouting at God because she was very heavy.'

'Wow! Then what happened?'

'He confessed to her that it was her weight which bothered him.'

'Oh! It is a dangerous thing to confess to a woman.'

'I know.'

'Then, what happened?'

'Days later, she caught him cheating. He was right in the middle of the act with another woman. In shock and anger, she packed her bags and just left.'

'Good move.'

'She now feels that time is passing by swiftly, her clock is also ticking.'

'What clock?'

'She was referring to her biological clock.'

'Oh. I thought an alarm clock.'

'Are you stupid or what? This is serious.'

'Ok, sorry.'

'As a result of this experience, she is very suspicious of men. She feels life has been unfair to her. And now she has also piled on the extra kilos. She feels marriage is only to have a kid. That is why she wants to marry and have a kid before the biological clock sounds an alarm. She feels after the initial period when things are rosy between a couple, problems will start and then there will be the inevitable break up.'

'She sounds quite disillusioned. What happened in her professional life to sour things?'

'She was fired from work in the recent past which made her lose confidence.'

'But I thought she was an artist full time?'

'No. She became an artist by chance. Post her engineering, she worked in a call centre for a few years. She was fired during the recession time. She was fired on the grounds of consensual flirting.'

'That's surprising. She doesn't seem the type who would flirt or talk with men.'

'Excuse me. I am good at flirting' Boardroom chipped in. She was back from the washroom.

'So looks like you have told him my entire life history' she told Bedroom, while wiping her hands on a towel.

'Yes' Bedroom replied.

'I have told you. Never confide in strangers.'

'Sorry about that. I asked her to tell me. But I would like to believe we are all friends now' I said.

'What happened with your boss?' I asked Boardroom.

'You really want to know?' she said.

I could see anger in her eyes.

'Yes. I do'

'One day at work, my boss was staring at my breasts as I entered his cabin. He told me to open it immediately. I knew he was talking about my shirt but he claims he was referring to the file I was holding in my hand!'

'Oh. Then what happened?'

'He being the man and me being the woman, I had to continue playing along to his advances as that call centre job was important to me. He then started praising my tattoos under my collar bone which is quite visible as you know. Incidentally, I also saw you staring at them in the cafeteria.'

The artists really had observed everything about me. It was scary yet exciting.

'I agree I was staring at them.'

'My boss even wrote a poem about them for me. It was seriously annoying. It was a typical display of arrogant male behavior. Obviously he thinks no end of himself and his supposed prowess in bed!'

'Oh.'

'And then many days later, during a night shift, I was having a dinner snack when he called me to his cabin. He was munching on a banana which was in his hand. He then dropped his pants!'

'What! That's disgusting!'

'Yes. He told me that going to bed with him would benefit my career. He was sitting with his pant half down. He then looked suggestively at the banana in his hand and then at me expectantly.'

'That's really shocking!'

'I went and complained to his manager.'

'And then what happened?'

'A few days later I was fired for being a 'non performer' and not a good "team player". That matter was hushed up conveniently. I was conveniently branded a *consensual flirt* with all men!'

'Oh!'

'Yes. When the boss looks at my breasts and talks, that is supposed to be all right but if I dress up and speak well it means I am a flirt. Smacks of double standards! Luckily, I came across this art school to keep me busy. I get a decent stipend to keep me going. Till I get my next job I shall continue with my sketching.'

'Good.'

'I mean what is a man's obsession with breasts anyways? I just don't get it.'

I kept my further excitable thoughts on this matter to myself.

'I don't know. I guess it's different.'

'It is just a goddamn body part like an ear lobe for instance. I don't know why it excites you guys so much. Just because I have big breasts does not make me smaller in the head does it?' she remarked, pointing at her brains.

'No, it doesn't.'

'Why can't men just accept me for who I am? The company accused me of sending out the wrong signals.'

'What signals?'

'They said my tattoos were sending wrong signals to the entire team.'

'Oh.'

'Like my tattoos are some sort of transmitters. It is very difficult to decode what men really think.'

'Talking of your tattoos even my boss had his views on them.'

I told them how HBS had also negatively commented on Boardroom's tattoos in the cafeteria.

'I want to teach him a lesson. He seems to be a typical Indian male. Outwardly modern but inwardly conservative and extremely judgmental' she told me.

I nodded, supporting her wholeheartedly.

'He tried very hard to impress me during our salsa dance. He also kept scratching as if a rabid dog had bitten him' Bedroom added.

I smiled. It was typical HBS.

'I guess in life so far I have been at the wrong place at the wrong time. An Indian man cannot handle this modern day, empowered Indian woman' Boardroom continued.

'I guess' I said.

'I am a woman of substance-modern, well educated and with a mind of my own. I am assertive, hardworking and intelligent. And guess what?'

'What?'

'My creep of a boss got promoted on basis of work done by me in that file. I was rejected and alienated at my work place. I have no issues about sleeping with one's boss. If I like someone, I will go ahead. But it should be a matter of mutual agreement. Not one of coercion.'

'That's fair, I guess.'

'It was then that I decided to pursue my passion for sketching. I am now a full time sketch artist. This is so creative, pretty stress free and quite lucrative.'

'Nice.'

'My parents though still think I am going to be promoted to become a manager at work.'

'Oh!'

'I don't plan to tell them till I get a new job.'

'Don't they know anything by now?'

'No they don't suspect a thing. They stay in Jaipur. I send them a part of my monthly savings from the sale of my sketches.'

'Ok.'

'After being fired, I went into depression. I began eating a lot—that explains these love handles of mine. My dogs helped me to overcome my depression.'

'Yes. I have heard dogs are awesome. They are just like human beings. In Bangalore, I have a client. He made a financial plan for his dog. He loves the little fellow like crazy.'

Memories of Giggles, the psychotic pug came flooding back to my mind.

There was silence for a bit.

'If you don't mind me telling you, think about losing a few kilos. It will boost your confidence and self esteem. Do it for yourself and it will make all the difference' I continued.

I knew I was on dangerous territory.

'Mind your own business' Boardroom told me curtly.

'I was just trying to be your friend, man.'

'First my boyfriend and then my company rejected me. The way my life has turned out, it can depress anyone.'

'But look at it this way...in spite of all the setbacks you are independent and working hard. You didn't take the shit your boss gave you. You have proved to yourself that you are a woman of character and above all, you have been honest with yourself.'

'Who cares?'

'*You* should care. Take pride in what *you* do. Stop bothering about what your neighbour thinks. It is you who has to face life. Not them. Always do what you feel is right. It is ok, if you make mistakes. They are *your* mistakes at the end of the day.'

'Well said. My... my...you are also understanding and sympathetic unlike other men. I am impressed' Bedroom added.

'How do you handle your boss? Do you follow your advice with him? Do you stand up for what is right?' Boardroom asked me.

'Not at all! My boss dominates me all the time. I guess I am better at giving free advice!'

'Thanks for your inputs. I shall reflect on it. Now let's get back to work.'

'Sure.'

'Understand the requirements for sketch 4- *The Act of Passion*.'

The sketch details read as follows-

"This sketch depicts the expected furious display of sexual passion between the fig leaf boy and his sweetheart in the bedroom under a starry night. The fig leaf boy stands on the bed displaying his waxed chest and his six pack abs."

'I like the way we have organized this sketch' Boardroom told Bedroom.

'Why do you say that?'

'The starry night sky in this will be in perfect contrast to the setting of the early morning sunshine in the earlier sketch.'

'I agree. This sketch will be quite intense.'

'We need you to shave your chest hair for this one' Bedroom told me as a matter of fact, casually.

'Shave! No way!' I replied, covering my chest which had a generous dose of chest hair.

'In this sketch we need a clean shaven chest. You agreed earlier.'

'Stop being a pest. The requirement of the sketch is to show the boy as being high on personal grooming' Boardroom interrupted rudely.

'But my chest hair grows very slowly. I don't have hair like a bear.'

'Remember the massage? Help us now. We need your support. Here take this razor and go clean yourself up' Bedroom said.

Her cajoling tone was enough.

I trudged to the washroom.

I was back. All clean shaven.

'That was not too difficult? Was it?' she asked me.

'No, it wasn't' I replied sadly, gazing at my clean shaven chest. I didn't want to make a fuss but I felt a sense of loss.

'It's all right. It is the metro sexual look.'

She ran her fingers over my bare chest. Her reassurance helped to an extent.

'I didn't notice this before, but you do have an outline of a six pack' Boardroom added, staring at me.

Was she mocking me? I had a fat stomach. But I was happy. This was the first time she was praising me.

'Well I do work out infrequently' I said.

I was happy that she had noticed something about me. She would be a great dominating teacher for me in the bedroom with her life lessons! But it was Bedroom who turned me on completely.

'Both of you lie down normally. Let me sketch. Remember don't get excited. Sketches are meant to inspire and create. Not titillate' she said.

'I shall try' I said rather uncomfortably.

'Stop tickling me' Bedroom told me with a shy smile.

'It isn't me. Maybe it is the soft satin sheets.'

We posed.

There was silence for sometime. Boardroom sketched busily.

'That's good. I like the energy' she told me.

'Thanks.'

'Do you want a break or do you want to continue?'

'Let's continue.'

'Ok. I am done with this sketch. Go through the requirements for sketch 5- *The Act of Disruption.*'

I went through the sketch details-

"In this sketch, the desired act of sexual passion has been abruptly cut short by the arrival of the girl's parents who are opposed to the union. A silhouette suggests their presence. The girl tries to shuffle between the bed sheets to try and cover her glistening hips. The moonlight reveals her face and other features. She has a beautiful face but has hairy armpits and a faint pencil moustache. The fig leaf boy looks on in horror. His hairstyle is however in place thanks to the hair gel which he has been applying. He is standing on the sidelines wearing handcuffs indicating his sense of helplessness in the situation."

'I want you to outline a moustache and darken your armpits with the black eyeliner' Boardroom instructed Bedroom.

'Ok. What a role reversal in this sketch. As a woman I am not supposed to focus on personal grooming at all!' Bedroom replied.

'What I need you to do is to spike up your hair with the gel. Also, I want you to stand by the side of the bed. It will give me an impression that you are looking at her' Boardroom told me.

'Ok.'

'Also wear this handcuff and act shocked in your expression.'

'Nice. For acting shocked, I have to just act like how I looked when I got caught by both of you tonight!'

'Yes. That's right.'

'Promise me you will not leave me' Bedroom told me displaying her well rounded hips.

'I promise I will not leave your hips.'

'What?'

'I am sorry. I promise I will not leave you.'

'All guys are the same. No feelings. You all…only want to get into our pants. Like how my boyfriend left me after getting what he wanted.'

She sounded serious. What had I said wrong? I had thought some feeble chemistry was developing between us.

'No…no…I was just kidding. I have the utmost respect for you. Anyway why did your boyfriend leave you? Surely he must have been a moron to do such a thing.'

I had heard Boardroom's story. This was interesting. I could not imagine someone wanting to leave Bedroom.

The floodgates of emotion seemed to open.

Both the women seemed like they had wanted a sympathetic, sensitive man for a long time to divulge all their secrets to.

'I am not at all ambitious on the career front. I had a boyfriend in college. I loved him a lot. He was a total useless fellow but I still loved him. I was willing to be just a homemaker and raise kids. We were to get married. But then things didn't work out' she replied bitterly.

'Oh.'

'I found out much later that he never loved me. He was a total mamma's boy. To top it off, he only loved my family's business machines and my wealth and not *me*.'

I nodded silently.

'My father never approved of him but I still wanted to give him a chance. That useless fellow let me down. He got another proposal from a richer family and left.'

She was getting emotional and was on the verge of tears. I still could not fathom how the daft boyfriend could have preferred money to this hot goddess.

'Get a grip on your life, woman! All men are the same. How many times do I need to tell you this?' Boardroom told her.

'I broke up with him a few months back. I am now in the recovery phase. Now…my parents are searching a guy for me, for an arranged marriage.'

'Oh…ok.'

'I will go with the flow. I will try to not let my past impact my present. Thankfully this art course has taken my mind off it. Marriage will most probably be at the end of this year.'

'That's good to know.'

'Let me have fun till it lasts. I actually wouldn't mind a fling.'

I sincerely hoped that Bedroom and I could engage in making love and not war. Love was the perfect antidote for hardcore anger.

'Once I am married, the routine of life starts.'

'What routine?'

'I will have to be dutiful wife, a good daughter in law, think about home loans, educational loans, think about giving my in laws a urinating infant within the first few years of marriage itself and so on.'

'A complicated and challenging life is ahead of you.'

'My parents are orthodox and have already told me to start thinking along traditional lines. They want me to start practicing things which I should do to make my husband and my in laws happy.'

'Like what?'

'For instance, my mother is teaching me the right way to keep a glass of milk on a tray for the first night.'

'Are you serious?'

'Yes. What will happen to my independence post marriage? What about my individuality? My happiness post marriage?'

I thought over what she said.

I honestly did not think an arranged marriage would work for her. If she needed someone to understand her, she should aim for compatibility and nothing else. She should look for a guy who understood her completely and someone who would never harp on her past. *Maybe someone like me!* But in a shallow sort of way I was not exactly concerned. It was not like I wanted any life long commitment! I hardly knew her! What I wanted was...to make love to her before the off-site was over!

'Ok good job, both of you. The sketches for the night are done. Thank you, for your cooperation' Boardroom told me.

'Sure. No problem' I replied.

'Why don't you take some time off during the day? We can hang out' Bedroom asked me. She was still emotional.

'I would love to but I don't want to raise any suspicions within my team.'

'Ok. So you don't want to spend time with me?'

'I want to but this is my company off-site, remember?'

'Well, I guess so.'

'I shall catch you guys tomorrow night. Is that ok?'

'That's fine. We will wait for you. Even we have some day time sightseeing of our own to do.'

'Great. And one more thing, I quite like this handcuff. Can I keep it for the night?'

'You can keep it.'

'What a night! And just to confirm...please don't blackmail me. I am a simple man with simple needs.'

Needs like sex on the rocks while sipping on scotch on the rocks!

'Don't worry. Once a commitment, it is always a commitment! Haven't you heard Salman Khan give this killer line in *Wanted*?'

'Actually, I have. I better get going before I am also on my company's wanted list. Thanks for the reassurance.'

'Here, take you your stupid Polaroid photo which we had clicked.'

'Thanks.'

Actually if you don't mind, shall keep it? It will remind me of *you* and this special night.'

'Good point. Please keep it.'

Bedroom looked at me naughtily.

I was very excited. Did I detect a promise in her eyes?

The night had been very exciting, unusual and memorable.

Not in my wildest dreams had I imagined such a night would ever happen in my bleak, routine life.

When I had left Bangalore, I had visualized 3 boring days. Now my days were exciting because of the Virgin's antics and theatrics and my nights were exciting because of the creative artists.

Both of them were a far cry from my college girlfriend whom I had known intimately.

I was now convinced that women of all shapes, sizes and experiences existed. In a sense, each one was an adventure with mysteries far beyond what appeared to the casual male eye.

I left Bedroom's room with the handcuff. I quickly checked the aisle passage to see if anyone was awake. No one was there.

I saw my watch. It was 3 a.m.

Thoughts rushed through my mind. Had I made a mistake in trusting them? For all I knew, in a matter of a few hours I could be the laughing stock and my position at WCA could be questioned. I was supposed to be unwinding and relaxing at an official off-site, not being a nude model for artists! Only time would tell if they would keep their pretty mouths shut.

I looked at my left hand. The handcuff was there.

That made the entire night's events worth it!

I entered my room. I turned on the light.

The Virgin was standing by the balcony door which was open. He was merrily urinating into the flower pot.

'*Tip tip barsa paani…* ' he sang rather aloud, rather merrily.

I was shocked by his act and by the fact that he was awake.

He was a confirmed psycho.

'Hey, how come you are up so early in the morning?' he asked me, turning around.

'Nothing… ' I replied, searching for a plausible explanation.

'Did you crack the case?'

'Which case?'

'Arre the murder mystery in which the sasuma kills her pota and then runs away to Mexico with the bag of gold?'

What was the psycho talking about?

'I don't remember exactly.'

'I think I need to contact the FBI headquarters to investigate. Or maybe I shall go undercover as a FBI officer, as a *female body inspector*.'

'I guess so.'

'I need an arrest warrant and a handcuff to capture the accused sasuma.'

'Well here is your handcuff' I said, removing the handcuff from my left hand.

'Sasuma, I am coming to get you' he remarked as he slapped the handcuff on his wrist.

All of a sudden, with a smile on his face, he started poking his finger on his head like a carpenter drilling a hole in the wall. He then slapped himself. He then started mumbling to himself. He bent on the floor and did ten pushups. He then stood up.

'Ah! I feel better' he told himself.

The truth dawned on me.

The Virgin was again in the middle of a post midnight, nightmare attack like in the train. He was in a state of some sort of psychotic tantrik trance where he behaved as though he was possessed by the soul of a madman.

Finally exhausted, he walked back to his bed and collapsed. He mumbled, grunted and started snoring and salivating.

I turned off the lights.

We had to be up by 5.30 a.m. in just over 2 hours.

An eventful first night at the off-site had come to an end.

PART 3- OFF-SITE-DAY 2

14
TIGER SPOTTING

My alarm rang at 5.15 am.

My head was spinning from a combination of lack of sleep and the crazy activities with the artists during the night.

I woke up the Virgin.

'Yaar, my head hurts. Too much booze' he told me shaking his head gently like a boxer in pre match warm ups.

I could not tell him my head was also spinning for a different reason!

'What the hell is this handcuff doing on my hand? Where did it come from?'

'No idea.'

'Strange. I didn't see it last night.'

'Maybe it is one of those football handcuffs which were used in the game.'

'It could be. But this one feels different. But how is it on my hands?'

'No idea, man. Get ready. We have to go downstairs.'

'I had a very exciting dream last night. Do you want to know about it?'

'Ok, tell me fast.'

'I dreamt that I was a horse and was being spanked and taken for a ride, by those hot chicks we met at the party. I hope it happens in real life some day.'

I remained silent.

I didn't want to discuss the artists and details of the night gone by. One thing would lead to another and the secret of the nocturnal activity would be out.

We reached the reception area.

The Virgin had undone the handcuff and left it in our room. In a satchel, he carried his binoculars, his Nikon digital SLR camera and a book on wildlife.

Our team was ready.

Some were scratching, yawning or just plain tired. What kind of scheduling was this by the Trainer-A drinking session the previous night and now an early morning jungle safari?

I looked at the team rather curiously with a sense of tension.

No one seemed to be giving me an odd glance.

The artists had kept their promise. Maybe they actually were sketch artists who just needed a nude night time muse to meet their deadline.

The jeeps were ready to drive us down to the Jim Corbett National Park which was a good forty five minutes away. The Trainer had organized this trip to engage in some animal and bird spotting. The idea of this visit was for us to appreciate the sights and sounds of mother-nature. It was also to inculcate in a team of financial animals, a fine appreciation for the real animals in the wild!

We set off in the jeeps towards the park.

'I am a certified tiger specialist' the Virgin told me in the jeep.

'Awesome' I replied.

'I had attended many wildlife camps while I was growing up.'

'Good for you.'

'Did you know that as per a recent advertisement, there are only around 1400 Tigers left in India?'

'And did you know there is only one real dumb-ass left on this planet?' Aunty no 2 chipped in looking pointedly at him.

'Keep quiet. Don't get me started early in the morning' he warned her.

After seeking the necessary approvals, we finally entered inside the Jim Corbett national park at around 7.30 am.

We were now in a different jeep from the one in which we had arrived.

The driver of our jeep told us that the chances of spotting a Tiger- 'the real king of the jungle' were slim but could not be ruled out. He seemed to speak from experience. He must have undertaken many trips into the jungle for the tourists. Also seeing him scratch the wild, unruly hair on his face, dense jungles seemed like a second home to him.

Twenty minutes into the park with the jeep curving through the narrow paths, the Virgin armed with his binoculars had spotted something.

'Look!' he said, pointing to something along the path.

'What?' Aunty No 2 asked excitedly.

'SAMBAR!'

'I didn't know there was idli for breakfast this morning.'

'Arre you are very silly.'

'What? You think you are more intelligent than all of us?'

'I am talking about Sambar, *the animal*! Look!'

'Oh!'

'We have come to see a jungle billi and you are talking about eating an idli. Show respect for the animals of our great country.'

'Don't talk to me.'

'I think it is time you stopped watching saas-bahu serials.'

'You mind your own business. I think it is also time for you to stop watching women's mud wrestling on ESPN.'

The Virgin was at a loss of words. He kept quiet. Aunty no 2 had silenced him for the moment.

The jeep slowed down considerably.

A few of us stood up, to view the animal from the open air jeep. In the distance, a sturdily built deer like creature with antlers and powerful hind legs peered straight at us. It was the Sambar-a very serious looking, mature version of the doe eyed bambie which appeared in cartoons!

It seemed like our date with spotting a Tiger would remain incomplete.

The driver of our taxi signalled that that the jeep had gone as far as it could inside the jungle. It was time to head back. There was not a Tiger in sight.

To however keep our spirits high, the Virgin provided nuggets of information about the wild life park. It was refreshing to see this knowledgeable side of him.

'The core area of the jungle is closed right now on account of the rains' he explained from his wild life book. The core area he explained was a separate section in the jungle in which a Tiger could definitely be spotted.

We were back en route to the entrance of the national park.

'Shhh…. ' the Virgin cautioned us all of a sudden.

He asked the driver to slow down the jeep. Taking out his binoculars, he zoomed in on something which had grabbed his attention.

'What happened?' the Aunty no 1 asked.

'Fresh tiger pug marks can be seen.'

'Tiger pug marks? Are you sure?' HBS queried who had been rather quiet until now.

'Yes I am sure. I can identify them! I have been associated with wild life camps since I was a teen' the Virgin replied with pride.

'Oh…ok.'

'I think a tiger just passed by here a few minutes back. It might return on this trail.'

In anticipation of the arrival of the lead protagonist, the supporting cast of the jungle also seemed to have risen to the occasion. Happy monkeys on the trees started howling in fear, birds in the air started their frantic fluttering, the mild breeze started intensifying and the rustle of the dry leaves was only getting louder!

'I think the Tiger will be coming back anytime now' the Virgin told us with excitement.

We all waited with bated breath.

With the excitement building up, the imminent arrival of the king was only a few minutes away.

This off-site was finally getting really thrilling!

Posing as a muse for hot artists during the night and spotting a Tiger live in action during the day. What more could a fat, bored, jaded financial advisor ask for?

'Shhh.... It is returning' the Virgin told us. He cautioned us to be very still and silent.

This was his moment.

The excitement on his face was palpable. He looked like a Harappan archaeologist on the cusp of finding something after years of toil! His time spent attending numerous wild life camps and watching Discovery and National Geographic channels would finally now pay off!

We were all silent.

Our eyes were transfixed on the proceedings, waiting for its grand arrival.

It was now show time.

In a swift move, a few meters in front of our jeep *it arrived and it moved.*

We stared in disbelief.

The King of the Jungle walked rather lazily across the path. It wagged its majestic striped tail.

This was however not the 'King' we had come to witness.

Instead of a real Tiger, we witnessed a rather small sized, ugly looking body double. It did not even look like a hyena. It was a scraggy, emaciated, weak looking *dog* with some sort of weird strips over its body and tail!

We all burst out laughing.

The Virgin looked embarrassed. He was all red in the face.

'How many wild life camps have you attended before?' HBS taunted him. This was his big moment to give it right back to the Virgin.

'I have been to many wild life camps before. This is the first time I have made a mistake' the Virgin replied, visibly downcast.

'Why don't you again reexamine the pug marks?'

'It's strange. The pug marks were very recent and fresh.'

'I am ashamed of myself that I actually believed your bullshit.'

The Virgin was silent.

To make him feel more miserable than he already was, the supporting cast which till now was nestled in the background again rose to the occasion.

'Look.... your friend on the tree' HBS smirked.

'Very funny' the Virgin replied.

A very happy monkey with a smiling face was howling in glee from a tree.

Our sightseeing tour had ended.

The jeep swerved through a final narrow passage and we reached the entry of the Corbett wild life park.

Our lodge jeeps were waiting to take us back.

15
VILLAGE TREK

'Is this supposed to be a relaxing off-site or a fucking army camp?' the Virgin asked me, wiping sweat off his forehead.

'Tell me about it' I replied.

'At least, I am wearing my khaki shorts and feeling patriotic. Jai hind!' he remarked with a salute skywards.

I could not agree more with him.

To begin with, a late night party, then an early morning trip to the Corbett Park and now a village trek for over six kilometers! After relaxing a bit at the lodge after the jungle visit, the Trainer asked us to get ready for this trek. The trek was to begin from a stream near our lodge and was to end at a Montessori school located in the middle of a secluded, godforsaken village.

Dividing us into the teams of the TIGERS and the LIONS like in the football game, the Trainer explained that the trek was slightly different from a normal trek. The only change was the Virgin was now in my team (the TIGERS) and HBS had shifted to the other team (the LIONS). The Founder decided to screw this sweaty trek and rather conveniently had taken a head start in a jeep!

In this 'HR style' village trek, the Trainer explained that each team had to work in collaboration and not in competition with the other. The objective was to observe the decision making abilities of the teams together in the absence of complete information. To identify each location, each team had to nominate a member to negotiate with a member of the opposing team to discuss details leading up to the concerned location. Each location contained a clue to the next successive location, which would finally lead to the final destination-the Montessori school. At the school, we had to observe a bunch of tiny tots in action, to learn the art of team work, cooperation and team building.

The trek finally started by a stream close to our lodge.

The teams successfully trekked across hilly terrain, also correctly assessed a couple of clues in a sandy terrain as well.

We approached a village.

The Trainer asked us to pause and observe the calm and serene village life, to make us realize that money is only a mere byproduct for a happy, fulfilling life.

A small bullock cart was merrily ambling at a slow pace with no tension or care in the world. A woman was carrying cow dung in her hand to her stove in order to prepare lunch for her family. Her husband was carrying bales of hay. He was perspiring. His chubby son was holding a thin, emaciated goat and was walking aimlessly. The goat was bleating. The son was laughing. The wife started singing some folk song. The son started thumping some beats on the goat. There was no need for an iPod. The father while lifting the bales of hay also started swaying to the beats of the folk song sung by his wife. All were happy. All in all, it was a simple, uncomplicated life which was a far cry from the stressful and hyper competitive world of wealth management at WCA.

'Yaar, I think I shall settle down in a village' the Virgin told me.

'Why?' I asked.

'I envy the lives of farmers. Most of these farmers spend their time with their families and also enjoy on the side with their rakhails! These guys have mistresses in different villages and buy property in their name.'

'Hmmm'

'Jokes apart, their lives are uncertain, man. It depends on the monsoon and all. Life is very difficult. Everyday is a challenge for them unlike our bullshit team building games in which we are forcefully trying to create some stupid "challenges".'

'I completely agree.'

I now had some new found respect for the Virgin. He was funny in his observations but was also pretty sensible and sorted in his thoughts. Barring maybe his occasional slip up while spotting a Tiger!

We trudged past the village.

The chubby son was now sitting on the goat like it was a little moped for running village errands.

The village trek was back in progress.

The way the clues were headed, it seemed like we were headed in the right direction towards the Montessori school. With only two clues left to be unearthed, at the negotiation round, HBS was selected from the LIONS team. After a bit of consultation within our team, the Virgin was chosen as the one to negotiate with HBS.

HBS and the Virgin stepped forward for the discussions.

The rest of the team stood by the side, waiting in anticipation for details of the next location to be unearthed.

'I am telling you, this clue directs us back to the hills to confuse us' HBS told the Virgin.

'No. I think it leads straight ahead, to a location towards the school' the Virgin replied.

'I disagree. We shouldn't go back that way towards the hills.'

'No. I think we should continue to walk that way.'

The Virgin pointed in the direction behind HBS's ass.

'Don't talk to me like that.'

'What do you mean?'

'Even my small nephew in Bangalore never talks to me like that! Talk with respect.'

'Why? Respect must be earned not commanded, ok?'

'You are new to this organization. And we know why you are in this organization. I am your senior. Learn to respect my decision.'

'WCA is a flat organization. There is no concept of senior or junior.'

'Don't question my understanding of the clue. Learn to respect me. And play the game in the right spirit.'

'You are not playing the game in the right spirit. I certainly am.'

The Virgin snapped right back at HBS.

This was getting interesting.

'Do you know how many cows we have seen so far?' HBS asked him.

'No' the Virgin replied.

'Do you know how many kilometers we have walked so far?'

'No.'

'Then don't question my understanding of the clue.'

'But what stupid questions are you asking? What does it have to do with the direction towards the school?'

'It shows that you don't use your head to think. The clues are designed to test your presence of mind. Don't mislead us like you did in the jungle.'

'Ok, let me ask you one question.'

'Yes. Go ahead.'

'How many times have you scratched your balls in the last five minutes?'

'You watch your tongue!'

'You mind your language. MIND IT!'

As if he was a younger version of superstar Rajinikant, the Virgin flipped a grass twig which he was carrying in his hand like a cigarette into the air. The twig did a quick gravity defying summersault in mid air!

'You are wrong. I am right. I know it.'

'NO CHANCE' the Virgin screamed.

The confrontation was getting intense.

HBS was staring down at the Virgin like he was sitting on a pile of hot coal, waiting to burn him down. Both were shaking their heads vigourously, disagreeing with each other. This was more than just a game. *It was about settling past scores from the beginning of the off-site.*

The other seniors seemed to be enjoying this 'senior-junior' confrontation. They were busy munching on bars of Kit-Kat distributed by the Trainer. After all, it was time for a break! The flare up had given them discussion points which the Founder might also use during the appraisal time for the both of them!

Sensing that the village trek was slowly fading away from being a game of friendly negotiations into a full blown ego war, the other team members also finally took sides and entered the warring zone. It was now, again a competition between the TIGERS and the LIONS, like in the football game!

I wanted to wholeheartedly cheer for the Virgin's decision but I knew that I would be meeting HBS formally in office again, a few days from now! I would probably meet the Virgin only during the next off-site.

While I was excited, both of them were silent.

The deadlock had not been broken. The egos needed to be massaged.

The Trainer finally realized this.

Small droplets of tension sweat and the frantic movement of his eyes seemed to suggest that this trek was blowing up into a full blown ego war.

He decided to step in to resolve the conflict.

He decided to adopt the safest route.

When in doubt be diplomatic. Satisfy the ego of both the warring parties.

'I think while you approached the game in the right spirit, your combative instincts were misdirected while dealing with a colleague' he told the Virgin.

HBS smiled. It was victory to him!

The Virgin shook his head vigourously in disapproval.

'However having said that, everyone in the organization at WCA whether senior or junior should welcome suggestions especially from youngsters' he told HBS.

The Virgin smiled! It was victory to him this time!

HBS seethed in silence.

'So let's shake hands on this positive happy note' he said, wiping sweat off his forehead.

HBS and the Virgin shook hands.

'Problem solved' he concluded triumphantly.

Seeing both HBS and the Virgin staring at each other with irritation, well the problem was not really solved!

The simmering undercurrents from the conflict still seemed to remain.

With the Trainer out of earshot, HBS cursed the Virgin.

'You wait and watch how your appraisal goes' he threatened further.

'You stay in Bangalore. If you dare come to Delhi, see what I will do to you' the Virgin threatened in return, breaking the grass twig into two pieces.

'We are all sick of you in this company with your daily naatak and nakras.'

'Why? What will you do?'

'I am going to ask the Big Boss to fire you.'

'Arre my uncle is the baap of this company. He gives the maximum business. You know that, right? How many times do I have to keep telling you?'

HBS was silent.

'The ball is back in my court' the Virgin said.

'Even I have balls' HBS screamed back. He obviously had not understood what the Virgin meant.

'That is obvious! You scratch it all the time!'

'You need to go see a doctor to get your head examined.'

'Take my advice! You need to go to a doctor to treat your scratching, you human plague!'

HBS was completely zapped. He clenched his fist.

Seeing this altercation between the both of them, it was hard to believe we were financial advisors at WCA! We should all have been street fighters instead.

The Trainer looked emotionally and mentally drained. The Aunties and I looked on expectantly. Unfortunately for us, no fist fight ensued. A fight would have been very interesting.

Who would have been the last man standing?

'*Dost dost na raha...*' Aunty no 1 started singing to Aunty no 2.

They both smiled at each other.

'We should sing for each other and also play antakshari sometime' Aunty no 2 replied.

'Sure. But just let's hope that, both of them first fight sometime. It will be a lot more fun.'

'Yes. Hope they fight like those aggressive women in mud wrestling.'

The Trainer looked desperate.

He decided to scrap the game and the search for the remaining clues. Instead, he asked us to follow him.

Like small little school boys following the head master, we followed him in search of the school.

This team building activity had gone sour!

As I walked, I was sure the conflict was not entirely resolved. I had identified two problem areas which went beyond the basic training modules of the HR Trainer-

1. Seniority based issues- 'Senior' versus 'Junior'.

2. Regional office location issues- 'Delhi office' versus 'Bangalore office'.

These problems would take time to sort out. And there was no easy solution!

We finally reached the Montessori school.

Our jeeps were waiting for us. Thankfully, we would not have to walk back again, after this school visit!

16

EXPERIMENTAL EDUCATION

'A child's mind is most productive when it operates in a creative, learning environment. Similarly each one of you at work, while working in the team, should strive to come up with creative solutions to meet your work challenges' the Trainer told us.

We all nodded in boredom.

Having concluded his gyaan for the moment, he directed our groups towards a giggling teacher who was in her late twenties. She was to take us on a guided tour of one of the Montessori classrooms to observe the tiny tots at work. 'Instructor, take it forward from here' he commanded her and walked away to join the Founder.

HBS was already in discussion with the Founder.

Maybe he was having a talk on how to improve the productivity of WCA which possibly involved firing the Virgin!

The Founder seemed to be in deep thought.

He was possibly evaluating the options-the Virgin was clearly a disruptive influence but his uncle was a big client.

But what was more important to WCA?

Having a dynamic, non-conflicting team? Or tolerating the Virgin and his antics because his uncle gave the big money to the company?

It was an uneasy situation to balance and manage!

With the giggling teacher in the lead, we approached a classroom. It was quite fascinating to get a first hand glimpse of the little kids working on different self directed pursuits. She informed us that the kids were in the age group between three to six years. Oblivious to the peering audience, some of the kids were crawling, some sitting, some walking, some talking, some reading and some were counting numbers on their fingers.

The Virgin standing in the row in front of me, readied his Nikon camera to click a few photos of the tiny tots in their colourfully decorated classroom. Standing behind him, I was able to obtain a picture perfect view of the tiny tots in action.

He began clicking away their images with effortless ease.

Image 1-The joys of team work- A small, skinny boy busy constructing a small sand castle was joined by his chubby friend who brought in a little heap of clay.

Image 2- The joys of stardom- In a corner of the room, a small girl was busy sweeping away with a broom and dust pan in hand. While taking rest, she also happily posed for the camera with a sweet 'baby beauty contest winner' smile!

Image 3- The joys of self discovery- In another corner of the room, an industrious boy was patiently learning to tie his shoe lace but was getting confused as to when to loop the lace and tie the final knot. He tried, retried and finally cried. He patiently tried to untangle the lace to restart all over again.

*Image 4- The joys of self learning-*In the center of the room, a seemingly precocious boy maybe of around five years, walked towards a table and picked out the English letter tablets to gain mastery over the language. He seemed to be an academic topper in the making.

*Image 5- The discoveries of nature-*A small, silent nature loving boy sitting by a window watched in rapt attention, the journey of an ant over a bean bag towards the wall.

*Image 6- The sound of music-*A small freckled girl sitting next to a bean bag was busy hitting her head on the bean bag. She seemed to wonder as to where the muffled thuds were coming from.

Explaining the benefits of the Montessori style of education, the teacher like a drug peddler intensified her distribution of the nuggets of school wisdom to us. Meanwhile, the skinny boy and his chubby friend were busy collecting sand from the sand pit located in the corner of the room for the construction of their castle. The skinny boy made small little round clay balls and placed it on the ground. The chubby boy flattened a bit of the clay in the shape of a long elongated erect carrot. The carrot was then placed between the little clay balls.

The visual image on offer did not make for good viewing.

They then, mounted the clay carrot, at a forty five degree angle along with the clay balls as companions on either side. All of a sudden, the distorted image looks remarkably innocent, childlike and refreshingly appealing. The creativity of the small boys was hard to dispute.

They had built a little clay cannon to protect their sand castle!

Post the castle pursuit, the chubby boy passed the sweeping girl and deliberately put some sand on her hair. She started crying. The freckled bean bag girl came to her rescue and cleaned her sand filled hair. She scolded the chubby boy, telling him that it was a wrong thing to do. The chubby boy however gleefully giggled at his skinny friend at the job well done.

As the freckled girl walked back to sit on her bean bag, the skinny boy this time, was coaxed by his chubby friend to indulge in some mischief. The skinny boy decided to put a pile of sand on the head of the freckled girl. This time however, the sweeping girl came to the rescue of her friend in the nick of time. The freckled girl turned around and overpowered the skinny boy. She removed the sand from his hand and put it in his shirt pocket. The chubby boy was very glum by the outcome. His skinny friend had been overpowered by a girl smaller in size than he was!

Undeterred by his previous aborted attempt at mischief, the skinny boy accompanied by the chubby boy moved to the corner of the room to disturb the nature loving boy. The nature loving boy happily watched the slow upward ascent of the ant onto the wall. The skinny boy offered the nature loving boy a small wrapped paper. He gleefully accepted it thinking it was a toffee inside. On opening the wrapper, he realized that it was actually a piece of clay! The tag team of the small and the chubby boy laughed out loud.

The precocious elder boy sitting in the middle of the room told the tag team to keep quiet. He appeared deep in thought. He was furiously arranging a set of letter tablets, which were scattered all around him.

HBLSLGVAIEIBA

After a pause, he rearranged the tablets.

IAHVEIGBBLALS

As he arranged the tablets, the industrious boy with his untied shoelaces accidentally stumbled over the arrangement! This scattered all the letter tablets. Out of sheer frustration, the precocious boy tied the lace of both the industrious boy's shoes together and pushed him to a side! The industrious boy started crying as he was not able to walk.

The precocious boy returned to his task. Angry at having been disturbed, he rearranged the tablets for possibly the final time. The final rearrangement read as-

I HAVE BIG BALLS

Standing in front of me, the Virgin let out a shocked gasp and placed his camera back in its flap. Even he was speechless for a change by the word arrangement! A small boy with small balls talking about big balls was certainly no laughing matter! The Trainer read the word arrangement in shock and interrupted the giggling teacher. Seeing the arrangement, the teacher shrieked. Hearing her shriek, the Founder also arrived. HBS

also trailed him to see what the fuss was all about.

With the teacher back in the classroom to attend to the children and to find out the probable source of inspiration, the Virgin could not keep his mouth shut.

'I am sure he must be the inspiration' he screamed, pointing at HBS.

All burst out laughing.

HBS immediately removed his ball scratching hand from his trouser pocket.

As we were walking out of the Montessori school, a pigeon perched on a twisted branch of one of the trees in the school complex decided to relive its tensions for the day.

The chosen one was HBS.

His cotton white starched shirt which was spotless, now had a few crimson shades to it.

'What a stupid crow!' he remarked in frustration.

'Actually it was a pigeon' Aunty no 1 said smiling.

'What a stupid animal!'

'Well, it is actually a bird.'

'Who the hell cares? Does anyone have a handkerchief to wipe this shit?' he shouted.

'Do you need help? But I will not help you' the Virgin stated rudely.

I wanted to burst out laughing but I did not. Somehow I had to step up and help out my boss cum mentor. The best I could do was to offer him my ten rupee handkerchief, one which I had purchased in a discount sale months ago.

'Thanks' he replied as he grabbed the kerchief from my hand.

Like a Picasso spreading his colours joyously from his palette, HBS spread the mess further across the expanse of his white shirt! His shirt now really looked like the stained, filthy shirts of adolescent boys which frequently appear in detergent commercials.

'Daag accha hai' the Virgin said, with a grin which almost split his face in two.

As we walked to the taxis to be driven back to our lodge, the Virgin started dancing. He started doing yet another vulgar dance. He started shrugging his shoulders vigorously while showing his posterior to HBS.

He started singing '*Masakali Masakali...*'

HBS kept his cool and muttered something under his breath.

'*Kabootar aa aa aa...kabootar ja ja ja...*' the Virgin continued in full flight.

We were all in high spirits.

This was what team building was all about- Having a good laugh and a good time.

We were ready to head back to the lodge.

17

RAPPELLING

The Trainer with his indefatigable reservoirs of enthusiasm and energy had organized a session of rappelling down a mountain cliff located by a stream near our lodge. It was an adventure task to face one's worst fears in the eye and to get out of one's comfort zone. It was slated as an optional session given the jungle trip and strenuous village trek of the morning. As it was optional, no one wanted to go for it.

The Founder however wanted to go.

Unlike us, he had unlimited reservoirs of energy. He had not trekked with us! It would be interesting to watch him excel at an adventure task. In the football game the previous day, he had kicked the ball rather gently. He spoke to us about his mother who did not like him pursuing adventure sports. Even at his age, he definitely listened to well meaning motherly advice like a true 'Indian son'! Maybe he was quite pampered like I was. Seeing the loose skin on his round circular face, maybe his mom still cooked oily aloo parathas for him! Maybe she also made him eat extra ladoos and halwa on Diwali to cement true mother-son festival love.

The Trainer wanted a few of the team members to also give the task a shot. Using a combination of exhortation and coercion, the youngsters of WCA had to also assemble in a line for the task.

As I made my ascent up the mountain, I saw Bedroom and Boardroom relaxing by the stream. Boardroom was in tights and a tight top while Bedroom was in a string bikini. She looked like a Kingfisher calendar model. If all the advisors had come to the summit, it would definitely have been a serious 'competition' of who could rappel down the fastest to impress them!

I reached the top of the mountain cliff.

The sheer drop was intimidating. I was scared!

The bubbling stream on the ground looked like a small water faucet diligently charting its course within the gigantic framework of the rugged terrain.

In front of me were the Virgin and our Founder.

A few of the Mumbai colleagues rather skillfully had rappelled down the mountain. It was now the turn of the Virgin. Strapped in his harness and with safety instructions from the safety expert, the Virgin looked down the sheer drop. 'What a drop' he gasped. With the safety team doing a double check of his harness, he seemed to have second thoughts about rappelling down the steep mountain.

'I don't think I will do it' he told the Founder.

'Are you sure you don't want to go down? Others have done it. Don't be scared' the Founder encouraged him.

'No. I am positive. I am scared.'

'Are you sure?'

'I am. I don't feel good about it.'

'Come on! Show some spirit!'

'This isn't a logical battle. This is a physical battle. I'm sorry.'

'You are a youngster. Get out of your comfort zone. This is the age to try new things.'

'Thanks for the encouragement but I shall maybe try it later on in life.'

'There is no later on in life! It is now or never. This is a chance of a lifetime. Have you changed your mind?'

'No. I am walking back down.'

'Ok, fine.'

The Founder shook his head, dissatisfied with the Virgin's meek attempt.

'Yaar, it is seriously scary. If I were you even I will walk off' he told me, untangling himself from the safety harness.

'Ok.'

'Those hot chicks are down there, by the stream. It was distracting me. That blue string bikini chick is awesome. The tattooed fat chick is also looking damn hot.'

'I know. I also saw them.'

'I don't want to die. I want to live for chicks like them.'

'Don't talk of death and scare me.'

'Ok. All the best! I shall meet you in heaven after twenty or thirty years!'

I was tense.

The Virgin started walking down the mountain back to the base.

It was now only the Founder and me.

'You want to go before me?' he asked me.

'No. I shall go after you' I replied meekly.

I was also really scared now.

I wanted to back out.

'I am going down now' he announced.

Rappelling down from the edge of the cliff, he was out of sight. I was the last man standing on the edge.

'There is nothing to worry. All the safety precautions are in place' the safety instructor assured me as he rechecked my harness.

He did not *sound* very reassuring though. Nor did he *look* very reassuring.

He was wearing a cheap, frayed half sleeve shirt. His left arm had the elbow joint protruding forward rather than backward like for the rest of us!

He also had only one eye.

The other eye was a green coloured glass eye. It was the sort which had either fallen out of the eye of a roadside cat or was a missing marble which a child had lost while playing a game of marbles with his colony friends.

I was really worried. It was moments like this when one really valued one's life.

I thought of my parents. I thought fleetingly of my ex-girlfriend. I also thought of the various unfulfilled pleasures of life.

I glanced down the cliff.

The Founder had reached the base. He looked like a little mosquito from the top.

It was my turn now. There was no backing out now.

'Sab theek hai' the safety instructor told me while checking the harness with his twisted left arm.

'Ok' I replied.

I now noticed that he also had a gold tooth in addition to his glass eye.

It really did not help matters.

Standing on the edge and with my harness firmly in place, I turned my ass on the edge of the cliff with my face towards the mountain. With the cable slowly being descended, I held onto the harness and started the slow descent downwards. I used my legs as shock absorbers, resting on the rough rock edges on my way down. Bouncing off the steep edges, I slowly reached the base.

The Founder was waiting for me.

'Was it difficult?' he asked me.

'It was challenging' I replied.

I was lying.

I was as scared as I could get.

'You should have tried too' the Founder told the Virgin.

'I told you, I was scared' he replied without a hint of any regret.

I admired the way the Virgin stood up to the higher ups.

I could never do it. I was born docile and subservient.

The next time I met my Mom, I wanted to ask her whether I had cried spontaneously at the time of my birth or whether I had to be whacked on my bum to do so.

As I made my way back to join the rest of the team, Aunty no 1 asked me what exactly had transpired on the summit between the Virgin and the Founder.

I told her exactly what had happened.

'He is definitely going to get a poor rating in his appraisal' she told me.

'But why?' I asked.

'Arre don't you know? They will use "fear of rappelling" as one of the qualitative aspects in our year end appraisal. It is all about getting out of the comfort zone. But this idiot is lucky. Not that the appraisal will matter to him but for the rest of us, it is good that the session was optional.'

'Hmmm'

'Especially since, the Big Boss tried his hand at the task and also successfully completed it.'

'I know. Thankfully I also somehow managed to complete the task.'

Aunty no 2 also offered her two bits of advice.

As per her understanding, non-rappelling down the cliff held the following implications at appraisal time for the Virgin-

1. He did not get out of his comfort zone.

2. He admitted that he was scared.

3. He was not a good sport and hence was not a good player.

4. If the Founder had the balls to do it, why could he not do it?

5. He may or may not have died (in panic...seeing the steep drop) but he should at least have tried!

All the negative conclusions meant that, despite the session being an optional one, the Virgin or any other team member who did not try was probably not suitable for a career in finance as a wealth advisor. It was time to look for alternate employment!

'Look at those women over there by the stream' Aunty no 1 told Aunty no 2 standing by my side.

'I know. Deliberately relaxing here to get all the men's attention' Aunty no 2 replied.

'They will first behave in a flirtatious way. Then when a man makes a pass at them, they will get irritated and blame him. I know these types.'

I did not know if I should agree with the Aunties or if I should support the artists and their freedom to live life on their own terms.

But I was clear of one thing.

The artists were hot! No denying that!

Seeing the other advisors also stare lasciviously at them, we were all the same! In such fast paced, stressful commercial times, it was debatable whether there was time to find the desired 'inner beauty' in a woman.

'I am sure they are up to something with the men from our team' Aunty no 2 continued.

'How do you know?' Aunty no 1 asked.

'My eye is twitching again. Do you know anything?'

Aunty no 2 looked at me searchingly like how my mom would.

'How will I know?' I replied fumbling for words.

'I was just checking.'

The Aunties walked away.

Maybe watching saas-bahu serials just like watching detective serials, did enhance one's sleuthing and investigative skills!

18
GOAL SETTING

Following the exciting events of the morning and afternoon, the evening time was reserved for a business presentation. The Founder was to present his 'vision' and 'mission' for WCA for the coming five years and beyond and also the road map that lay ahead to achieve these goals.

The presentation would be all about vision, mission, clients, group targets, business growth, future prospects, improvement of existing systems, better time management, coordination, enhanced efficiency, strategies, leadership and overall feedback on running the operations-complicated long winding terms which one would get to read in management books.

No wonder the Trainer slated it as a two hour session.

We were given pencils, note pads to scribble relevant questions, and a 500 ml bottle of mineral water to prevent us from getting dehydrated. As advisors, our job was to listen carefully and offer intelligent feedback, if any.

The presentation began.

The Virgin put his hand over his face and pretended to be listening. He was actually sleeping. The exhausting village trek had taken its toll!

It would be interesting if he would also begin to snore.

'In 3 years from now, we should scale up both in terms of clients and in terms of revenues..... ' the Founder waxed eloquent.

'What a waste of time' Aunty no 1 sitting to my immediate left told Aunty no 2 sitting by her side.

'I know. Total bakwas. All management gyaan' Aunty no 2 replied.

'Why can't they just mail us the presentation and bring on the booze?'

'What about the first and second year? How did he jump to the third year directly?'

'No idea. I don't care. See this drawing of mine.'

Aunty no 1 showed a drawing she had made on her note pad. It was a caricature of the Founder delivering the presentation. It was like we were back in school.

I had never suspected this humourous streak in Aunty no 1.

'....In the long run, such a strategy would pay off.... ' the Founder ranted identifying the means to achieve the end goals.

'What long run is he talking about?' muttered Aunty no 2.

'May the next ten years?' Aunty no 1 replied.

'Why don't they project growth over the next hundred years also?'

'Who cares about this presentation? In the long run we are all dead!'

'Plus even saas-bahu serials don't run that long!'

'Well said!'

'But I am sure, we would still be listening to this sort of bullshit at some fucking off-site, some hundred fucking years from now also' the Virgin said.

He suddenly was awake!

But then having made his point, he went back to sleep, resting his head on the desk. He started drooling on his note pad.

I thought to myself.

It was the Founder's job to give such 'goal oriented' pep talks to keep us motivated. It reminded me of my school Principal who spoke to the students just before the 12th Board exams, to motivate us to stay focused during the exams. He explained in a cutting tone that exam marks were an apt indicator of success for a student in the journey of life. As he spoke, it became clear that, more than making our parents proud, it was about making the school proud! The school could then publish an advertisement in the newspaper listing the meritorious students- student 1- 97.6%, student 2- 96.6% and so on and thereby hike the fees for the following year's new admissions! If we could not make the school proud, then as students we should get the hell out and dare not return to attend any of the school alumni parties!

The thought of being for 100 'fucking' years at WCA made me think. 100 years was a lifetime to be in a company!

By then, I would be 126 plus years old. I would be an old man, with all my body parts literally collapsing. I would be using a walking stick as an aid to walk, two steps an hour towards the office to meet my existing high net worth clients. The clients would also be really old, in the age bracket between 130 to 180 years. They would also be facing their own respective health problems. HBS would *continue* to remain my self imposed mentor. He would continue to scratch his old age balls. He would continue to remain fit and fine for a really long time. Words would come out of his mouth really slowly. Despite the old age, he would however have not lost his argumentative and scratching streak. However unlike the present time, arguments (especially with the Virgin) would take days if not months, to be resolved on account of the slow pace of old age.

In 100 years from now, the Virgin would still be arrogant and in command. That was because his Uncle would still continue to remain the biggest client in the Delhi office. The Virgin's Ramu Kaka would have reached heaven or would still continue to work, hobbling on one leg with the aid of a gold plated crutch to help his beloved master.....

Auntie no 1 jolted me from my futuristic reverie.

'Hey, so how do you like the Bangalore office?' she asked me.

'It is good' I replied.

'So how is it, to work with him?' she asked as she dangled the pencil in the direction of HBS, who was sitting diagonally across us.

'It is a good learning experience.'

'Are you serious?'

'Yes, I am.'

I had to be careful. What if she went and sneaked? After all, I had to go back and work in the Bangalore office!

'But isn't he very dominating?'

'I guess he likes doing things his way.'

'He is as dominating and obnoxious as this bloody idiot sleeping here.'

She pointed at the sleeping Virgin.

I just smiled.

'Anyways, good luck to you.'

'Thanks.'

'....In five years, I think our practice will be of a critical size and scale such that we can look at penetrating tier two and tier three cities as well. Let's make WCA... the most admired, desired, cherished and loved finance company pan India and across Asia!' the Founder concluded.

The ambitious five year plan for the company had been comprehensively outlined!

'Let's do it!' the Trainer said, raising his glass of water as a toast to this ambitious plan.

'Hey guys! How about a thumbs up...raise your glasses please' he told us.

Taking the cue, the 500 ml bottles of mineral water were raised in solidarity to achieve this grand 'vision' and 'mission'.

The Virgin also stirred and held his bottle of mineral water.

He also raised his middle finger up in the air.

No one noticed.

The group started to break up.

With the session having concluded, it was now time to hit the makeshift bar for a second night of drinks and dinner.

HBS was talking to the Founder. They were near me.

'How did you like the session?' HBS asked me.

'Very informative' I replied.

'Even in Bangalore...as a team it is very important to follow *my* vision and work towards goals.'

Wasn't team goals all about 'our' and not 'my' vision?

'Hmmm'

'Given my track record, I am sure we can plan ahead and work towards getting more clients.'

'Sure.'

In short- HBS was the best! Doing and trying to say all the right things to get the best financial advisor of the year award!

'Oh...you guys are already strategizing and working on goals? Good. Keep it up.'

The Founder looked at HBS appreciatively.

'I always tell my team to think out of the box.'

'Good job, guys. Keep it up.'

The only box in Bangalore was our office, which was a small match box sized office!

'It is important to keep leadership on the same page. Once leaders across the board think alike....'

I coughed.

The Founder again launched into one of his elaborate explanations.

Maybe he was drawing on extra bull shit from the book which I had given him on his birthday!

Wasn't the two hour session enough?

I was getting late.

They kept talking. I was tired of keeping an interested face. I had to eat and rush for the remaining sketches with Bedroom and Boardroom! I had to strategize my time and meet the client deliverables required by them!

HBS and the Founder finally finished talking after a while. I excused myself.

I had a quick, light dinner and finally left the hall.

I rushed to my room.

The Virgin was already in the room. He was arranging his bed in all readiness to go to sleep. I did not tell him about my plans with the artists. I was planning on telling him that I was going for a night walk around our lodge.

'My fucking legs are going to collapse. First my testicles got damaged and now my knees and my ankles are hurting. I am going to kill them both' the Virgin said, referring to HBS and the Trainer.

'Why, what happened?' I asked.

'How much we walked today. I haven't walked this much in the last one year put together. I think today I have lost at least 2-3 kilos.'

'Are you serious?'

'I am.'

'I am actually going for a night walk right now, around the lodge.'

'Kitna walking karega? Hero aur size zero dono banega kya?'

He laughed at his own remark.

'No reason in particular. The weather is nice.'

'Kiske saath jayega? Making new friends in WCA? Going for a walk with them without me?'

'I'm going alone.'

'Oh, for time pass. Do you want me to come?'

'No, man. You relax. Your leg is paining right?'

'Yes, yaar. You go. Take a torch. It is very dark outside. Also take our room key.'

'Sure.'

'Can you also keep the balcony door open? The room is so stuffy.'

'Ok.'

'Have fun.'

Did he mean anything by *fun*?

I went and opened the balcony door to let in some fresh air.

The room was actually very stuffy. The Virgin was all tucked in to sleep. He covered his entire body from head to toe like a dead body. He started to gently snore. I saw the handcuff, the one which he had slapped on his wrist in the wee hours of the morning.

I picked it up to return it to Bedroom.

I wrapped my hands around and it and I walked out of my room. Hopefully it would be a satisfying night up ahead with the artists!

19
THE FIG LEAF COLLECTION-2

I knocked on room 310.

Boardroom opened the door.

'Oh, you are back?' she asked me. Her voice expressed a tinge of surprise.

'Well I am a professional. I like to keep up to client requirements' I replied.

'My… my…. so you did enjoy posing for us last night?'

'Yes. I like the temptations and the perks that come with it.'

I wanted to finish the sketches quickly and give Bedroom a good enjoyable massage.

'So let's get on with it then. I am also sorry for the way I behaved last night. You did give me some good weight related advice which I shall try to implement.'

'No problem. I am treated worse at work. But before starting, do you have anything to eat? I am hungry. I had a very light dinner.'

'Room service will be closed now. Plus I don't think you want the room service guys to see us the way we are now.'

Boardroom turned away and went to the table to get the sketch requirements ready.

'Do you want some oranges? They are nice and juicy' Bedroom asked, pointing at the fruit basket.

'Sure. Why not? I like them juicy and firm' I replied, staring at her breasts.

She noticed me staring.

'You are repressed and sick.'

'I am not sick...just a little repressed and honest. After all, I am an Indian male who gets more action on the stock markets than in bed. I have told you that.'

I lapsed into some unrelated thoughts as I grabbed two oranges.

According to the annual sex surveys published by leading Indian magazines, sex seemed to be everywhere. Indian society had opened up. Surveys indicated that cricket statistics and a woman's vital statistics were the only two things on an Indian man's mind. Couples had become less coy and had become more experimental in their desires and actions. The sexual revolution was happening right here right now in India, in the 21st Century ...but I had seen nothing of it. People were supposedly humping wildly in schools, colleges, offices and elsewhere.

But why the hell had I been so unlucky? Was I scared of rejection from a girl again? Did I suffer from low self esteem issues?

Was I destined to be a late bloomer in matters relating to sex?

With my college girlfriend, our indulgences were limited to the odd kiss, awkward moments of PDA (like we were a gawky teen couple!) and copious amounts of 'love filled' emotional dialogues. Aspects which one normally associates when one experiences the first flush of love. After a point, I wanted them to end and things to lead to something more physical

It somehow never did!

Boardroom was ready to sketch.

I gathered my thoughts for the sketches lined up.

I hurriedly finished the two oranges.

I placed the handcuff which I brought back from my room, on their bed.

I was ready.

The artists' room was nice. In comparison to my room, it had a warm, reassuring 'in love with nature' kind of atmosphere. Lining the corner of their room next to the balcony door were potted artificial plants. Despite the plants being artificial, caterpillars, centipedes, millipedes and other small creatures of the soil were slithering in an out of the pots, rather merrily.

'Here understand the requirements for sketch 6- *The Act of Defiance*' Boardroom told me.

I went through the sketch details-

"In this sketch, with the fig leaf boy's union with his sweetheart being opposed to by her parents, the fig leaf boy takes on a new avatar. Replacing the innocent, well groomed appearance is a certain brutal coldness to his appearance. The gelled hair has been replaced with a dishevelled look. The clean shaven facial look has given way to a rugged stubble look. The shaved chest makes way for a sprinkling of chest hair. The red sneakers are missing and have been replaced by army boots. Slinging on his shoulder is an AK-47 gun. It seems like the fig leaf boy is taking to violence to seek revenge against the girl's parents and to also fight for the other ancillary problems which plague the Indian society."

I got ready to pose for the sketch.

Bedroom messed up my hair. She gave me army boots to wear which fitted me perfectly.

She used her black eyeliner to dot my face and chest to give me the rugged look. She gave me the black coloured toy gun which was to be the AK-47.

I was all ready in character.

Boardroom started sketching.

'I love this sketch. A rebel is born' Bedroom remarked, gazing at my transformed appearance from the sidelines.

'This is the sketch which portrays the untold angst of the fig leaf boy against the girl's parents. This sketch also captures activism at its zenith. It is very relevant in today's times of terror' Boardroom added.

'Interesting interpretation' I stated.

The three of us silently reflected on further possible interpretations.

'Go through the requirements for sketch 7-*The Act of Sacrifice*' Boardroom told me after some time.

I went through the sketch details-

"Unlike the personal angst and anger of the earlier sketch, this sketch displays the sacrificing side of the fig leaf boy. Realizing that his love is too pure for his sweetheart and given that she cannot be his in this lifetime, the boy discards the AK-47 and instead decides to give up his life rather than take someone else's. In the sketch, he is shown lying down on a railway track along with a tube of his favorite hair gel which he has stopped using. He is waiting to be run over by an oncoming train."

'In this sketch, I want you to feel a sense of loss. I want to capture the fragile nature of the human spirit. Think of the times you had spent with your girlfriend and how she was married off' Boardroom said to me.

I started to feel a little emotional. Time had passed but the moments I had spent with her felt like it was just yesterday.

'Lie down on these lines which she has drawn. They are the train tracks which is an important part of the sketch.'

Bedroom had drawn chalk marks on the floor. I lay down on the ground uncomfortably as Boardroom started to sketch.

'Also hold this tube of hair gel' Bedroom told me.

'But where is the train?' I asked.

'You don't bother. You focus on your angles. I like the way you have got into character. This sketch depicts true, unconditional love as opposed to the extreme wild side of revenge in the earlier sketch' Boardroom said.

'Unconditional love was something which none of us were given by our past lovers' Bedroom added rather grimly.

Boardroom continued to sketch.

'I am done with this sketch. Good job. Now go through the requirements for sketch 8- *The Act of Nervousness*' Boardroom told me, a while later.

I was sitting stark naked on the bed. I was about to go through the sketch requirement.

Boardroom had begun to sketch a rough outline.

The doorbell rang, all of a sudden.

'Who can it be?' Bedroom asked.

She sounded nervous. So was I.

Wasn't the 'Do not disturb' sign firmly in place on the door knob?

Was it a waiter? Was it someone from WCA?

My heart started pounding. I wanted to get away from it all. All my dreams of being a nude model and getting the benefits attached, if I completed the sketches with the hot artists…vanished.

'Wait. Let me go check' Boardroom said.

She walked up to the door and peered through the peephole in the door.

'It is not good news. Something is up' she told me.

'What? Who is it?' I asked.

'It is your off-site Trainer.'

'Shucks! What does he want? What is he doing here?'

'No idea. Hide somewhere!'

'But where can I hide?'

Even as a kid, I was not good at 'hide and seek' sort of games. And now at this age, I wondered as to where I could hide my fat body. Should I hide in the bathroom? What if the Trainer wanted to use it? I finally decided that hiding under the bed was the best option.

'Hide under the bed.' Boardroom said, seconding my choice.

Suddenly it dawned on me that I was in my birthday suit and was exposed.

'But I am naked. Please protect me.' I sounded like an infant who needed his mom to change the baby diaper.

'Stop whining like a baby. Let me see what he wants. You just hide.'

'But all the props and all...?'

'Just hide!'

I obeyed. I hid under the bed.

It was dusty. The damn room cleaners had not done a good job. I hoped I would not sneeze.

Bedroom stood in front of me to offer a feeble second line of defence. I could see her legs.

I heard the door being opened.

'Oh, hi...how come you are here? Rather late isn't it?' Boardroom asked the Trainer.

'Well I am really sorry to disturb. I just stopped by to ask for a favour. I got your room number from the receptionist' he replied. He sounded as though it was a normal thing to drop in so casually and so late in the night in people's rooms.

'What kind of favour?'

'Well as you are aware, I am conducting this off-site for WCA.'

'We are more than aware of that.'

'Well tomorrow, I am having a role play contest for my team in the conference hall, at ten in the morning. I was just wondering if both of you would like to attend the same? WCA's Founder had asked me to check your availability.'

'Sure. We will be there.'

'Ok, great. I wanted to ask you something else.'

He obviously had not yet left. I could not peer out.

'What? Go ahead.'

'Everyone in the company makes fun of me, my voice and my mannerisms.'

'So?'

'Can I come inside and discuss my problems with you?'

'Unfortunately tonight is not a good time. How are you placed tomorrow night?'

'I am leaving with the team back to Delhi tomorrow evening.'

'Oh!'

'I really hate this job as an off-site trainer. It is so demanding and all the men make fun of me.'

'Then I guess you have to grin and bear it. All of us have our problems.'

'No one even wants to listen to my problems.'

I heard the sound of someone crying. Was it the Trainer?

'Don't get emotional. Be practical. Life must go on. Let's meet tomorrow sometime, if possible. Ok, bye.'

'But...'

'Bye for now. We shall be there tomorrow. Thanks for the invite.'

I heard the noise of the door being slammed.

'You can come out now. She has shut the door' Bedroom told me.

I came out. I removed a cobweb from my hair.

'There are four of us *now*' Boardroom announced.

'What! Where is he? I thought he had left?' I asked in complete shock covering my modesty with a pillow.

'I was joking. What's with Indian guys not having a sense of humour?'

'Oh, thank God. You gave me a real fright.'

'I love to scare you. You are such a gullible guy.'

I did not say anything.

As long as my end objectives were met, I did not mind remaining a gullible fool for them!

I just prayed that the night would be uneventful henceforth except for the ultimate moment after the sketches.

'Ok, let's continue with the sketches. We have work to finish. Lie down on the bed' she instructed me.

I started reading the through the requirements for sketch 8- '*The Act of Nervousness*'-

"In this sketch, with the light beams of the speeding train fast approaching, the fig leaf boy starts panicking. He drops his tube of hair gel on the railway track. There is an expression of fear all over his young face."

Boardroom started to sketch.

'Here, I have shifted the table lamp to give the appearance of the light beam' she told me.

'Ok.'

'In a sense, the train lights represent the brutal parents waiting to run over the boy.'

'Just an observation- How come these tracks are so clean? I thought Indian railway tracks always have dung. This track is refreshingly clean.'

'Good point. Let it be open for interpretation later on.'

'Ok. I am also placing the hair gel by my side.'

'Great! I think you really are in character. You look scared. Good that the Trainer had come!' Bedroom said.

My heart was actually still pounding because of the Trainer's unexpected arrival.

'We are progressing at a good pace tonight. Only two sketches left to go' Boardroom told me.

The artists were on a mission. There was no time for a break.

I read through the requirements for sketch 9- *The Act of Union.*

"In this sketch, the fig leaf boy's sweetheart is lying down on the same bed in which she had engaged in an aborted act of sexual passion with her former lover (the fig leaf boy). At the door of her room, stands her new lover with some stock market related investment applications in his hand. It is the lover to whom she is being forcefully married off by her parents. Tonight is their first night as a married couple. Placed on the bedside table, is a 'dowry' cheque readily signed by the girl's parents to ensure the acceptance of their reluctant daughter by the new lover. "

'Money is the root cause of all evil' Boardroom remarked.

'I agree even though I am a financial advisor!' I said.

The mood was sombre. My attempt at a witty remark had not gone down too well. I had recovered from the Trainer's unexpected arrival and I was now in a relaxed mood anticipating moments of pleasure which would hopefully begin shortly.

'The concept of dowry is very regressive but still so widely prevalent. My boyfriend left me for bigger machines. No one can understand this issue better than me' Bedroom chipped in.

'Who will play the new lover in this sketch?' I asked Boardroom.

'No idea. I will probably have to ask the receptionist tomorrow in the morning. I will make him a *Godfather* kind of offer which he cannot refuse' she replied.

'Do you have anyone in mind?' Bedroom asked me.

I could ask the Virgin or any of my other team mates. Who would not want the chance? But the cat would be out of the bag. I could be in trouble.

'Ideally we need someone who is money minded, practical, authoritative, very low on emotional intellect and who monetizes every second of his life' she continued.

I could think of only one and only one such person- HBS!

'I can think of only my boss' I replied.

'That... scratching salsa guy?' Boardroom asked me.

'Yes.'

'That could be difficult. It could get you into trouble. I think I shall ask the receptionist.'

'That will actually be better.'

Bedroom lay on the bed. I watched her. I did not know whether she realized the effect she had on me.

Boardroom sketched keeping a portion of her sketch sheet blank.

The receptionist's part in the sketch had to be added later on.

'Wow! We have reached the final sketch. This collection has been so much fun. Go through the requirements for the final sketch-*The Act of Cowardice*' she told me a while later, with a sense of achievement.

I read through the sketch details-

"The sketch sheet has been split three ways with three separate images woven together. At the extreme left of the sheet- the fig leaf boy with fear all over his face, rolls away from the railway track. The train speeds past him, flattening the tube of hair gel which he has left behind on the tracks.

In the middle of the sheet- the fig leaf boy's sweetheart while continuing to lie down on the bed, takes out a bottle of acid from the bedside table drawer and pours it on the right side of her face, disfiguring it permanently. On the left side of her face, she places a face pack to enhance her 'fair and lovely' beauty quotient in readiness for some love making. This way while she may consummate her new marriage, by scarring her face, she reaffirms that her love remains true only for the fig leaf boy.

At the extreme right of the sheet- there is a look of sheer shock on the new lover's face. The shock is not on seeing his wife's grotesque appearance but it is because a part of the acid has fallen on the dowry cheque, thereby ruining it beyond recognition! As a result, the cheque cannot be presented to his bankers and he therefore cannot invest the money in the stock market as he had secretly planned."

'I need to sketch this one differently. It's tricky. This sketch has all the trappings of a Greek tragedy. There is a sense of melancholy on account of an impending tragedy which is waiting to unfold. I shall finish your part first. And then I shall sketch the remaining portion with the receptionist' Boardroom told me.

'Ok' I replied.

'All you have to do is to roll on the floor outside of those lines. I will do the rest' she told me.

'Ok, sure.'

'I think an art lover might enjoy the contrast between the acid and the moisturizer cream.'

'If in future you have a girlfriend and acid chars her faces, would you still love her?' Bedroom asked me.

It looked like she would decide on a lot of things based on this answer. This was the time for me to show my high levels of empathy and sympathy.

'Of course' I replied instantly.

'You are lying! All men are shallow. All they want are these' Boardroom interrupted pointing to her big ones.

'No, I disagree. I do have a heart and I do respect beauty on the inside and outside' I stated.

She looked at me skeptically.

I would say any bull to get some action.

My portion in the sketch was completed. It was now Bedroom's turn.

She placed her body across the sheets as Boardroom sketched her.

I watched the creative artists in full flight.

'You know something?' Bedroom asked me, as she lay on the bed.

'What?'

'You should take up modelling sometime. I mean *nude modelling*. You have a nice body and most importantly you pose well.'

'No! I shall stick with finance for a few years.'

I did not say anything.

I was excited that these compliments could now possibly be leading on to something better! Finally!

'Ok, then! I am done' Boardroom exclaimed triumphantly.

'Great! So you did manage to meet your targets' I said.

'Yes. Only the reaction of the new lover is left in sketch 9 and 10 which I shall finish tomorrow.'

'The time has finally come! For the massage!' I exclaimed.

'Look at him...how excited he is getting' Boardroom told Bedroom.

'I like my man to be excited!' she replied.

'Yes!' I exclaimed pumping my fists in delight. I started playing with the kinky handcuff on the bed.

'I think I heard someone again knock on the door. Who the hell is it? It is so late in the night' Bedroom said.

I was tense. And very worried.

Who was it this time?

I could see my career crumble in front of my eyes. My career was certainly fragile!

'Let me go check' Boardroom announced.

She walked to the door.

'Oh. I think this time we have a real problem. It is your scratching boss' she said, peering through the peephole.

'What! My BOSS! What is he doing here?'

'No idea.'

'Don't open the door. Pretend that you have gone to sleep.'

'But he is ringing the bell like a madman. It must be something urgent.'

'Ok. By any chance, does he think that this is my room?'

'How will I know?'

'I am screwed. Please help me.'

'Is your balcony door open?'

'Yes. It is. I kept it open before coming here.'

'You can walk along the ledge and enter your room.'

'And fall into that big ditch? I am too young to die.'

'Ok. Then just hide somewhere. I shall talk to him and dismiss him quickly.'

'Ok. Please scatter my clothes, hide my shoes...'

'Calm down.'

'Oh my God! This handcuff has got stuck to my hand. My hands are locked! I can't rush across the ledge.'

'Then just hide under the bed! Quick!' Boardroom told me. 'And you please wear some clothes' she told Bedroom.

I hid under the bed.

I was naked. And my hands were handcuffed. Rivulets of perspiration were lining the worry lines on my forehead. My heart was beating really hard. The only thing left for me was to get a heart attack.

I could imagine the following news headline-

NUDE FINANCIAL ADVISOR FOUND DEAD UNDER THE BED

Before I embraced death, I wanted the answer to one important question.

What was HBS doing here?

20
THE LATE NIGHT VISITOR

'I was wondering if I could talk to you' HBS announced in his usual overconfident manner.

'Regarding what?' Boardroom asked.

'I actually wanted to introduce myself.'

'But isn't it kind of late?'

Her voice clearly expressed her displeasure and anyone would have taken the hint to go, but not HBS!

Hiding under the bed, I could imagine his over the top, aggressive, alpha male style.

'As you are aware, I am from WCA. I am also the head of the Bangalore branch.'

'Ok. So?'

Her cold tone was sure to bring any man's confidence to ground zero.

'I am in room 105.'

'So? How can I be of help?'

'Actually if you don't mind, I have been observing you ladies from the party last evening when we met. I didn't really get a chance to speak to both of you properly.'

'Speak to us about what?'

'I also think both of you have been looking at me and are interested in me.'

'No! But what gave you that impression?'

'I saw you looking at me from a distance when I was doing the salsa dance with your friend.'

'Please stop this nonsense. You are not Tom Cruise, Brad Pitt or Salman Khan for me to admire from a distance.'

Boardroom's voice now dripped with sarcasm.

'Ok. Let me be fully honest. I like you ladies. Both of you make me feel young again.'

'What!'

'Yes. But please don't misunderstand me.'

'Then what should I understand?'

'That….'

'What that? Aren't you married? Why are you covering your wedding ring on your hand?'

Boardroom sounded outraged.

'My marriage is stifling me and bringing me a lot of suffering. There is a lot of tension in my life about loans to pay, targets to meet and the expectations of clients. I want to feel free for at least one night. Will you or both of you come with me for this night?'

'WHAT? I am sorry. I think you have formed the wrong impression about us.'

I could sense how angry Boardroom would have been to hear such a confession! Even I was shocked. I always knew HBS was a hypocrite. But right now, he was dangerously crossing a well defined matrimonial line.

'Don't be angry. I just felt that I should share my thoughts with you ladies.'

'What did you think we are? We are artists… not some random street side prostitutes!'

'Ok. I am sorry. At least I feel lighter having told you what I felt.'

'Who the hell cares whether you are light or heavy?'

'I wanted to express one more thing which had got my attention.'

'What?'

'I like your tattoos. I really like that scorpion under your collar bone.'

'Oh. You like it?'

She sounded surprised.

In the cafeteria, HBS had told me that the scorpion tattoo distracted him and he hated it! I had communicated the same to Boardroom while sketching too!

'It is very different to look at. It excites me.'

'Ok. But by the way, how did you get our room number?'

'I got your room details from the receptionist.'

'Ok. Not from the Trainer?'

'No…not from the Trainer. He is very weird. We hardly speak. But why did you ask? Did he tell you anything about me? I think he is jealous of my success.'

'Relax. I just asked. Stop connecting random dots.'

'Ok.'

'Are you always judgmental like this?'

'I don't know what you mean. But I am smart. Today I am the head of WCA Bangalore. I am a big financial advisor in Bangalore. Advisors my age are still struggling in their careers. I am an achiever.'

'Good for you.'

'So can I come in now?'

Trust HBS like a good financial advisor cum salesman to push his case if he detected the slightest leeway!

'No!'

'Ok, I am sorry for the confusion then. I was of the view that women love the power and the position an achiever like me has. Please keep this conversation among ourselves. I shall leave now.'

He sounded a bit deflated. He certainly was trying hard to push his luck. As if…women were lusting for an overachieving scratching salsa champion!

'Ok, bye.'

'Actually it is good I came to your floor, now. I think…I shall go meet my subordinate who is next door in room 309.'

That was me! Clearly HBS knew my room number.

'Who is that?' Bedroom chipped in, in her sweet voice. She was standing in front of me like my protective screen.

'He is my office subordinate. He is a very hardworking fellow. He has good values instilled by me. Also talks very little. He does all the extra work I give him without too much of questioning.'

'Oh…that's nice. I think I remember him. Was he the one who was carrying that drunkard after the dinner party last night?'

'Yes, he is the one. But I have been noticing that he has become a little confident. He tried to air kiss you in the party. It was something I never expected him to do!'

'Oh, yes. He did try to kiss me. But don't you think it is rather late in the night to meet him?'

'Not really. I always call him up at any time. I do that in Bangalore also. He is not married, you see. I like him to be well prepared always.'

'Ok.'

'Many times, I deliberately give him work on a Friday night and tell him to mail it to me by Sunday morning for a meeting which we may or may not have on a Monday. This is to teach him that focusing on work should always be top priority.'

'How cruel are you?'

'No, I am not cruel. I think he enjoys it. He is a hardworking fellow.'

'What are you meeting him for?'

'I have to discuss about a quiz and a role play with him. As a team, I love to win. Winning is everything. I need to discuss some strategies so that we are ready for tomorrow.'

'So you are planning to go meet him right now?'

'Yes, I have to. I would have given him a call right now but I have left my phone in my room. Since I am here, I might as well go and meet him face to face.'

'What if he is asleep?'

'I shall ring the bell and wake him up. He is used to my style of working.'

Please God no! HBS would ring my room doorbell.

The Virgin was asleep. He would wake up due to the noise. He would open the door. HBS would ask for me. The Virgin would say I had gone for a walk. HBS might come in search of me or he would ask nearly a hundred questions about my whereabouts!

I could get into trouble.

The tension I was feeling right now was much more than what I had felt when the Trainer had come in. HBS was my damn boss!

'Oh! So you are going to meet your subordinate right now in ROOM 309?' Boardroom asked again.

She was talking quite loudly.

Was it some sort of signal for me?

'Yes. But why are you shouting?' HBS asked.

'Actually, would you like to spend some time with us?' Bedroom asked, all of a sudden.

'Me? I thought, both of you just said you were not interested?' HBS replied.

The excitement in his voice was obvious.

'Don't you remember? We need a new lover for our last two sketches?' Bedroom commented.

'Oh, yes! How could I forget?' Boardroom replied instinctively.

'Ask him, if he would be interested to pose as the new lover. We can wrap up the sketches tonight'

'What new lover? I am confused' HBS said. *Knowing HBS, he must have thought that the artists were reconsidering his proposition of being a lover!*

'Only the THREE of us for the sketch…no hidden strangers, please' Boardroom stated loudly.

Was this some sort of a hint for me again?

Were they trying to prevent HBS from meeting me in my room by creating this diversion?

'Excuse me... but why are you shouting again and what sketches are you talking about?' HBS asked.

'As you know, we are artists. Would you be interested in posing for us?'

'Posing for a sketch?'

'Yes'

'Ok. I am on. Good opportunity. I love challenges. What should I do?'

'I will give you the brief. Just pose. I shall sketch and do the rest. But if you are not too comfortable to pose, we don't want to push you too much. We can ask someone else.'

'NO! I want to do it' he protested.

HBS fell for the bait like how I had fallen for it, a night ago! The thought that the opportunity could go to someone else had made him insecure!

'It was so sweet of you to compliment us earlier' Boardroom told him.

Her voice sounded surprisingly gentle and inviting.

'Thanks but how come all of a sudden?' he asked.

'I was just thinking. You are right. No man has praised me in a long time like how you just did. Come in.'

I heard the door slam shut.

I heard footsteps. I could feel HBS's disgusting, authoritative presence. He was walking towards the bed. I could make out by the appearance of his dirty black sandals which he was wearing. I heard a noise above my head on the bed. He had comfortably seated himself on the bed.

He was quite literally on top of me!

'Hey, are those oranges? Can I have one of them?' he asked. *He probably was referring to the oranges in the fruit bowl.*

'Sure, go ahead' Boardroom replied.

'I like them firm, juicy and ripe.'

'Are *all* of you so horny?' Bedroom interrupted.

'What do you mean by *all*? Did I say anything wrong?' he asked.

I feared the worst. I hoped that she would not blurt out something about me.

'Forget these silly questions and answers. Have the orange' Boardroom said.

I heard sounds of hungry eating. It was HBS, the greedy Somalian boy once again, busy eating free food.

'You have a lot of props…a toy gun. Wow!' he continued.

'It is supposed to be an AK-47' Boardroom replied.

'Can I see some of your other sketches?'

'Why?'

'Just to get an idea on how I should pose.'

'Ok. Here have a look-'

Why was she doing that? I had expected her to be more secretive.

'In the sketches, why are there no clothes? Why are the boy and girl all nude?'

'Well we are mostly landscape painters and sketch artists but we also do nude sketches and paintings sometimes.'

'In Bangalore, a few of my HNI clients have purchased paintings of famous painters and also invest regularly in art funds.'

'Ok.'

'By the way, you know what? These sketches remind me of someone. I am not able to place the person's face properly.'

'The boy in the sketch is actually a professional model.'

'You know what? In some angles it looks my subordinate too.'

My heart sank. The truth was going to be out in the open. My career was over.

'Which subordinate?'

'The one I was telling you about earlier.'

'What is this obsession about your stupid subordinate? Let us focus on your sketches.'

'Ok.'

'Hey! What are you doing?'

I heard Boardroom scream all of a sudden.

'Why did you drop your pants?' she shrieked at him.

HBS had dropped his pants!

From under the bed, I could see his pants had reached his ankles!

'Oh. I am sorry. I thought you said nude sketches. So I decided to get ready. I like being a self starter' he replied nonchalantly.

'But silly, she never said she wanted to sketch you in the nude. By the way, why are you wearing a cricket abdominal guard strapped around your waist?' Bedroom asked, laughing out loud.

Even Boardroom started to laugh.

I was panicking and sweating.

There was too much of tension!

But why was HBS wearing an abdominal guard?

'This is nothing to laugh about. It is for safety reasons. I want to protect myself from that drunkard, my subordinate's roommate. To teach him a lesson, I had kicked a football into his balls when we had a football contest.'

The damaging TT 'on' and 'off' shock treatment!

'Ok, so?' Boardroom asked.

'I am afraid that he might try to kick me back. So I am trying to protect myself.'

'Are you serious? But it is now night time!'

'I know. But prevention is very important.'

'Ok, so you believe that it is better to be safe rather than sorry at all times?'

'Yes. I completely agree with you. Even when the stock market crashed, the investors had not taken enough protection. But I informed all my clients to take the necessary steps to safeguard their portfolios.'

He was lying! He never did that!

'Maybe all investors should also consider wearing one! But on a more serious note, do you always wear a cricket guard?'

'No. Actually I got my entire cricket kit along as I thought we would be playing cricket during this off-site. I also really wanted to play badminton. But my stupid driver didn't pack the racquets! Plus anyways there are no facilities here for the same.'

'Enough about your cricketing encounters. Let me sketch. And please pull up your pant.'

'Ok.'

'Please go through the requirements for sketch 9 and 10 from this pamphlet.'

'I will. I like this title- *fig leaf collection.*'

'Ok. Now please read it fast. Let's get this done with.'

The room was silent for a few minutes. HBS had not yet pulled up his pant. It was still by his ankles. All of a sudden, the abdominal guard fell to the ground in front of me. I could see his ball scratching right hand bending down to collect it.

'WAIT! Let me pick it up for you.... ' Bedroom said.

She bent down. I could see her. She looked at me. She was laughing. I signalled for her to get rid of him quickly. I could do little else.

'...And here is your cricket guard.'

'Thanks. I don't know how it fell down. The sports guy told me it had a good fitting on my body.'

The artists burst out laughing again.

HBS sat on the bed again. Clearly he was not going anywhere.

'Ok, I am ready' he finally announced.

Thank God, the sketches were going to begin. Finally!

'I am starting to sketch' Boardroom announced.

'Sure. Apart from sketching, how do both of you earn your money? I mean, there is not a lot of money right?' he asked.

'That's right. But creativity is an expression from the soul. I don't think in terms of money' she replied.

'That is what all artists say. If you don't have the money, you talk about complicated things.'

'Excuse me?'

'Not in a bad way but what I am trying to say is that there is no money in art unless you are really famous. I make lots of money in finance.'

'We don't care. We really enjoy our work. We do it for our personal satisfaction and treat each of our completed works as a personal victory.'

'Do you want me to take both of you, from the small league to the big league? I can recommend you to my HNI clients and my friends. Interested?'

'No. I have told you, we sketch and paint for only our personal satisfaction.'

'But when will you make money? Sketching, painting and all…honestly are for people who have lots of free time. The world is run by people who make money.'

'Ok, if that is the case, do you want to leave right now?'

Boardroom sounded irritated.

'No…I want to stay! Don't get angry with me. I am giving my opinion, that's all.'

'Let me concentrate while sketching. Talk if you want but stay still.'

As she sketched, I felt a movement on the inside of my fat thigh.

Something was merrily gliding on my thigh trying to make an unauthorized entry into not so friendly private places. I felt uneasy.

It was an itchy sort of sensation like it was the bristles of a paint brush brushing against the hair of my inner thigh. Could it probably have been a caterpillar or a small centipede which had made an entry from the artificial potted plants by the balcony?

It was a little difficult to move. My damn hands were handcuffed. The itching persisted. I wanted to run to the washroom.

The slithering creature had entered strictly private, restricted areas.

I moved my body a little and I saw what was happening on my thigh. Earthy sons of the soil were up to some mischief. Moon walking across my thigh was a little caterpillar with its childhood friend, a millipede. I finally managed to move my handcuffed hands a bit. I stopped their dance moves in mid flight. I took them in my bare fingers and flung them away. They slowly but steadily glided away into a crevice.

Reality resurfaced.

HBS was still around.

But at least the caterpillar and his friend were out of my thigh. And that was a relief!

'I am done. Thank you for your cooperation. All good things must come to an end' Boardroom announced.

'It is all over? It was so much fun' HBS said.

'It was. Bye for now.'

'By the way I must say that I have a new found respect for both of you. You both are absolute professionals. I always thought women would love to be associated with someone as successful as I am and enjoy the benefits.'

'Thanks. Now we think you should get going. Good night.'

'Ok, then. See you around. I am off to room 309.'

'Oh! You still want to meet that subordinate of yours?'

'Yes, I have to go meet him. I am goal oriented. I believe in working hard and partying harder. I just enjoyed. So it is now time for work. I have to discuss strategies with him.'

I heard footsteps.

I could hear HBS walking towards the door. The door opened and slammed shut.

'Come out! He has left' Bedroom told me.

'Can you first please undo this handcuff and give me my pant?' I replied.

She gave me my pant and undid the handcuff. All it required was a simple move of an un-cooperative lever.

'You better rush through the ledge and enter your room. You have no other choice now' Boardroom told me with a sense of urgency.

'Ok. I shall try' I said.

'I shall rush to the hallway and talk to him if he is there.'

'But where is my shirt?'

'I don't know. Now just go!'

'In the meantime, I shall stand at the balcony till you enter your room' Bedroom told me. She accompanied me to the balcony.

She pressed my hand and whispered 'All the best'.

There was no time for love-*Only survival.*

I saw the deep ditch below. I prayed to God. The image of the one eyed rappelling safety harness man flashed past my eyes. I gained confidence. I walked well within the lines of the narrow ledge. If I lost my job as a financial advisor, I could certainly try my hand as a circus trapeze artist.

My room's balcony door was open. I gave her the thumbs up.

She smiled. I had reached.

But had HBS already reached my room?

21

CARNAL CONFESSIONS

I entered my room through the open balcony door.

The Virgin was awake!

I was surprised. When I had left the room he had been fast asleep!

He was now watching something on his laptop. He had head phones plugged on. His hand was in his shorts.

The door bell was ringing.

'Yaar! Where are you coming from? Where is your shirt? What are those black dots on your face and chest?' he questioned, seeing me.

He removed his head phones.

'I shall explain later.'

'I was worried. When I got up, I couldn't find you. I thought that the mountain dog had bitten you. For a moment, I also thought you had been kidnapped or something. I was about to call to check where you were. What is going on?'

He looked at me suspiciously.

'I shall explain later. Please help me' I muttered under my breath.

'Ok. By the way, a nice scene is coming up in the porn movie which

I am watching. The girl is telling the guy to unleash his hidden powers.'

'Dude, help me! This is serious.'

'Ok, sorry. What happened? By the way… who the hell is ringing the door bell?'

'Boss is at the door. Open after a few minutes.'

'That fucker? But why has he come so late in the night to meet us?'

'I will explain everything after he leaves. Don't tell him anything about me. If he asks, tell him I am in the bathroom. I shall change and come.'

I took a shirt from my suitcase and ran to the bathroom. I locked it from inside.

I washed my face thoroughly till I looked as spotless and blemish free as a model in the fairness cream ads.

From inside the bathroom, I heard the noise of our room door being opened.

'Why did you take so long to open the door?' I heard HBS asking the Virgin.

'I was watching a movie on my laptop with my headphones on. I didn't hear the door bell' he replied.

'Ok. Where is he?'

'He is in the bathroom.'

'I want to speak to him. I shall wait.'

'Ok. But how come so late in the night?'

'You mind your own business.'

'Ok, I will. I am tired right now. I have no energy to fight. But maa kasam you are highly irritating.'

I came out of the bathroom with my shirt all tucked in. With my scrubbed face and clean shirt, I must have looked as if I was going for a page 3 party.

The Virgin was back to watching his movie.

'Oh! Hi!' I greeted HBS as though he was my dearest pal in the universe.

I was thankful that he could not hear my heart pounding. He also seemed tense.

'Why are you breathing so heavily?' he asked me.

'Not really.'

'Why are you all dressed up? You also look different.'

He was looking at me suspiciously.

'I just changed.'

'But still.'

'You wanted to meet me?'

'Oh yes.....oh yes.'

'Regarding the quiz?'

'Yes. As a team we should win it!'

'We should. I shall try my best.'

'I also have some insider news. The Trainer is holding some sort of role play session in the morning. This information is power.'

'Ok. So?'

'He will be dividing us in teams. We should be well prepared and we must create a good impression.'

For the next few minutes, HBS pulled me to a corner of the room and we discussed some moronic strategies to win the quiz. Winning the quiz was getting a little obsessive for my mad boss. He also removed a piece of paper on which he had scribbled down a role play topic which we had to enact. He gave me a quick brief on which he wanted me to work.

We finally finished our discussions.

'Ok, I am leaving' he told me.

'Sure. I shall keep your valuable advice and strategies in mind' I replied.

'You should. Ok, let's meet tomorrow.'

He finally went.

I do not know how HBS was impacted after meeting the artists and posing for them.

This I would never know and he would never know that I was under the bed the whole time. Maybe I could say something in a later casual conversation to make him jittery. I could ask him questions like- 'Do you think oranges are good to eat?', 'Do you think women make better artists than men?'

I knew I would never have the guts to ask any of these questions but the possibility of asking him felt good.

I was finally free. The night had been eventful to say the least.

'I want to know exactly what is happening' the Virgin demanded. He jumped on me as eagerly, as a man in a lungi jumping on a coconut tree in Kerala.

'Get off me. I will tell you everything' I told him.

He jumped off me and squatted on the floor. He now looked like a man shitting in an Indian style toilet eagerly waiting for a magical story to while away his time as he finished his toilet business.

I told him the full story.

Everything from how I met the artists, to how I posed and the nature of the sketches. What I did not tell him about however was the arrival of the Trainer or HBS in the room. He was capable of tackling HBS head on and that would bring everyone down.

There would be no secrets left.

'But when the asshole came to our room, how did you know he had come?' the Virgin asked me. He was critically analyzing my late night encounter.

'Your favorite-the tattooed fat one heard a doorbell ring. She opened her room door. Then she caught a glance of him standing in front of our room' I replied feebly.

'Oh. So is that why you had to rush through the ledge?'

'Yes.'

'Why did you come rushing back? You could have come in aaram se after some time from the front door. He would have rung the bell and gone off. We are not crazy idiots like him to stay awake so late.'

'No, man. He would keep waiting till we opened. I know him.'

'What if I had closed the balcony door?'

'I guess I would have called you on your mobile to open the balcony door.'

'What if my mobile was switched off?'

'Dude, what are you…a CBI or an FBI officer to ask so many questions?'

'No, yaar. I thought I shall just check.'

'I thought you were sleeping. How come you got up?'

'I wasn't getting sleep. I was getting some weird dreams. I just got up like twenty minutes back. So I decided to watch this kick ass porn movie to relieve some stress. The chick in the flick is just too awesome.'

'Ok.'

'One more thing, the handcuff on my hands before the jungle safari belongs to the chicks, right?'

'Yes. It belongs to them.'

'I was searching for it right now. I couldn't find it.'

'I returned it.'

'Yaar, I am really sad about one thing. I think we have no dosti left.'

He sounded emotional.

'Why?'

'You lied to me. You were with the chicks the full fucking time and you didn't tell me?'

'Dude, it got complicated.'

'But I am your friend. We have shared a lot, man. You know me better than most people do. I didn't expect this from you.'

'Ok. Stop overreacting. What do you want?'

'Just like I helped you, I think you can help me.'

'How can I be of help?'

'Remember my dream which I told you in the morning?'

'Which dream?'

'Arre the dream in which I am a horse and the hot chicks are spanking me.'

'Ok…that one!'

'My life will be complete if these artists spank me, man.'

'What!'

'I am a small school boy who needs corporal punishment. I have never been very good in studies. I need to be taught a lesson. When I was a kid, a sexy teacher hit me on my ass and I still remember the happiness I felt. I just saw a similar scene in the movie right now. It brought back happy memories.'

'Are you serious?'

'Yes. Can you please ask them?'

'Let me try. No guarantee though.'

'You are the best. You are a friend for life. I mean it. This will be the best night ever!'

'Ok. You stay here. Let me go check with them.'

I was taken aback by his audacious request.

But I decided to try. If they acceded to this request, I could also push for something more than a just lotion massage.

I checked the aisle passageway for any human activity. No one was there. I knocked on room 310.

Bedroom opened the door.

'Oh! You are back! What happened?' she asked me, as I entered their room.

I told them everything.

'You poor baby…thankfully you managed.'

'Your boss is disgusting. What a proposition he made. I still can't get over it' Boardroom remarked.

'I told you.'

'He thinks he is some sort of hero. He kept staring at my breasts while eating the oranges. All you men from WCA are the same!' Bedroom added.

'I have something which might interest you' Boardroom said.

'What?' I asked excitedly.

'I took a Polaroid photo of him, standing only in his abdominal guard and posing with the toy AK-47! You can threaten him that, you will send it to the main office if he does too much of boss giri.'

'Are you crazy? No....I can never do that. Doesn't he know that you took his photo?'

'No, he didn't notice me clicking. He was too busy admiring himself while posing with the toy AK-47.'

'Oh.'

'Keep it. It might come in handy in future.'

I took the photo rather unwillingly and put it in my pocket. I noticed that Bedroom (a rather hazy outline of her) was in the background, in the photo. Her shapely hips though were clearly on display.

'I need a favour. I don't know how you will react, though' I spoke a bit tentatively.

'What kind of favour?'

'My roommate-that psycho drunkard wants to meet both of you. I told him, all about the two of you.'

'Oh! You did?'

'Yes.'

'What does he want?'

'Well it is an odd request. He wants to be spanked.'

'Spanked?'

'Yes.'

'Ok, send him across. It has been a long time since I have hit someone. It will be a good way to let off some steam.'

Boardroom sounded elated.

She smacked her thigh in delight. She seemed very casual in her response. Placing the request was easier than I had thought.

'No problem, right?'

'Don't worry. We shall handle it.'

'He is crazy. Be careful of that. And please don't discuss our conversations and the presence of the Trainer and my boss with him.'

'We won't. The encounters will be kept a secret' Bedroom said.

'Thanks.'

'Aren't you forgetting something for yourself for all the hard work you have put in?'

'Oh yes… the massage. I am quite stressed right now. Let's do it later.'

'You are the loser. I gave you a chance.'

Bedroom gave me a tight hug.

'Ok then, send that drunkard now. I am waiting' Boardroom said. She sounded excited. She had the whip in hand.

I left their room and went back to my room.

I saw the Virgin.

It was obvious that he was excited. Even the little strands of hair peeking out of his mole were quivering with anticipated excitement. He was writing something on a sheet of paper. It was like he was writing down equations to mug up before a maths exam.

'Position 69, doggie style, man on top, woman on top….' he said, talking aloud to himself.

He saw me.

'What did they say?' he asked excitedly.

'They agreed rather quickly and happily to your request.'

'I was praying to God that they would.'

'By the way, what are you writing?'

'Sometimes I get these short term memory losses. I am writing down the various sex positions just in case I forget.'

'You have got to be kidding.'

'I am not kidding. You never know when opportunities stop by you. One thing could lead to another....'

'Hmmm'

'Wish me luck. Hopefully it will be the best night of my life.'

He was off.

The sheet of paper having the various sex positions was tucked in his shorts.

After he went, I had conflicting emotions. Should I have let him go? What was happening in the room? I imagined him screaming with joy each time he was spanked. Maybe even I should have told the artists of my clear intentions once I had posed. I should have been more brazen and outspoken in my thoughts. Each time, the artists kept telling me it was a strictly professional engagement and that I should not entertain any further thoughts.

I had obeyed them faithfully. I had complied with every command and order like a true gentleman. Had I let a dream opportunity slip by?

Did the artists prefer aggressive, dominating men? If that was the case, why did Boardroom refuse HBS's offer? He was persistent enough. Women...they certainly were difficult to understand in matters relating to sex and the heart.

With my mind cluttered, I worked on the role play brief which HBS had asked me to work on. There was so much work to do, even in the middle of the night, in the middle of the off-site!

There was more tension than relaxation in this off-site!

The Virgin returned grinning like a Cheshire cat.

I looked at my watch. He had been in their room for almost an hour.

Had he had more than a spanking?

'*Ever night in my dreams...I feel you...I need you...my heart will go on...*' the Virgin sang like Celine Dion, while happily stretching his arms out like Kate Winslet on the deck of the Titanic.

He hobbled towards me and hugged me. He had a handcuff in one hand. The same one, which I had returned and was then handcuffed in later under the bed, when HBS had arrived!

'This has been the best night ever! God is great! Mazza aa gaya!' he hoarsely whispered to me.

'Oh!'

I wanted to know what happened.

'I don't see ghosts anymore!' he declared triumphantly.

'Really?'

'Yes. Also, dreams do come true! I am no longer a school boy. I am now a big boy!

'What happened with them?' I asked, the one question which was simmering within me.

He gave me a huge, broad, satisfied grin.

He did not answer.

He walked to the wall and started hitting his head. After a few minutes, the realization of the real world had set in, that his head would definitely crack like an egg to make an omelet but not the wall.

'Dude, what were you doing?' I asked.

'Thanking bhagavan-our uparwala, our raksha karnewala' he replied, rubbing the temples of his head. He rubbed the lines on his forehead. The lines of sexual prosperity also seemed to have been finally ignited.

'You are thanking God by hitting your head on the wall?'

'Yes, yaar. I am finally making my beginning towards big bangs with chicks in the future.'

'Congrats. Good for you.'

'I want to be spanked and enjoy like this more in the future. I am so selfish. But I can't help it. I love those women. Item hai. Maal hai.'

All of a sudden I felt really insecure.

And definitely jealous! The artists were my friends! Just when things were looking bright for me, this guy had swooped in conveniently and got the best deal. *Life really was not fair.*

I had an interaction with a caterpillar and he had an interaction with the hot artists, even though I was the better looking! The world was coming to an end. This indeed was a sign of the kalyug times.

Did he have sex with them? He was keeping silent on the issue. Who was it? Was it Bedroom? Was it Boardroom?

Bedroom liked me. So if he did have sex, it had to be Boardroom. I found it hard to believe but it was quite possible.

Even as I drifted uneasily into sleep, I thought of the vagaries of fate.

The Virgin was still speaking about how selfish he was and how God deserved to punish him some more in the future. His next request was to be whipped continuously for two hours, non stop.

The crazy second night of the off-site had also come to an end.

PART 4- OFF-SITE DAY 3

22
ROLE PLAY

'I have never had the chance to be *really* good at foreplay but I think my role play will rock' the Virgin told me. We were seated in the conference hall.

Did he mean the foreplay of the night?

I was not chummy with him at the moment.

I felt like kicking a football straight into his nuts to damage it temporarily like how HBS had, during the football match.

He appeared more confident and appeared as if he had been injected with a few extra vials of testosterone than normal. After the suspicious spanking of the previous night, he was actually glowing. I was pretty sure that he would now be totally out of control and display his new found confidence at every given occasion.

I thought to myself again.

Why had I introduced him? What was wrong with me? A friend in need was a stupid friend indeed. How could any of them have had sex with him *and* not me? I felt used. I had been with the artists for a longer time. I had obeyed them fully. I had never crossed the lines of decency though Bedroom and I were nude on the bed for a majority of the time. I had also had felt the vibes between us. I had shown the highest artistic restraint even though I wanted to make passionate love to her.

I was also definitely better looking than the Virgin.

What did he have that I did not have? Was he pushier? Was he more appealing? Did he pay them money? He definitely had the money. But....no...he would not do that. He wanted true love and acceptance. Not the kind that one got through money. If that was the case, he could have gone to a pro a long time back. And most importantly, the artists would never accept money.

These thoughts kept plaguing my mind. I tried to concentrate on what was happening.

The Trainer had organized a session of role plays to understand various issues facing us as financial advisors while we worked with our HNI clients to meet their expectations. He had set up a make shift stage, in the hall for us to enact the role plays in front of the entire team.

The idea of the role plays was to highlight the various issues impacting our business by enacting the situations in front of our team mates. Also the objective of the role plays was to check the thinking capabilities coupled with the presentation skills of the various team members. He had given the teams close to an hour to do some on the spot brainstorming. HBS and I were paired up.

HBS was going through the role play skit which *we* had prepared (which I had sat up in the night to work on, but which he modified conveniently to suit his requirements!). Our theme was on '*Working with HNI clients and strategies to reach a HNI client to recommend our services*'.

The artists arrived and seated themselves in the audience.

They looked as composed as ever and displayed no signs of the night time revelry. Their arrival increased the general excitement in the hall. Everyone wanted to impress them. All the teams were now preparing for their role plays seriously which had not necessarily been the case earlier! I expected a special look from them but nothing came my way. They were acting nonchalant. HBS also did not seem too perturbed by their presence in the audience. It seemed to me that I was the only one who was bothered by the happenings of the night.

The various role plays got underway.

A team from the Mumbai branch discussed effective ways of dealing with competition. Another team spoke about the marketing and promotional events with clients which should be undertaken to enhance visibility of WCA among the investment community. The Aunties in their role play spoke expertly on various investment products to be recommended to clients. Like skilled ballerinas moving across a dance floor, the Aunties glided through the various investment avenues they proposed for clients.

HBS and I took center stage to demonstrate our role play- '*Working with HNI clients and strategies to reach a HNI client to recommend our services*'.

HBS began by explaining the concept of *cold calling*.

A strategy of unsolicited *cold calling* typically adopted by pesky credit card agents is not a very effective medium to reach a HNI client. Clients in this category are very particular about an encroachment into their dimensions of space and time. A *direct referral* approach- getting an introduction from an existing client or a person who knows the HNI is a more appropriate way of getting to meet the HNI client. This is a faster approach as it at least generates some sort of response from the HNI client and might actually lead to a first investment meeting with them.

To demonstrate the ineffectiveness of cold calling as a strategy to reach a HNI client, we decided to enact this phase of the role play.

'Hello, is this Mr.....? I am calling up from....' I said, playing the role of a pesky mutual fund agent.

'Hello! Hello! Yes, I am.... Who is this....?' HBS answered, playing the role of a prospective client.

'Sir, actually I represent a boutique wealth management firm called...'

'How did you get my number?'

'Sir, actually...'

'How did you get my number? I don't want a credit card!'

HBS thrust an imaginary phone down.

The call had been disconnected by the HNI client.

I tried again.

'Hello sir...I am calling from...' I said.

'Didn't you just call me a while back?' he asked.

'Yes sir, I did'

'I DON'T WANT A CREDIT CARD. Do you understand?'

'But...but....'

'Don't you know that, as per a recent Supreme Court judgment you cannot make these telemarketing calls on a mobile? Give me your name and number! I shall complain to the authorities!'

'But sir...'

'What is your name? Where is your call centre? Is it in Delhi, Bangalore, Noida, Jaipur or Gurgaon? Don't tell me lies!'

'Sir, please listen to me-'

'This is a real nuisance. This time, I am definitely filing an official complaint against you and the call centre.'

'SIR, I AM NOT A CREDIT CARD AGENT.'

I screamed out loud in front of everyone.

'WHAT? Then who the hell are you? How did you get my number?'

'Sir, I got it from our data base.'

'Don't call me ever again! I don't want a home loan, car loan, personal loan, insurance or any further credit cards. Do you understand?'

'Sir, you are mistaken. I am not an agent.'

'Then who or what are you?'

'I am actually a mutual fund advisor. I want to recommend good mutual funds for your portfolio. Can we please meet some time?'

The call was disconnected by the HNI.

The first phase of our role play ended.

The entire team was clapping.

I thought I had played my part pretty well despite my troubled, betrayed state of mind. Maybe I had the basic qualities to be a good actor just like the office assistant in Bangalore!

We walked to our table to grab a glass of water.

The Virgin smiled at me. Did I detect satisfaction on his ugly face?

'I hope you never have the status to use a credit card!' he screamed at HBS, all of a sudden.

HBS glared at him but maintained his cool and kept silent.

'I also hope that you never have enough bank savings to afford a debit card. Bikhari saala!' he continued. He contorted his face like a roadside urchin.

Everyone laughed.

We were back to continue phase two of the role play.

It was now time to demonstrate a better, more effective way to acquire a HNI client.

I gave a brief to the gathering.

In most cases, the financial advisor had to take an appointment with a rather well endowed, sexy looking secretary in a corporate set up. In case the client belonged to a family run, non-MNC sort of office, a client meeting had to be usually scheduled with a rather grumpy looking, middle aged secretary who would be more bothered by her own set of health, digestive and marital issues.

'Can I have volunteers to play the role of the secretaries?' I asked the audience.

HBS and I had prepared the skit, visualizing the Aunties to be playing the role of the secretaries. However, Bedroom and Boardroom put their hands up in a flash! HBS looked on with excitement.

He had not expected this.

'Please come onto the stage' I said, with some coldness in my voice to not show any familiarity with them.

If they could be cool about the happenings then I would be cold! I hoped I would get a chance to ask them the most important question about what happened with the Virgin.

'Even though I am not that old, I will play the part of the middle aged secretary' Boardroom announced authoritatively.

The audience laughed.

'I will play the MNC secretary' Bedroom announced sweetly.

The artists joined me and HBS on stage.

'I have been trying to get a meeting for the last few months' I said innocently as the role play got underway.

'Oh!' the artists remarked in unison, reading from the draft script I had prepared for the secretaries.

'Each time the meeting gets postponed.'

'Well you can come on Monday at around lunch time. No…no…wait! On Monday, I have to go to the doctor with my husband for his annual health check so I will not be here to help you. I will shift your appointment to later this week. Just call up on Tuesday to confirm' Boardroom read out from her script.

This was the inconclusive approach which was not definitive in resulting in a client meeting.

'The meeting has been fixed for Monday' Bedroom playing the MNC secretary announced authoritatively in a saucy yet business sort of voice, taking over from Boardroom.

'Thanks. You look nothing more than twenty' I said.

Given her svelte figure, I really meant it!

All laughed in the audience.

'You are a very naughty advisor! Flirting doesn't help! In your case however I will make an exception. If possible, I shall reduce the time lag further and slot your meeting by pushing it ahead on the boss's calendar' Bedroom announced.

'Thanks.'

'Do you want *me or* the meeting?'

'Which one should I choose?' I asked the gathering.

Bedroom pretended to blush in front of everyone. Everyone laughed again except Aunty no 1 and Aunty no 2.

They were staring at Bedroom comparing everything from vital stats to skin texture! They had seen her bikini hour glass figure during the rappelling session. Their combative, catty instincts were resurfacing. Their reaction seemed to suggest- "You bitch... you think you are hotter than us? Ten years ago, even we were hot. You may be beautiful from the outside. But we are beautiful from inside. So what if no one cares or stares at us? It is their problem. Not ours!"

HBS was back on stage. The brief role as the secretaries for the artists was over.

I focused back on the role play.

The focus now shifted on the client meeting.

The meeting had been fixed. It is now up to the advisor to promote his 'highly recommended' wealth management services on offer.

'You have ten minutes'- take me quickly through what you have on offer' HBS, the client said, reading from the script, making his time as always sound very important.

It looked like I could not escape him being my boss whether it was a role play or whether it was in real life!

'But sir, I thought it was a half an hour meeting' I said.

'You are wrong. You have only ten minutes!' he remarked, glancing into an imaginary watch.

'But my presentation itself is for twenty minutes!'

'I don't care.'

'Ok....ok' I said, fumbling over the keys of an imaginary laptop to reach the more important slides of my business presentation.

'Show me what you have got!' he said, threatening me in this role play as well as he often did in real life as well.

The lines between role and real life were fast blurring!

'Yes...yes.'

'One minute to go.'

'Ok. I shall explain about our mutual fund product offering...'

'I don't think there is anything new to offer in your presentation- the same old mutual funds and investment products. I want something new and fresh. I want something that will excite and tempt me.'

'But...but.'

'Do you want him to scratch like how you do or what? Do you want him to show you a third nipple or what?' the Virgin screamed from the audience, all of a sudden.

This was definitely not in the script prepared by me!

'Keep quiet. Please maintain silence' the Trainer chipped in.

'Maybe you want an orgy. Threesome! Maybe a foursome! More the merrier!' the Virgin screamed again. He zipped his mouth with his fingers.

Everyone laughed.

'Shut up!' the Trainer shouted.

I was also a little happy with the Virgin's unscripted support. But was he talking about threesomes, because he had enjoyed one last night? Oh my God! I was really jealous.

'I can explain our good products in mutual funds' I continued with difficulty, getting back to the role play.

'No more time left. Your ten minutes is up!' HBS shouted.

'But....'

I acted startled.

'This meeting is over!'

We now enacted a successful meeting.

'I am so sorry. I had been travelling like crazy. I am back. Would you like to have a cup of tea or coffee?' HBS asked me at the resumption of our client-advisor meeting.

'Looks like, I might get my thirty minutes of presentation time' I told the audience.

All clapped.

'Why don't you tell me about your company services?' he asked me as we both sipped on imaginary cups of coffee.

'At WCA, we believe in a long term, client centric approach' I began.

'But give me reasons to work with you, over say an MNC bank.'

'We liken ourselves to be like a trusted CFO to you, to manage all your financial affairs just like a company CFO is for a company.'

'Your company services sounds interesting.'

'Thank you. Banks are exploiting your choice of convenience. By working with us, the fee which you will be paying is only a small price for the quality advice which you will be getting.'

'Tell me more.'

'A good advisor is one, who generates revenues for his company but not at the expense of the client. Client centric advice should always come first.'

'I think both of them deserve an Oscar! Kya mast dialogues hai!' the Virgin screamed again from the audience.

He was unstoppable. Again this was certainly not scripted.

HBS kept his cool. He did not react to the taunts.

'The services on offer seem interesting. Very different from how a bank operates' HBS told me post the Virgin's outburst.

'It sure is.'

'I am travelling for a bit. Let me think about this for a bit.'

'Travelling again?' I asked.

All started laughing.

'Ok, I am sorry. Enough of this "catch me if you can" attitude which I have been displaying. I will be interested in working with you at WCA.'

'Thank you! Yes!' I said, showing some fake excitement.

'Excellent! It was very entertaining' the Founder remarked from the audience.

He got up and gave me a standing ovation.

'I advised him to prepare the role play in this manner' HBS stated conveniently, stealing my thunder.

'Which is the best company in the world?' the Founder asked us.

'Wealth Capital Advisors!' I screamed. Everyone clapped.

Hopefully the additional dosage of sycophancy might help during bonus time!

My role play had ended.

HBS was very happy with the response. Bedroom looked at me and smiled.

We got off stage and took our seats in the audience.

The next role play to be enacted was by the Virgin-the ever enthusiastic candidate for attention.

He explained the contents of his role play to us.

The role play was on '*Wealth management being a competitive field and the need for speedy, timely client servicing*'. He explained that in the event a bank was tardy in handling a client's affairs, as competing financial advisors from WCA, we had to step in to deliver timely client services to the client and try and shift the business away from the bank to our end.

He took center stage.

He was playing the role of the financial advisor at WCA. He was accompanied by Aunty no 1 who volunteered to play the role of a client in the role play. He handed her a paper on which he had prepared his script.

The role play began.

'A couple of my fixed deposits just matured recently. I want to reinvest the same in mutual funds' Aunty no 1, the client explained to the Virgin, the financial advisor.

'Fixed deposits matured? Oh!' he reacted with a nervous start.

'The fixed deposits matured and my banking advisor didn't even inform me. I wasn't even aware. I just found out that the money is parked in my savings account' Aunty no 1 continued.

The Virgin acted shocked.

'What! This is unacceptable' he said.

'I know. I thought for such big amounts my banking advisor would be proactive to my finance needs.'

'A client should never lose interest on his investments. You should park the money right away in liquid funds without any further delay.'

'What's that?'

'Liquid and liquid plus funds are very short term debt funds for the temporary parking of your money. The funds invest in short term debt papers.'

'Ok.'

'Most importantly, you will be earning higher interest than what you are getting in your savings account.'

'What! I am very irritated with my bankers. They haven't shown any interest in managing my portfolio.'

'If you are comfortable, let me at WCA invest this money for you for the time being.'

'That makes sense.'

'And also, our interaction is more regular.'

'That's correct. I think I will escalate this matter with my banking advisor. I have lost valuable interest on my money.'

The first part of the Virgin's role play had ended.

Now the setting shifted towards the banking side, to see what really happened. This time, the Virgin took on a new role of being the banking advisor who was guilty of the oversight and Aunty no 1 took on a new role of being his reporting superior in the bank.

'Do you realize what you have done?' Aunty no 1 screamed at the Virgin.

He remained silent.

'You have lost us business! You deserve to be punished.'

She explained the oversight committed by him and how the client's money had gone to a competitor which was WCA. To display his wrongdoing, the Virgin handcuffed himself! The entire team started laughing.

It looked like the handcuffs which had been used during the football game.

'How many times have I told you that a good banking advisor should be able to handle any client meeting?' she continued.

'Sorry madam. I am really sorry.'

'The client had so much confidence in our bank. Now she is being advised by some advisors at WCA. This is too much!'

'Sorry.'

'This is an act of financial rape! You deserve life imprisonment.'

'Guilty as charged, your honour. You are right. I deserve to be handcuffed and spanked again and again…. the really *hard way* till I learn from my mistakes for the crime committed.'

The Virgin stared lasciviously at the artists- *As if last night's spanking was not enough!*

'I will definitely beat you on behalf of all woman kind' Aunty no 1 threatened.

This did not seem scripted. It sounded real.

This was probably retaliation for all the sasuma and idli-sambhar jokes!

Aunty no 2 sitting in front of me started whistling.

The Virgin pretended to be dejected with the handcuff remaining on his hands.

The role play ended.

We all clapped.

'How was my role play?' the Virgin asked me as he took his seat near mine.

'Very entertaining' I replied.

'Thanks. I improvised a lot.'

'Where did you get the handcuff? I think I have also seen a similar type of handcuff somewhere else' HBS asked him, cutting short our discussion.

Was he referring to the handcuff in the artists' room?

'Tere baap ka nahi hai. It is none of your business. I was wearing it during the football game, remember?' the Virgin replied arrogantly.

'Don't get personal again. Stop it!'

'I will start, continue and never stop. Tu kaun hai rokne wala? Chal abhi kalti mar le.'

'Let's see who wins the quiz and the best financial advisor of the year award.'

The fight was on.

I was sandwiched yet again in the argument. But it was fun.

Wealth management was indeed a competitive field.

Two financial advisors fighting over the legitimate ownership rights for a handcuff-They had now descended to a new level by calling each other a urinating dog and threatened to tie each other up to a street lamp post.

The quiz that was to start shortly would definitely be exciting.

Would *Amirchand Express* win?

23
QUIZ

'You will see how I am going to perform in this quiz!' the Virgin told me with a smile on his face.

He did not seem to notice that I was pretty dull. But thankfully I was in a better mood than I had been during the role play.

We were sitting in the banquet hall of the lodge which doubled up as the quizzing centre for the day.

'Also if I win the big prize- the home theater system, I will give it to you.'

'Are you serious?' I asked with some reawakened interest.

'Yes. You know that I have the money. It is now, only because of you, that I am also happy in life. You are the friend I never had.'

I seethed...I could not speak. I felt like the Ancient Mariner's crew whose throats were parched.

'I guess I am that *friend*' I said finally mustering all my faculties of decorum. My fists were paining from all the clenching I had done while listening to my large hearted 'friend'.

I felt like a total fool. A movie should be made about my foolishness and shown on the home theater system.

The Virgin moved away to join a Mumbai colleague who was pairing up with him for the quiz. I sat with HBS, my quiz partner. I did not know whether my limited brain cells would work during the quiz. I missed the night time sketching with the artists. HBS was so excited that he did not notice that I was unusually quiet and was not even giving my usual 'hmmm' and 'ok' to his various observations.

We were all waiting for the prelims to start.

The Trainer arrived in the hall. He had the quiz cards in his hands. He explained the rules of the quiz. The quiz was going to follow a two stage format. The prelims round which was the first round was a written round of thirty questions. On the basis of the scores in the prelims, the top six teams would go on stage, to fight it out for the home theater system.

The prelims started.

The questions were a mix of business awareness, entertainment, sports and current affairs. For each answer which he knew, HBS scribbled down the answer and made me use both my hands to cover the answer pad. This was to prevent some prying competitor from copying our answers! This was one of the stupid strategies which we had discussed during the night! I felt like an overachieving stupid school boy who tried to ward away competition but I ultimately did as instructed.

For a couple of questions, I knew the answers.

'....I think the answer might be...' I mumbled into his ear with all my fetid bad breath. 'You are too loud! Someone might hear! Write it down' he whispered back into my ear with worse bad breath than I had.

'....I think I might know the answer for this question as well...' I said.

'What did I just tell you? Don't speak. Just write!' he replied.

The prelims were over.

The Trainer was giving out the answers to the various questions. The wait for the results was now on.

'I think we are going to be on stage' HBS told me excitedly.

'How many do you think we got right?' I asked.

'I think we answered eighteen out of the thirty questions correctly.'

'That's pretty good.'

'It now depends on how the others have done.'

'I have the list of finalists with me' the Trainer announced.

The first team called on stage was *The Wealth Sizzlers*. The team had mauled the prelims round, securing twenty seven correct answers! It was the team of the Aunties- Aunty no 1 and Aunty no 2! They were greeted with loud, wild cheers from the excited audience.

'Unbelievable!' HBS screamed.

'I know' I said.

It was a quite a surprise.

The second team on stage was another Delhi team, *The Alchemists* with a score of twenty six points. Following them was a team from the Mumbai office, *The Financial Mavericks*. They had scored twenty four points. The fourth team on stage was again a Delhi team, *The Contrarian Artists*. They had scored nineteen points.

'We still have a chance' HBS stated.

'Let's hope we make it' I said.

The tension was mounting.

'Ladies and gentlemen, the fifth team securing a position on stage is AMIRCHAND EXPRESS from the Bangalore branch! Please give them a round of applause!' the Trainer stated.

The moment we had waited for, had arrived. We were going on stage!

I could sense HBS's relief.

For a moment, he was in a trance. The home theater seemed so much closer. Getting up from his chair, he embraced me in a bear hug with his smelly hands clasped round my broad frame. 'Come on! Let's do it! Let's win!' he told me.

With a gentle round of applause greeting us, we walked confidently towards the stage, with HBS in the lead. I adjusted my shirt which had been crushed during the bear hug.

For me, the quiz was just all about having fun. For him, this quiz meant much more - it was a matter of winning! He seemed quite clear on what a victory could mean for us- A victory could enhance our branch's goodwill. It was also another opportunity to impress the company Founder. It would prove the brains of HBS and his protégé!

'....Ladies and gentleman, the sixth and final team on stage is *Apna Sapna Money Money*' the Trainer concluded. It was the Virgin's team!

I wanted to rename his team as- *Apna Sapna Sex Sex* or *Apna Sapna Hot Spanking* or *Apna Sapna Fulfil Ho Gaya* or *Apna Sapna Happy Threesome.*

We reached the stage.

We took our positions at the table assigned to us. HBS seated himself to my left. I saw a large glistening image of the home theater system strategically placed in my eye line. The aspiration of owning the system was also getting to me!

The final was divided into three rounds.

The first round was a simple Q&A round with a total of twelve questions with the questions passing to the next team in a clockwise manner. It was ten points for a correct answer with no negatives. If none of the teams knew the answer, the question was going to be passed on to the audience.

With a press of the bell the first round was underway.

The Aunties from *The Wealth Sizzlers* seized the early initiative by not only answering their direct questions correctly, but also the passed on questions. *The Alchemists* closely trailed them. We were yet to get a point on board. HBS was getting increasingly agitated.

At the end of round 1, the scoreboard for us did not make for good reading. The only reassuring point was that the Virgin's team, *Apna Sapna Money Money* and *The Contrarian Artists* gave us company with no points on the board.

The second round was a visual round.

It followed the format of the first round. Kicking off proceedings, the first direct question was directed at *The Contrarian Artists.* It was a visual on some monument which was in the news.

'I know the answer!' HBS said.

His eyes lit up. He was excited. Our first points seemed in sight.

However the excitement was short lived. *The Contrarian Artists* answered it correctly.

'What the hell!' he screamed in frustration.

The second question addressed to *The Wealth Sizzlers* was a visual on some landmark geographical event.

'I know the answer' HBS told me again, cautioning me to be silent.

It was again too late! *The Wealth Sizzlers* had answered correctly.

'Our bloody bad luck' he muttered under his bad breath.

The possibility that the other teams may also know the answer to the question did not seem to strike him!

Our direct question finally came.

'*Amirchand Express*-Identify the actress on screen' the Trainer asked us.

As the visual emerged on the screen, HBS with incredible alacrity picked up the mike and answered.

'Well done! That is indeed the correct answer. 10 points to *Amirchand Express*! With that, they have finally opened their account' the Trainer announced.

HBS was excited.

In a display of 'positive team spirit', he slapped me really hard on my upper left shoulder. He also nearly dislocated the digits of my left hand while giving me a high five!

The remaining questions in the round were accompanied by further frustrated shrieks from HBS. *The Wealth Sizzlers* and the *The Alchemist* were answering most on the questions on offer.

The script was not going as planned for us.

The astrological stars were misaligned, shifting us further away from the path towards the prize! The score ticker at the end of the second round indicated that it was going to be a two horse race for the top two and for the bottom two positions! *Amirchand Express* was fast hurtling southwards towards the bottom!

The final round was a buzzer round with negative marking in place.

As per the rules of the round, if a team pressed the buzzer and answered correctly, it would get plus twenty. If it answered incorrectly, it would get a negative ten. Unlike the earlier rounds, this round had only six and not twelve questions.

With minutes before the third and final round was to start, HBS briefed me on the strategy we had to adopt-

'If you know the answer, immediately go for the buzzer' he ordered.

That was the problem- '*If*' only I would know the answer to a question.

'We are still in this quiz. We have a chance to win. Let's go for it. It is now or never' he told me. Similar words were stated by him also during the football match. Hopefully this time, we would emerge at the top and not remain at the bottom of the heap!

The Trainer asked the first question.

HBS rammed his palm into the round red buzzer just as the question was completed. He answered.

'That is the correct answer! Plus twenty to *Amirchand Express*!' the Trainer announced.

'Come on!' HBS shouted.

He slapped me again as a part of the team bonding. This time, I was prepared for the camaraderie and moved away in time to escape the full impact.

The Trainer asked the second question. 'Identify this cricketer in the visual' he said.

I had vaguely seen the face of the cricketer in question. I slammed my hand into the buzzer with full force to contribute to our team cause. 'And the answer is....?' he asked.

HBS looked at me expectantly.

I looked into space. *The answer was....that the Virgin possibly had sex and that I had not! No...that was the answer to the other question which plagued me. Not this one!*

I could not remember the answer.

The only thing I could see was a blind spot.

'...Minus ten points to *Amirchand Express.* The question passes to the *Wealth Sizzlers...*' the Trainer said.

As the question was passed on, the answer came flooding back to me. It was however too late!

'WHY DID YOU PRESS THE BUZZER? What have you done? We could have won!' HBS howled at me.

The home theater dream faded far away. We were back at twenty points.

The third question was clinically answered by *The Alchemists.* The fourth question was answered by *The Wealth Sizzlers* which effectively sealed the victory for them. From this point on, they could not come second, only unless *The Alchemists* got the remaining two questions correct, thereby pushing the contest into a final tie breaker.

The Trainer asked the fifth question.

Just as the words rolled out from the back of his tongue, HBS with all his might smashed the buzzer with his palm, to answer.

'THE BUZZER IS NOT WORKING! IT IS JAMMED' he screamed.

Simultaneously three other teams also went for the buzzer.

The correct answer was given by Virgin's team.

The Virgin looked at us and laughed loudly.

'This quiz is rigged in favour of these bloody Delhi and Mumbai branch people' HBS shouted.

I remained silent.

A few drops of his frustrated spit dropped straight onto my face.

With *Apna Sapna Money Money* answering correctly, *The Wealth Sizzlers* team broke out into an impromptu congratulatory hug. The Aunties were grinning ear to ear.

They had won against all odds! They were being cheered on by our Founder sitting in the audience.

The final question was a mere formality to conclude the quiz which was answered by *The Contrarian Artists* who finally seemed to get out of their slumber.

The final scores as per the ticker read as follows-

The Wealth Sizzlers-110 points, *The Alchemists*-50 points, *Apna Sapna Money Money*- 40 points, *The Financial Mavericks*-30 points, *Amirchand Express* –20 points and *The Contrarian Artists*- 20 points.

The Virgin's team had come third.

We occupied the last position jointly with *The Contrarian Artists*. This was reinforced by the Trainer. 'You didn't quite live up to your "rich" team name, did you?' he asked HBS jokingly as he shook hands with us.

With confetti and streamers descending on the grinning Aunties, HBS and I stepped down from the stage in search of the main door of the banquet hall.

HBS reflected on the lost opportunity of not having coming 'first' rather than acceptance of the bitter truth that we had come 'joint last'.

'If only you had not pressed the buzzer we could have won' he told me again.

I kept quiet.

This was only the beginning of the blame game. I was pretty sure he would blame me for days to come as well!

He walked out of the hall.

'Yaar, I am sorry I let you down. No prize' the Virgin told me at the exit door of the hall.

'No problem' I replied.

'Need to work on my quizzing skills.'

'At least you guys came third.'

'You guys came last…all because of that asshole!'

The Aunties walked towards us.

'We won! Yes!' Aunty no 1 told Aunty no 2 displaying the gift voucher for the home theater system which they had won.

'Congrats' the Virgin said.

'Well done' I added.

'I read, I write, I work, I run a household, I watch sports and I love saas-bahu serials. I am not ashamed of watching those serials. I now have a prize to take home for my small kids. Everyone always underestimates my potential' Aunty no 2 said.

'Sorry for always making fun of you' the Virgin said.

He sounded apologetic.

'It's ok. But learn to be more understanding and empathetic towards people.'

'I will try. I do understand that beneath all the layers of fat, you are actually a woman of substance whom I have made regular fun of. Sorry.'

'I am not less than anyone especially you- you rich, arrogant, spoilt loafer. And you don't have a perfect figure to call me fat, ok?'

'I am not a loafer, I am a lover. I am a love machine' the Virgin clarified without losing his cool.

He smiled.

'Chup kar, tum aadmi nahi, bandar ho' Aunty no 1 added.

We all laughed.

The quiz had made me a bit philosophical!

I had learnt an important lesson of life. Never underestimate anyone's skills ever, even if they put you off guard with their comical saas-bahu antics!

Another lesson which I learnt was that, in such fairly promising stock market times, instead of moving northwards like a runaway train on a one way track, *Amirchand Express* had derailed quite spectacularly off track! And this was after having done all the detailed planning right from the start of the off-site!

24
PRIZE DISTRIBUTION

The last event scheduled for the off-site had begun.

It was the prize distribution ceremony to felicitate the deserving, meritorious financial advisors of WCA. Like in all award ceremonies, the biggest award was reserved for the last.

In this case, it was the award for the "best financial advisor of the year at WCA".

The shortlist for this award was done on the basis of the revenues and new clients acquired by the advisor for the company over the previous year. Five advisors were in the reckoning with HBS being one of them. If he were to win the award, I was sure that I would be hearing about his 'greatness' in the Bangalore office, for days if not months to come! If he were to lose, he would crib and act like the Gods had conspired against him!

Before the awards however, the Trainer informed us that the Founder wanted to give us a brief talk.

'Ladies and Gentlemen, please put your hands together in giving a warm round of applause for a truly 'great' individual. He is like a towering '*God father*' for all of us. He is a '*Miracle worker*', a '*Saint*' among individuals. He is the one and only….' the Trainer stated, holding the mike in his hand.

He stopped his introduction abruptly.

He looked at the Founder standing by his side. He touched his feet in reverence!

The Founder was quite taken aback by this impromptu show of respect!

Seeing this act of Indian tradition, the gathering however broke out into a round of applause.

All the attention was now focused on the Founder.

He had the mike in hand.

'Thank for such a wonderful introduction' he said. He took over the proceedings.

'It gives me immense joy and happiness in sharing with all of you a piece of news' he told us.

'The news that he is pregnant?' the Virgin remarked, cracking up at his own stupid joke.

'I am making a formal announcement with regards to a dream project of mine- *The Centre for Excellence*.'

'What's that about?' the Virgin asked me.

'I don't know. Listen to him.'

'It must be quite an adaptive challenge for all you youngsters, especially after the technical challenges at the college level, right?' he asked, looking at the youngsters in the organization like me and the Virgin.

I did not even understand what his question had meant. I glanced at HBS. He was busy rubbing his head, lost in his own problems.

'Through the process of setting up WCA, I have found my true purpose in life.'

'That he is a woman and is...pregnant?' the Virgin asked me and laughed again.

'Please keep quiet. We will get into trouble' I mumbled.

'I was in the rat race. I made my wealth. Then I quit and set up WCA on my terms. If you are in the rat race, you still are a rat. I would suggest that, all of you search for the higher meaning in your life and determine the reason for your existence.'

'That's true. Look at him. That's his special purpose in life. He has found his reason' the Virgin told me, pointing at HBS, who was scratching his balls.

I smiled.

'When I stretched out of my comfort zone, I finally had the conviction to set up a personally fully funded, fully furnished *Centre for Excellence* for children....'

The Founder went into details of his proposed philanthropic venture.

The *Centre for Excellence* was a school of sorts. He explained that he wanted a part of his sizeable wealth to be utilized for a child centric school like the school we had visited after our village trek. A school which would give equal opportunities to all kids irrespective of which section of society they came from. The venture clearly seemed like a deeply cherished cause for him to pursue. It was quite a difference from the 'Founder' I knew at WCA. Away from the world of corporate targets, stress, competition, undercutting and most importantly leading someone else's dream, the Founder seemed happily perched at the 'self actualization' level in the *Maslow's* need hierarchy chain.

Holding the mike in his hand like it was an Oscar statue, the Founder had rambled on for close to forty minutes. He finally finished his lengthy speech.

All of us dutifully clapped.

The Trainer took over.

'It was this man's steadfast dream to give back to society. If it had not been for him, this project would not have been possible and we would not have been gathered here today. I urge more individuals to come up with such initiatives and to hold such beautiful off-site sessions' he said.

The Founder seemed touched by these kind words.

I could not help but notice that the Trainer, by having praised the Founder, had pushed all the right buttons for getting possible future off-site events from WCA!

My few years in finance had taught me a valuable practical lesson which did not involve any finance jargon or equations. The lesson was- *flattery goes a long way in corporate life.*

The Trainer had done his bit, by praising the Founder to be 'The Miracle Worker', 'The Saint among individuals' among other titles during the public forum! From his perspective, he would hopefully be rewarded for such flattery with a life time full of material riches!

It was time for the awards.

After all, in this moment of the higher meaning of life, self actualization and living for others and all, the Founder should not forget the regular people of his office- the financial advisors who were in the constant pursuit to make more money! For advisors like us, the pursuit of money was an essential stepping stone towards the pursuit of happiness!

HBS was gearing up for the big awards coming up. The excitement was palpable on his face.

'How am I looking?' he asked me.

'Nice' I replied.

'I am asking because I might have to go on stage to collect the prize.'

HBS actually looked pretty well dressed in his dark navy blue Reid & Taylor suit. It was unlike the casual and fairly sloppy dresser I had known him to be. He must have spent a small fortune to look so dapper.

The Trainer started with the small awards to keep everyone happy.

I won a prize for 'entertaining role play' and was awarded a book.

It was a leadership book! *Why was everyone obsessed with leadership books?*

The one I had given the Founder on his birthday had 600 pages. This one had 170 pages. The book had phrases such as-

"....a good leader should always treat his subordinates well..."

"...a good subordinate always looks up to his boss/ leader as a role model to follow..."

"...a good leader always understands and empathizes with his subordinate's problems...."

I closed the book-The contents were not relevant for me. I would prefer being spanked by the artists in room 310. That would be a better gift any day.

The Virgin won a table cloth as his gift for being 'Mr. Outspoken with different opinions on any issue'. He showed his displeasure at the choice of gift by wiping the table cloth on his posterior as a sign of protest.

I would have preferred the table cloth to the book. I could have given it to my mom. She loved freebies *especially* the ones related to home furnishings.

It was finally time for the big award.

'Finally to the big award of the day.... any guesses as to who will be the financial advisor of the year?' the Trainer asked, screaming into the mike.

Other than the concerned 'Famous Five' who were in the running for the award no one else seemed really interested.

The Trainer opened a sealed envelope.

'The competition is so fierce that all of you seem confused. The winner is.....' he screamed.

As he announced the name, the sound system went blank. He was talking into the mike but we could not hear the name of the winner!

But the result was out!

An advisor from the Delhi team stood up.

He was the winner of the 'soundless' financial advisor of the year award! HBS had come a close second as per the murmur doing the rounds.

In life like in sport, no one remembers who comes second. It is a self soothing cliché for a runner up to state that it is the race that matters and not the winning. The winning matters! That is because the winner takes it all! In this case, the winner was actually taking quite a lot of goodies home!

The advisor from the Delhi team walked onto the stage.

He was being given a fully paid, ten day holiday to China! However for a few days during the trip, he had to also attend a wealth management conference! It was an interesting way of mixing business with pleasure! Seeing the happiness on his face, he did not seem to be complaining!

With the announcement of the win, the Delhi advisor was swamped by his colleagues who seemed genuine in their praise for him and the efforts he had taken in the previous year. HBS offered his congratulations while making a really constipated, shitty sort of face- a face of discomfort when the pressure builds up while shitting in the morning but when the toilet paper, water or a combination of both have run out.

'Let's however not forget his commendable efforts in spearheading the Bangalore branch to new heights…' the Trainer stated, reserving a special mention for HBS.

This was classical management speak at work again.

Praise the runner up as he anyways was not getting any monetary reward! This specially earmarked praise paled horribly, in comparison to the fully paid holiday to China!

'…..There is a lot to learn from his excellent work ethic which I am sure the team in Bangalore will agree with' the Trainer continued.

Many eyes were looking at me, seeking my opinion.

'He is a great mentor. Also a truly inspirational leader' I replied diplomatically.

All clapped.

HBS seemed crushed. In a sense, his spirit was also broken.

'What a life the Big Boss has' HBS told me a while later speaking aimlessly and a bit incoherently.

'I know' I replied.

'He lives in Sainik Farms, has other property in and around Delhi, he drives a BMW 7 Series, helps children and most importantly has lots of money.'

'And also plays golf' I added.

'He has a complete life. I have NOTHING!'

I did not say anything. I did not know the right words to use to console HBS. *For some strange reason I felt bad that he had not won.* He was obnoxious, irritating and authoritative but was definitely a worthy contender for the award.

'I have worked so hard and the award goes to someone else. I have won nothing! I am not going to give up. I think even we should reach our goals and targets.'

'I agree. It is important to focus on personal goals.'

'What are you talking? I am not talking about some stupid personal goals. I am now talking about our FINANCIAL GOALS…OUR COMPANY TARGETS for this coming year! I will show them that I am the best. I will die but I will try.'

Clearly even I would die under the crushing workload!

'Oh…Ok.'

'I will get maximum clients and business this year. They canno stop me from next year's award.'

'I agree.'

'We need to strategize once we reach Bangalore. I will do so much business and client acquisitions that they cannot deny me next yea Maybe I will start my own company and show them!'

I was glad HBS was back to being his normal self.

He walked away.

The off-site had concluded rather unexpectedly on a whimper for him. However he was pretty resilient in the face of failure! A quality of a true scratching champion to take on challenges!

I would certainly have to bear the brunt of these challenges! Lucky me!

So much work was planned, that I could bid goodbye to one more year of my life!

However this was not the time to argue with HBS.

It was time to pack and leave for the station.

25

PACK & RELAX

'I am thinking of becoming an artist' the Virgin told me in our room as we packed.

'Are you serious? You want to be an artist?'

'Yes. Especially after last night, I have this new found appreciation for creative people. Even when I was in college, I hated this bull shit finance.'

'Is it?'

'Yes. Finance is only for boring people with no social life who want to lead a life behind the scenes. It is so boring. Chicks love someone who is creative.'

'So why don't you do something about it?'

'Maybe I will. I shall put my MBA plans on hold for the moment. I think I shall paint or sketch by the side or I shall try to join the hot chicks full time in Delhi.'

'Go for it.'

'I will be happy if I even get one thousandth of the respect and love which M.F Husain saab or any of the other great artists enjoy.'

The Virgin was really quite optimistic about his artistic talents!

He went to take a shower. I finished my packing and rushed to the artists' room.

I knocked. Boardroom opened the door. I wanted answers.

She smiled but I found it difficult to be normal. The room also looked quite uninviting. I found it difficult to imagine that it had been a place of intense sketching, me being in the nude, me enjoying the presence of the artists. It had been a room full of promised passion. Now it was just a room. In one corner, I could see the sketch book with one of the sketches on display.

This reminded me that the nights had indeed happened.

'Don't you have to leave right now?' she asked me.

'Yes, I have to in sometime. But I want to know one thing.'

'What?'

She was now joined by Bedroom.

'What happened when he came last night?' I asked Bedroom.

'Why do you want to know? Are you jealous?'

'Not really. But I thought we were close and if anything had to happen, it should have been between us.'

'What gave you that impression?'

'Let's not pretend. We spent two nights posing for the sketches together and at times even you were getting turned on. I would like to know what happened.'

There was no answer. Something did not seem right.

Bedroom turned away.

'We haven't been entirely honest with you' Boardroom told me.

'About what?' I asked.

'What if I tell you that…all along this has been a setup by us?'

'You said it was not…..'

I felt scared.

'Well, we lied. The Trainer had involved us in this to see how advisors react to temptations.'

'What? I knew it! This was too good to be true! I knew I couldn't get so lucky in life.'

'Don't get emotional. We are in command. We will blackmail you. That's all.'

'Will he also get into trouble?' I asked about the Virgin.

'We will see.'

They smiled wickedly at me. There was silence in the room.

I felt exposed.

I felt cheated.

I felt weird.

I felt irritated.

I felt they had liked me.

This betrayal was not acceptable among friends. The song- *Love, sex aur dhoka darling…love, sex aur dhoka*…started buzzing in my head.

Boardroom spoke something to Bedroom. I could not hear a word even though I was quite an eavesdropping expert.

They were probably planning on the final execution.

They finally spoke.

'You idiot! You are so gullible!' Bedroom screamed.

'What do you mean? What is going on?' I asked.

She began circling around me.

'We will do nothing to you. I was just joking. I just wanted to see your reaction, one final time before you leave. You are really a repressed, scared guy. You are always low on confidence, high on over the top talk. Be a man!' Boardroom stated authoritatively.

'Just relax' Bedroom told me, hugging me.

'Nothing has changed from the time you first met us. You are always scared! What do you want to know?' Boardroom continued.

'You win. Women on top! Are you happy? I want to know what exactly happened last night with my room mate after I left. He is not telling me the complete details' I said.

'You really want to know?'

Boardroom sat on one of the plush chairs in the room. She crossed her legs like Sharon Stone in *Basic Instinct.*

'Yes.'

'We spent some time talking to each other. Once the ice was broken, the stuff began.'

'Oh. What stuff?'

'He first came to our room. He revealed that he was a very horny virgin. He said he had lots of money. But girls showed no interest in him as he was ugly. As he spoke, something strange happened.'

'What?'

'A note fell out of his shorts.'

'Oh! Are you talking about the one with the sex positions?'

'How do you know?'

'I saw him scribbling something before he left my room.'

'Yes. He had written in great details about the positions he liked. I like a man who is well prepared.'

'And then?'

'He started talking dirty. He spoke about how he suffered from some memory loss and how he wanted to be spanked like a schoolboy. He then begged us to teach him the real thing. He said he needed both high school and college training to become a man.'

Even I needed the training!

'Hmmm'

'He said he had sent a lot of friendship requests on Facebook to girls who were in his school and college. All declined his requests. He even keeps a count of the number of rejections.'

'Oh. How many? I am just curious.'

'It was 17 girls from school and 44 girls from college as of last week.'

'Wow. Then what happened?'

'I felt sorry for him. He stripped. His ugliness didn't matter. His mole also looked quite proud standing all alone in the vast expanse of his ugly face. He looked so vulnerable and defenceless. The rest I will not say.'

'What? You felt sorry for him and so you acceded to his requests?'

'Yes. I did impart some real world education.'

I was totally stumped now. I needed a glass of water.

'In my case, you told me clearly everything had to be strictly professional while posing and in his case it became personal straight away! Why?'

'I am an independent, new age woman. I will use my sexuality the way I please. I don't have to explain anything to you.'

'Oh.'

'He expressed his naked, honest ambitions and got what he wanted.'

'What did he want?'

'I told you as much as I could. I cannot tell you more. It was in strict confidence. I keep secrets.'

'Even I am not aware of what happened' Bedroom added.

'Why don't both of you feel sorry for me also? Even I want to become a man. I also want some pity sex.'

'Don't get me wrong. You are more of a 'nice guy'. Actually you are more like a 'brother' to me especially after all the weight loss and relationship based motivational talks which you have given me, over the past two nights.'

'BROTHER? I DON'T WANT TO BE A BROTHER! I WANT TO BE A LOVER!'

Oh God! I felt a sudden pain shooting through my heart. Yuck! I was a nice guy. Nice guys do finish last. A bit of chivalry and Boardroom thought I was a brother type.

'You are the caring, boring and sensitive type. I realized that there could be too much of emotional baggage while dealing with a guy like you.'

'No, I don't agree. I like a no strings attached fling' I defended myself.

'No, you don't.'

'Ok, fine. What do you know about me? Are you my mother?'

'See. I think you answered your own question. You are still immature and sensitive.'

'But so is he!'

'Whatever.'

'But what was he doing in your room for over an hour?'

'A lot can be achieved in a moment…an hour is a lot. Because you have no experience you are probably not aware of this.'

'So it happened?' I wanted to confirm.

I only got a non committal smile. Boardroom actually blushed.

Sensing that I was jealous, Bedroom came to my side.

'Naughty boy, come to me. You looked great in the buff' she said, while clasping me tightly.

If I was a naughty boy then why was I not honoured like the stupid Virgin?

'What was your part in it?' I asked curiously.

I was curious as the Virgin had spoken about 'threesomes' during the role play. Was I a brother like figure for her as well? If she said yes, it was better for me to get an on the spot heart attack and die!

'I wasn't a part of anything. I was just the score keeper initially.'

She was not a part! Thank you God!

'Score keeper? But for what?'

'For the number of times he was spanked. Let's just say that he will never forget the numbers from one to a hundred in a hurry.'

Spanked hundred times! What the hell!

'Where were you when all of this happened?'

'After the spanking, I left both of them in the room. I don't know what happened. I was having a relaxing bubble bath in the tub in the bathroom.'

'You were having a bubble bath so late in the night?'

'Yes. Last night was hectic.'

'Hmmm'

'I think you are feeling low. My back is dry. I could do with a massage right now. Do I know anyone in the room who can help?'

'That's me! So finally…I am getting something for all my efforts!'

'Do you think I am as sexy as Megan Fox?' Bedroom asked me, as she arched her back. I emptied nearly half the bottle of lotion on my hand and started to rub her back.

The best part of the off-site was unfolding.

Thank you, God for having put me in Room 309 away from the entire team which was stationed on the ground, first and second floors!

'Do you think is it a good time to invest in the equity markets?' she asked me. I was impressed. I did not expect her to have stock market views.

'It depends on your asset allocation and risk profile' I replied.

'Ok.'

'In our company research at WCA we still have reason to believe that the fundamentals in India are very strong.'

'Oh, the economy is that strong?'

She turned around and tugged on my biceps.

'Yes. It is. There are many good books to learn about the stock markets. If you want I can give you a list.'

'Talking about books, the drunkard was telling us last night that he is planning to write a novel' Boardroom told me.

'A novel?' I asked curiously.

'He said that you will be a hero in his stupid novel. The entire time he was here last night, he kept talking about you and praised your efforts in motivating him for the journey of life.'

'Oh. Is it?'

'He really considers you as his good friend. A kind of friend he never had. For a moment, I wondered if he was more interested in you than in me.'

She laughed out loud.

My anger and irritation towards the Virgin was fading away. Every dog has its day and last night was obviously his.

'Ok. Enough of the back massage. I think it is time for you to leave' Bedroom told me.

'It is' I replied, glancing at my watch. The massage had come to an end so quickly. Damn. But it was totally worth the wait.

'Thanks for the massage. It was so relaxing. I feel better.'

'I should be the one thanking you!'

'I also have a gift for you. Open it.'

She took out a packet from below the bed and gave it to me.

I opened the packet.

There were two gifts. One was a sketch of me. The other gift was a whip.

'The whip is actually for… ' Boardroom interrupted with a happy smile on her face. She blushed again. '….Can you give it to him?'

'Sure.'

'When did you sketch this?' I asked Bedroom.

'Last night after you had left, I thought of you and sketched. Do you like it?'

'It's awesome. Thanks a lot.'

'I hope you remember us by these gifts. Thanks for all your support. You gave us a lot happy memories. I shall send you an update on the *fig leaf collection*. I have your contact on your business card.'

'No! Please send it to my personal email id.'

I gave them my personal contact details.

'I think the time has come for you to leave. Always remember. This is our little secret. Take care and good luck with everything' Boardroom told me.

'Sure.'

'I will miss you' Bedroom told me.

She kissed me.

'I will miss you too' I said.

For a second, I felt like I was in instant pop corn love with Bedroom, the kind that sets an instant flutter in one's microwave heart and then splutters away. The next time I was in Delhi or if she ever was in Bangalore, we could meet and take it forward. Most probably, she would be married soon. Even I would have made progress in the matrimonial search, courtesy my Mother and the constant prodding by my relatives. Would these artists tell the guys they married later on about these crazy nights and encounters? Would they be honest? Or would they hide this and start life anew? If they did indeed confess to the guys, would an Indian guy be nonchalant about their past and deal with it coolly? Deep down was a modern Indian male still very bothered about his wife's sexual innocence when it came to the time of marriage?

One thing was amply clear. No one could dictate terms to these artists...whatever they did, it was because they felt like it.

I walked out of the room in a daze. No one would believe what had transpired over the two crazy nights. When I had reached Kyari, I had not expected such things to happen to me.

I reentered my room. The Virgin had finished his packing.

'Dude, I have something to give you' I told him.

'What?' he asked.

'Here, take this packet.'

'What is it?'

'Have a look.'

I gave him the packet containing his gift- the whip. I slipped my gift and even put HBS's Polaroid photo which the artists had given me during the night, in my suitcase.

'This is fucking awesome. Who gave it?'

'The artists gave it to me to give it to you.'

'It's awesome. Today is the best day ever! I however don't need this to remember them. I will keep this whip on my bedroom shelf. The true gift they gave me is the gift of "self confidence" for all my future affairs with chicks.'

'Hmmm'

'Whenever I am low on confidence, I am sure the time I was given last night will motivate me. I am not ugly anymore. If women as hot as them can tolerate me, I can score with anyone in future.'

He had tears in his eyes.

Now, that was a first.

I thought to myself.

Nothing was planned last night. Things just happened. But the effects would be far reaching in the Virgin's life. The artists may or may not remember how they restored confidence in him. They may be quite unaware of the fact that if he became less arrogant and more approachable and successful with women, they would have had a major role to play. To begin with, the chances were- his dressing sense would surely change!

We walked down to the reception area with our suitcases.

The chained mountain dog growled at us. Maybe it wanted more dog biscuits.

'Does that kutta also want some biscuits?' the Virgin asked me, pointing at HBS.

I just smiled remembering the biscuit mix up episode which had happened, a couple of days ago.

The Virgin patted the mountain dog one final time. He had a quick mini bath in front of us with the dog licks. He also hugged the scared waiter from a few nights ago like he was his long lost brother.

We walked out of the lodge.

In the fading light, the jeeps were waiting to drive us down to the Ramnagar railway station.

PART 5- RETURN

26
TRAIN TRAVAILS

The entire team was in the train.

The mood was quiet. Most of us were tired and were dreading the thought of going back to work.

The train would be reaching the Old Delhi station by around 6 in the morning. It was the early part of the night and the landscape outside was getting increasingly difficult to view.

The Trainer was meeting each team member to solicit feedback and also to click photos for the company off-site album.

HBS was lost in his own thoughts and was sitting separately in a side berth away from me. He must have been wondering about how he would tell his wife about his sad tale of defeat.

The Aunties were also away in discussion with the Founder in a separate compartment. Post their victory in the quiz, there was some new found respect and importance for them, from team mates all around them.

I was sitting with the Virgin.

'Yaar, I am planning to write a novel' he told me.

'A novel?'

So this was the novel, Boardroom was telling me about which the

Virgin was planning on writing!

'The novel will be titled "*The Horny Indian Revolution 2020.*"'

'What kind of title is that?'

'Come on! It is a good title. My story will be about two nights, two cool guys and two possible wives. I want to focus on the unexpectedness present in everyday life.'

'It sounds very interesting.'

'The tag line of my book will be the two best mistakes of my life. And the novel will show how mistakes can actually benefit a person's life.'

'What mistakes are you talking about?'

'The first one was that I got drunk during the party because of which you met the chicks and the second one was my sex note falling out of my shorts in the chicks' room.'

'Oh.'

'I think I shall start writing my novel. I think it will become a national bestseller.'

'Go for it.'

'It is based on our experience, man. Both of us will be the heroes in the novel.'

'Thanks, man.'

'I hope it will become a movie some day. Maybe Rajini sir and Ghajini sir-Aamir Khan can play our roles. I hope they agree. Then the movie will be a super duper hit all over India.'

'Maybe they will. But keep a complete, bound script ready for them to read.'

'I will keep a script ready. I am happy that I have my maa ki dua and my baap ka pyar from heaven. I am sure they will be proud of me.'

'Yes, they will be proud.'

'I have also written a quick poem. Do you want to read it?'

'Ok.'

The Virgin gave me a piece on paper on which he had scribbled his poem. It read as follows-

Love, Loins, Lust & Longing

-A poem straight from a horny man's heart which is in transition during the journey of life.

Earlier when I would look at hot women

My body would shiver with nervous tension

My heart would suffer palpitations

My forehead would moisten with droplets of perspiration

The rocket between my trouser pockets would however rise in anticipation

Like an upright, anxious, honest old man in search of his monthly pension

But alas! I would get no fucking action

But now of late…

In a rather surprising positive turn of fate

I have now become the big baap of carnal sensations

This being quite remarkable, especially since I encountered a rather painful off-site football episode of testicular tension

But now finally, I can say with confidence… that in days to come…

I will be the heart throb for chicks at all my school and college reunions.

So dear readers of my wonderfully self indulgent yet sensitive poem

Please don't forget to come on the day

When I do decide to enter the binds of holy matrimonial union!

A day when it is a new beginning for me in my journey of life with a modern day Indian woman!

A woman for whom I shall have the utmost respect, affection and deity like devotion

A woman for whom I shall give up all my horny thoughts and vulgar observations

As I make the transition and become a married man who makes only mature grown up decisions

A man who discusses EMIs, onion prices and the general impact of inflation

A man who sings old romantic Hindi songs and a limited number of double meaning songs for the missus while she rather voluntarily cuts vegetables in the kitchen

A man who forgoes watching a cricket match coming live on television

And discusses whether or not to make an investment in gold, which I know being a financial advisor is a rather good hedge against inflation

Post the dinner, I shall talk romantic things and do goofy things to get her attention

To get her in the mood for a night of steamy passion

On the following morning, post a night which whizzes past like a T-20 match with exploding sperm balls of passion shot out of a human cannon

I shall enter office and face a working week dreading the fucking 24/7 cubicle tension

A migraine also makes an unexpected guest appearance out of hibernation

A mini mountain of paperwork greets me and stares at me right in the face

Paperwork which I should speedily execute to move ahead in this cut throat corporate rat race

The tension strains the muscles of my face

As I curse my fate

This my friends…is the journey of my life

Mull over my journey which I shall open my tiffin and munch on a low calorie muffin

My proposed journey from being a vulgar directionless man to becoming a focused, stressed out yet a committed married man

The poem was pretty graphic. I was not sure whether the Virgin's grandfather in heaven would approve of such raunchy poetry. Why would the Virgin suffer from cubicle tension? He was rich and his Uncle was a big client. He was and would continue to lead a comfortable life. I wanted to ask him, but I kept quiet.

It was however not the last I heard of the raunchy poem. There was more to come. There was a rap version in line. The Virgin insisted on rapping the poem for me. He shifted his pants down below his waist to give himself the loose, baggy rapper appearance. He thrust his hands out in front of him and started to rap. A cap and a fleece hood were missing. He sounded like a desi Eminem.

He finally kept quiet after his poetry rap.

I was also getting inspired in our small little creative train compartment.

To write a novel- the working title would be '*3 financial advisors and the search for sex in their non happening lives.* It would be a story spread over two nights and three days! In addition to the three advisors, the story would also have two hot artists. The artists would be confident modern Indian women who were well aware of their sexuality, unapologetic about their choices and were clear with whom they would choose to enjoy their sexual encounters. No one could take them for a ride. The first advisor's character would be that of a fairly decent looking, docile subordinate who wanted to get laid. He would be someone who was too decent and afraid to express his desires. Maybe a past relationship with a girl had dented his confidence. In spite of all his efforts in helping the artists with their sketches that too in the nude, all he would get to hear was that he was 'too nice' and like a 'brother' type to them. He was more of a nice guy in whom they could confide their issues and problems. As a result, he could not achieve his goal. The second advisor, an ugly rich man with a bloody mole would be a character who would enjoy the fruits of no labour by getting spanked and much more...possibly his first sexual encounter by conveniently playing the pity card which won favour with the artists. Finally, the character of the third advisor would be that of an obnoxious man in his thirties who was already having sex in his married life but wanted to enjoy the temptation of the casual, post marriage, one night forbidden fruit which was denied by the women.

HBS entered my compartment. He looked serious.

'I just received a call on a new fixed deposit issue' he told me.

The fun times were over! He already had dived into work! The off-site was technically not yet over!

'Oh. What are the terms like?' I asked in my subordinate mode.

'The Tamil Nadu Electricity Corporation is coming out with a fixed deposit issue. The interest and principal payments are being fully backed by the Government of Kerala.'

'But...'

'Why will a fixed deposit issue by Tamil Nadu Electricity Corporation be backed by the Government of Kerala?' the Virgin questioned.

'Listen, the off-site is over. Please keep quiet and stay out of it' HBS told the Virgin curtly.

'But what did I say?' the Virgin protested.

'What are you saying? How can the fixed deposit issued by one state be backed by another state? Pay attention!'

'What do you mean "What am I saying?" You just said that the fixed deposit is backed by the Government of Kerala' the Virgin replied, staring at HBS.

'Did I say *Kerala*?' HBS asked me for confirmation.

If I favoured the Virgin, HBS would get angry with me.

If I favoured HBS, my friendship with the Virgin would be disrupted.

As long as I was in WCA- the Virgin was an important tool to have in my professional arsenal of friends. He could confront anyone and everyone.

But I had to adopt a diplomatic stance. Something which I learnt quite effectively from observing the Trainer during the off-site!

'Well actually I didn't hear too clearly. What were the terms again?' I asked.

'Forget it. We shall discuss it later' HBS said.

'Ok.'

'Please listen to me carefully…forget this off-site…this party time. It is because of you that we lost the quiz! You are losing your concentration!' he told me curtly.

'Hmmm'

'Focus on business! This stupid party time is over. We have to meet targets this time! I don't want to lose because of working with you again.'

HBS walked out. I remained silent.

I felt really irritated.

I had felt sad for him when he lost.

Not anymore.

He deserved it! If he had won, he would have been insufferable and would have acted more authoritatively. God had certainly chopped his wings for a while.

'What just happened?' the Virgin asked.

'What?' I asked in return.

'Yaar, tu na darta bahut hain. React! How can you let this guy blame you for no fault of yours?'

'It's complicated.'

How could I explain that it was in my nature to take shit? How could I say that I was non confrontational and tried to stay clear of all controversies and trouble? The artists had also told me about my non-daring nature.

'It isn't. It is time you speak up or you will always be a pushover.'

'Dude, it is easy for you to say. You are a big guy in Delhi. I am not.'

'Arre, I know I am a big shot but I didn't mean it that way, man. What I meant is that he is pissed but he cannot blame you for something you didn't do right?'

'I guess so.'

'Remember this always-once a pushover you always remain one. Once you become a fighter like me, you will become a winner.'

'Thanks. I shall keep that in mind.'

'Good. Either get hit on the balls or take it on the chin like a self respecting man.'

'I can't, man. I think he is just grumpy because he lost and is trying to vent his anger.'

'He can do that but he shouldn't blame others for his failure.'

'That's true.'

'The idea of this stupid off-site was to give you the confidence to face your fears.'

'It is all gyaan, man.'

'It is for you to think out of the box, strategize, brainstorm and all.'

'You are kidding right?'

'Yes, obviously I am joking. From tomorrow, all of this will be back to normal. All this is just bullshit time pass. But you shouldn't be a pushover.'

'Thanks for the advice.'

I liked the determination in the Virgin.

It sounded like fun to teach the boss a lesson, a challenge fraught with extreme risk though.

Who was I kidding? I was scared.

Was it because I was scared of a public dressing down by HBS? Was I scared that if I retaliated I would be rendered jobless and would have to face my dad's wrath? Was I scared, that if I expressed my opinions, I would be termed as an aggressive employee and not be given my share of the yearly bonus?

Was it wishful thinking to believe that I could fight the system, challenge the boss and come out on top?

The Trainer arrived with his note book and a digital camera. He told us that the learning from the off-site should be implemented by us in our office work and we should monitor our performances for superior results. He spoke about having a plan to integrate the off-site goals with team goals which in turn were to be integrated with overall company goals. The overall 'integration' would be beneficial for the growth of each individual.

The Virgin yawned.

The Trainer got the hint and stopped his lecture. He gave us a feedback form which was meant to be anonymous in which we had to describe the off-site and how much we liked or disliked it. In the form, we also had to describe each member in terms of an adjective which best summed them up during our interaction with them during the off-site.

I termed HBS as 'persistent' and the Virgin as 'confident'.

The Virgin wanted no anonymity. He put his name right on the form and also autographed it like he was a celebrity or a cricketer! He termed me as 'creative and 'hardworking'. He termed HBS as an 'obnoxious asshole'.

'No bad language please' the Trainer told him.

The Virgin scribbled the words out. He replaced it with 'bastard'. He scratched it out again and then wrote 'scratching dumb fucker'.

'I give up' the Trainer conceded.

'Good' the Virgin said.

The Trainer asked a boy sitting in the aisle side berth to click a snap of the three of us with his digital camera.

'Let's please stand together. These are snaps for our annual company off-site album' he told us.

The Virgin, me and the Trainer posed together for the camera- The Miss Universe, Miss World and Miss Earth! This beauty contest was well and truly over.

Well not quite.

The Trainer hugged the Virgin and clasped him around his hips. It reminded me of the dance party in which he had felt electricity from the Virgin's ass!

'What the fuck, man? How many times have I told you not to touch me or my ass?' the Virgin shrieked in discomfort.

'Sorry...I didn't know that you would notice. It wasn't deliberate' the Trainer replied innocently.

'Back off.'

'If I am invited again by WCA and the stock markets do well, I will push for an international off-site next time...maybe to Singapore, Thailand or Egypt.'

'Sure. Sounds exciting' I replied.

'There will never be a next time. Now...just get out' the Virgin said, pointing at the aisle passageway outside our compartment.

The Trainer was off.

Why the Trainer only clasped the Virgin's hips and ass would remain a mystery. Maybe he was trying to get friendly with the Virgin after possibly finding out that he was a very rich man. But sadly the Trainer ended up irritating him, big time!

The dinner arrived. The night passed by uneventfully.

It was around 5 in the morning.

In close to an hour we would be reaching Old Delhi railway station.

HBS was in the toilet taking a shit.

The Virgin was brushing his teeth by the washbasin. I was standing by the coach door next to him breathing in some early morning air.

'Want to have some fun?' he asked me.

'Sure' I replied.

'You wait and watch.'

He ran up to toilet door in which HBS was shitting and started banging on the door. HBS started shouting something from inside but could obviously do nothing!

A few minutes later, the Virgin ran up again and started banging the door. I began laughing. It was like I was back in some school picnic or hostel with these juvenile pranks. It reminded me of the incident in which the Virgin threatened to tie HBS with the dog leash on the first day of the off-site.

'Let's go back to the wash basin' the Virgin told me.

He rushed to the washbasin and began again to brush his teeth. I rushed towards the door like nothing had happened.

HBS came out of the toilet. He glared at us. But he had no proof.

The Virgin had toothpaste all over his face.

I pretended to be observing the outside sights.

'Nice breeze blowing' HBS told me pushing me to a side and breathing in some fresh air.

His BlackBerry started to ring. He put his hand in his track pant pocket to pick up the phone to attend to the call.

I stepped aside.

'Kick him on his ass!' the Virgin muttered to me.

'No…No' I replied.

'Kick him. He will go flying out. You will permanently get rid of his torture. Go for it!'

'No ways, man! Don't be silly.'

'….Arre jaanu kaise ho? I love you jaanu. Chotu kaisa hai? There is too much of noise in the train' HBS croaked on the phone.

I glanced at the Virgin. He was grinning.

'His wife and son' I told him.

'….WHAT! Chotu again has gas and constipation problems? Even I have a stomach upset and some gas problems. See you in Bangalore.'

HBS hung up the call.

'Bahut gas hai kya? No wonder you fart all the time' the Virgin muttered under his breath.

'Did you say something to me?' HBS asked him.

'Yes. But I cannot repeat it. Can't help it if you are deaf' he replied.

I stood still though I wanted to burst out laughing.

'I am warning you. YOU ARE GOING TO BE FIRED FROM WCA.'

'Not as long as my uncle is a client!' the Virgin stated arrogantly.

The train eased in to the Old Delhi railway station at 6.15 a.m.

We had to take a taxi directly to the airport to catch our 7.45 a.m. flight. The scheduling was a bit tight but thankfully with very less early morning traffic, it was not going to be a problem.

Our entire team got off and bid goodbyes to one another.

I once again congratulated the Aunties for their quiz victory. They also wished me luck for everything and walked away. Their husbands would possibly be waiting to eagerly hear all the news. HBS was haggling with a porter to carry his luggage. He was returning back to his usual self. The sadness at not winning the award seemed to have been forgotten.

'Yaar, stay in touch. Add me as a friend on Facebook. I will never forget what you did for me' the Virgin told me as it was our turn to bid goodbye.

'Some day tell me the full story, ok?' I replied. I would then know if the two versions tallied- the artists and his version.

'I will. Wait for my novel. It will cover everything. I will call you for the book launch. I will definitely hold a reading at a Crossword or a Landmark store. Meanwhile you keep me updated about that scratching asshole.'

'Of course, I will.'

'If I get a girlfriend or if there are any developments in my love life, I will tell you. I now have a lot more confidence to get chicks. This wouldn't have been possible without those hot chicks and your friendship.'

'Thanks, man.'

'Do you think I should get the hot chicks, diamond rings?'

'It is a decision I leave entirely up to you.'

'Ok. Call me any time if you want property in Jor Bagh. You know that I have solid jugaad.'

I did not have any money to buy a new house in Rajender Nagar or in Karol Bagh let alone Jor Bagh!

'You have told me that ten thousand times!'

We laughed.

We embraced.

His Ramu kaka was waiting to pick up his luggage.

The Virgin hugged his kaka and broke into a quick railway platform *'Jai Ho'* dance with him like Dev Patel and Frieda Pinto had in *Slumdog Millionaire*. The kaka seemed surprised by the sudden outburst of sweaty railway platform love.

The Virgin walked off. There seemed to be an extra swagger in his walk. Was that swagger on account of the newly found confidence he now had because he was finally laid?

27
ROAD RAGE

En route in a prepaid taxi from the dirty Old Delhi railway station to the Delhi airport, HBS spoke to me at length on having come second at the awards function.

He sounded bitter.

He clearly had still not forgotten the loss.

He kept telling me that it was a loss to 'us' as a team as he had not been awarded the prize.

I maintained a really sad artificial expression on my face to sympathize with him.

Our taxi driver was merrily motoring to the airport at a gentle speed. It was very unlike a typical Delhi driver. He did seem to have a care in the world. It was like he had accepted life's vagaries and had come to terms with it. His speed was so gentle that a couple of early morning cyclists on their geared cycles and a teenage boy on his moped rushed past us.

We passed a roadside display which read- 'Lingerie that supports and reflects a woman's hidden inner sentiments'. It was a display of a local brassiere manufacturer. I wondered if Bedroom used this brand.

I also wished that I had some sort of support in the taxi-whether elastic or otherwise.

The reason was that there was not enough room in the taxi for my suitcase.

The driver informed us that the boot was already filled with his personal belongings. It could not store any more items. The taxi also did not have the overhead stand to place the luggage. In the front, in the passenger seat next to the driver was one of HBS's suitcases along with his cricket kit. In the back, HBS was seated comfortably with his other suitcase in the middle of the seat. He asked me to hold on to this suitcase, as he opened up a box of fruits to eat which he had picked up the station. Rather than challenging the existing status quo, I continued to hold onto his suitcase and balanced my suitcase on my thighs and stomach.

As I maintained my balancing act, a white Toyota Corolla swerved rather violently from the middle lane to the left lane in front of our taxi. The car did not flash the left indictor nor did it slow down. Our driver in his own world of slow reflexes did not brake in time. As a result, our taxi bumped rather ferociously into the car's rear bumper resulting in a fine dent. Our driver was however not to blame. The car driver had flouted the rules.

At this moment, an angry voice was directed at us, at our taxi driver in particular. It was the voice of the angry car driver shouting from his damaged car in front of us. He instructed our driver to halt the taxi by the side of the road.

He walked towards us.

He seemed to have dedicated his life to body building. Maybe he was in a real hurry to reach his gym for a morning workout. He was dressed in track pants and a tight T-shirt meant for a small fourth standard boy. His rippling biceps burst through his shirt. Seeing the seething anger on his face and his muscular appearance it was a time to make peace and not war with this gym toned muscular Rambo.

The North Indian Rambo reached our taxi.

He stood by the driver's seat in front of me. He started hurtling abuses in a thick Hindi accent. The North Indian road rage blood within him was boiling. Veins of anger were sprouting at various points on his forehead and branching merrily across his broad forehead. Our driver also began abusing in Hindi. The anger in the Rambo was intensifying. He wanted an immediate payment for the damages.

'Just keep quiet. Let me handle it' HBS told our driver.

'Saab, just because he yells at me, does not make him a better driver' the taxi driver shouted in Hindi.

HBS silenced him. Our driver gave in and decided to observe the proceedings from the taxi itself.

HBS stepped out of the taxi to sort the situation.

Instead of diffusing the situation with a quick apology, he decided to spice it up, making it more combustible with an aggressive retaliation. He engaged the angry Rambo in a discussion to explain that it was his and not our driver's fault. The angry Rambo was not willing to listen. He continued hurling abuses.

Even though we had a flight to catch, HBS decided to get more aggressive in explaining the exact sequence of the car's movements. He was like a small, aggressive bull dog in the face of this majestic, angry elephant. He however did not seem to mind. He also started shouting aggressively. He liked a good confrontation. Apologizing in a combative situation to a stronger enemy was a sign of weakness as per the HBS rule book. However in this battle between a small, scratching man and a muscular, angry man, I would put all my money on the muscular, angry man.

The Rambo was losing his cool.

He was rubbing his fists on his track pants, creating some sort of warm friction. Maybe HBS was going to be punched straight in the face. *He had pushed his luck too far!* If it was to happen, it would be a day of celebration for me at WCA with him finally going to be out of action!

The punch which I was expecting did not happen. Instead, the Rambo just pushed him. HBS lost his footing, hit against my door and then finally fell to the ground.

The Rambo walked away.

'What is the matter with you? Why did you not catch me?' HBS screamed at me.

'But...how could I? I have all these suitcases to hold' I said.

'What is more important? Holding onto these stupid suitcases or holding me, your boss?'

The suitcases any day!

'You are more important.'

'I have been noticing for last few days... you have been taking work and life very lightly.'

But it was meant to be a relaxing off-site!

'Hmmm'

'I want you to focus on work again.'

What did he mean by 'again'?

'Hmmm'

'You can't even make effective on the spot decisions and you call yourself a financial advisor who manages HNI money? All of you are INEFFICIENT and USELESS.'

Me, the Virgin, his Bangalore driver, this taxi driver, the office assistants....the list was endless!

I was pissed.

The Rambo meanwhile had reached his Corolla which was in front of us.

HBS walked back towards him to settle scores. He was not going down without a fight.

Hopefully the Rambo would just gently break his head like a man breaking a Marie biscuit with his morning tea or vigourously break his head on the road like a man breaking a coconut before Lord Ganesh in a temple.

At that very moment I got a random, lengthy telemarketing text message on my mobile which read as follows-

> Are you an honest, hardworking employee who despite being servile and having good intentions always ends up in heated discussions with the boss, who is hell bent on making nonsensical strategic decisions?
>
> You may have done your Masters in Financial Management. But do you know the art of conflict management?
>
> Don't fret! We are there. We love you unconditionally like your parents do.
>
> We will help you achieve superior corporate success (in the competitive rat race) and turn you into a company VP, CFO, CEO or MD before you turn 35! All you have to do is call us on this number for *real tips*...
>
> 100% success is guaranteed!
>
> We also have astrological and other career guidance services!
>
> Call us...call us fast!

I made a note of the number in the text message. It could come in handy for the future. I also corroborated the advice in the message with what the Virgin had told me in the train. More than corporate success, what I wanted right now was some good old fashioned justice and a modicum of respect.

I had to step up and fight against injustice. I had to stand for what was right. I had to teach HBS a lesson albeit a slightly risky one.

I had to stop thinking only of my salary and the good bonus as the only reason for work. The Naval Commander had quit, the Virgin did not take nonsense. It was now my turn to stand up in my own little way.

I could not take the HBS shit anymore. I had to stop being docile. I had to assert myself.

It was time to fight a scratching system.

I thought over my plan again.

The idea seemed good. I was getting nasty.

I went for it.

I removed the instant Polaroid photo from my suitcase which the artists had given me of HBS standing only in his abdominal guard and nothing else, while holding the toy AK-47. I put it in the side pocket of his suitcase which was next to me in the back seat.

This was my way of getting back at him. I still lacked the guts for an open confrontation.

Was it an intelligent thing to do? Deep down…I knew it was a spineless, slimy thing to do…which could possibly wreck a marriage. But I somehow wanted to assert myself.

I visualized his wife unpacking his suitcase and discovering the photo. She would be shocked to see her husband dressed only in an abdominal guard! What would shock her even more would be the shapely hips of a woman (Bedroom) in the background of the photo. Her mind would start to imagine the ugly possibilities. She would realize that her husband possibly had had extra curricular activities during the relaxing off-site which crossed the sacred matrimonial lines of commitment, truth and honesty! In anger, she would shout at him! HBS would get a dose of his own medicine!

His lily white reputation would be in shreds!

If HBS unpacked and found the photograph himself, the chances were he would suspect the Virgin with whom he had fought all through the trip. If he did check with him and the Virgin denied knowledge of the same, but did confess to giving me this idea of standing up for my rights, all three of us would be in trouble.

If as an extreme possibility HBS somehow did check with the artists (as the photo was taken in their room), the matter would be hushed up or blown seriously out of proportion by them. If he asked me, directly about the photograph I would ask him other questions leading up to the artists and his presence in their room which he did not know I knew about.

I felt powerful.

I never knew I had such a vindictive streak in me.

It felt good.

I really did not care whether my action was the right one or not.

HBS was still in conversation with the Rambo.

A woman stepped out of the damaged Corolla. Maybe it was the Rambo's pretty wife.

She joined in support of him. I could see her talking to HBS.

HBS changed completely in her presence.

For each of her questions about the collision between the vehicles, he replied looking straight back at her breasts and then at his watch.

Running out of time and left with no other choice, HBS rather grudgingly muttered something to the Rambo's wife's breasts! She seemed to accept the apology with minimal fuss and did not ask for any sort of payment for the damages.

The problem was solved.

The Corolla moved away slowly.

HBS was back.

'I sorted everything out. I am sorry I lost my cool with you. You are a really good guy' he told me.

He actually sounded apologetic.

'It's ok' I replied, making my artificial sad face again.

'I have been really disappointed since yesterday. I hope you understand.'

'I can understand.'

He pushed his suitcase to the front seat to make more room in the back.

The additional suitcase on top in the front seat started to shake uneasily. It came perilously close a couple of times to falling off the seat.

All of a sudden, HBS showed me a set of his family pictures on his BlackBerry. He was standing with his wife (not slim but certainly not plain looking) and his small son in various poses. It certainly looked like a happy urban family. I noticed HBS putting his finger in his eye. Was he getting emotional thinking about his loved ones?

I noticed some serious commitment towards his family especially his little son. In light of this, I found it hard to believe that he actually had propositioned the artists.

I felt guilty again. But the damage had been done.

The photograph was in his suitcase! There was no way to retrieve it! If it led to something more serious than a marital fight then I possibly would think of stepping in. Till then he had to face the music!

We were reaching the Delhi airport.

28
UP IN THE SKIES

We were a bit late.

We checked in our suitcases quickly. *With that, the photo was also checked in for good!*

HBS quickly dashed to an airport store selling semi precious jewellery. He returned with a packet which he put in his handbag. Probably it was a guilt-gift for his wife. Maybe his wife in turn as a gift would take him to a good dermatologist for his scratching related body issues.

We rushed through the security check and finally boarded the aircraft.

Inside the economy class of the airline, HBS and I had taken aisle seats in the same row. He was to my right. As yet, no one had occupied the window seat next to me. The in flight captain announced that the flight would be delayed for a few minutes on account of some air turbulence.

In front of me, there was turbulence of a different sort.

In the seat in front of me, an infant started to cry. To its right, an elderly man burped. Someone in the same row had put some balm which made the entire row smell of the 'hospital smell'. And finally, someone opened a plastic bag from the overhead locker out of which a slippery box of slimy soap fell right onto the aisle passage! The only thing actually missing right now was the presence of a washer woman who could squat, fasten her sari, add some detergent, remove her scrubber and start washing some clothes!

While low cost air travel was certainly in, right now travelling by train would certainly have been more fun!

'I am the bloody boss. They should at least upgrade me to business class! This smell is too much' HBS told me covering his nose.

I covered my nose as well.

'I don't get the best advisor award nor do I get to fly business class!'

Thankfully I could not be shouted at, this time. Blame the HR policies followed at WCA!

Giving some sort of semblance that we were in an aircraft were the airhostesses who in their tight blue skirts were standing on their toes, projecting their perfectly fleshy yet toned backsides as they closed the overhead cabins.

Watching the airhostesses certainly refreshed the both of us.

HBS seemed to be in a better mood now and seemed to have finally forgotten about the loss and the hot headed Rambo for good.

An airhostess smiled vacantly in his direction. His face lit up. He sensed an opportunity!

'I am sure you are thirsty' he told me, smiling at me.

'No… not really' I replied.

'I know you are thirsty' he announced again. His ball scratching right hand went vertically into the air. It pressed the overhead switch to make a request for water. Such sudden concern for me, the subordinate was very surprising! What was not surprising was this feeble, desperate attempt at flirting with the airhostess. *Maybe I was wrong about HBS and his commitment towards his family!*

Expecting the arrival of the airhostess, HBS adjusted his crumpled shirt and shook a bit in his seat in anticipation of the brief tête-à-tête. With a smile hanging out of her angularly pouted mouth, the airhostess instead of stopping by our row, walked past us, smiling at a fat man seated three rows behind HBS!

Instead, attending to HBS's request was a muscular steward!

'How may I assist you, sir?' he asked HBS.

'Oh. Can I have some water?' HBS asked meekly.

'Sure, sir' the steward replied, projecting his ass in front of HBS as he closed an overhead locker above me.

HBS was back to being his grumpy self. He had lost interest.

'We should have won' he continued reflecting on his lost opportunity. Or maybe he was reflecting on his lost *opportunities*- the rejection from the artists at the off-site, not winning the best financial advisor award and now the failed flirting attempt with the airhostess!

As he cribbed, adding colour to what had already been an eventful day was the late arrival of a really pretty woman. She looked quite similar to my ex-girlfriend with her wavy hair and attractive features. She was dressed in a pale green kurta and black leggings. She wore ethnic jewellery and looked gorgeous.

All eyes were fixed on the pretty woman as she moved in search of her seat.

She came as a breath of fresh air amidst all the odd people assembled inside the aircraft.

She smiled at me. I could not believe it.

I glanced at my watch. It was 7.40 a.m. - A moment to be preserved for posterity.

It was an electric sort of smile which could light up any morning- The kind which could turbo charge an individual through the drudgeries of life.

'Excuse me... that's my seat' she said, pointing to the window seat next to me.

As she moved past me after putting her bag in the overhead cabin, her hand grazed my left bicep. It was a real pity that I had no time to flex it!

She was so close to me, I could actually feel her breath.

'Hi! Myself.... ' HBS sitting to my right on the other side of the aisle suddenly tried to introduce himself to the pretty woman.

'What are you saying? I am not able to hear you' she replied back to him.

'Pssss....can you move to my seat?' HBS whispered to me as he wanted to flirt with the pretty woman. My close proximity to the woman was being challenged. The smile reserved for me, by her, was being threatened.

'Why?' I asked.

'She cannot hear what I am saying' he told me.

'Neither can I' I stated assertively for once. *Was it the Virgin's effect?*

HBS looked grumpy. He flipped through the in flight magazine for some entertainment.

The pretty woman settled down to read *The Fountainhead* making it clear she did not want to be disturbed *especially by* two financial advisors who were fighting for her attention! She seemed like a reader of serious, thought provoking writing. I enjoyed lighthearted reads. That just about ended my chances of any further conversation. I grabbed the *Economic Times* from the rack in front of me to scan for the latest financial headlines to get back into work mode.

I switched off my mobile. The last received call was from my mom on the first night of the off-site. I was pretty sure my mom, in the months to come, would go on the offensive with her marriage talks and proposals for me. I would have to wait and watch as to how that would progress.

The flight had started to gather speed.

With turbulence of all sorts out of the way, the flight taxied off the runway up above into the morning sky. After this crazy off-site, I could not imagine spending my time managing the portfolios of HNI clients. But then such was life. In a few hours...I would be back in Bangalore and with that a return to the drudgeries of office work. The overworked office assistant with his sad emotional stories from his mechanical life would greet us at work and with that my office life would resume.

⫶ *Abhay Nagarajan* # 271 # ⫶

We reached Bangalore.

We collected our suitcases and came out of the terminal.

HBS suddenly screamed. I turned to look at him sprinting in the direction of a woman with a plump, cute kid in her arms. It was his wife and little HBS. They both looked so happy to see him. Little HBS quite literally jumped out of his mother's arms wanting to hug his dad. Even though he was just over a year old, he did look intelligent enough to read all the leadership books his dad would buy for him in the years to come.

It was nice to have someone waiting for you, in spite of all your imperfections and transgressions. I said my goodbye to HBS, who said he would step in to work, later in the day.

I got into a prepaid taxi all alone to head back to my PG.